ODDS

William Peter McGivern was born in Chicago. He began his writing career in the pulp magazines and soon graduated to more sophisticated markets like the *Saturday Evening Post*. He served in the US army during World War II and was awarded the Soldiers Medal in 1944.

After a stint as a newspaperman, he successfully turned to crime writing in 1949 and enjoyed much acclaim, with ten of his novels adapted for the screen. Foremost was *The Big Heat*, which Fritz Lang turned into an all-time classic in 1953, starring Glenn Ford, Gloria Grahame and Lee Marvin. McGivern also turned to screen-writing in the 1960s.

Although he is better known as a writer of crime fiction who covered the whole gamut of crime – police corruption, detection, crooked cops and homicidal psychopaths – McGivern also wrote war and espionage novels.

His other crime novels are *But Death Runs Faster*, *Heaven Ran Last*, *Very Cold For May*, *Shield for Murder*, *Blondes Die Young* (as Bill Peters), *The Crooked Frame*, *Margin of Terror*, *Rogue Cop*, *The Darkest Hour*, *The Seven File*, *Night Extra*, *Odds Against Tomorrow*, *Savage Streets*, *The Road to the Snail*, *A Pride of Place*, *A Choice of Assassins*, *The Caper of the Golden Bulls*, *Reprisal*, *Night of the Juggler*, *Summit*, and *A Matter of Honor*.

William P. McGivern died in 1982.

Also available in the Blue Murder series

The Big Clock Kenneth Fearing
Whatever Happened to Baby Jane? Henry Farrell
Solomon's Vineyard Jonathan Latimer
Somebody's Done For David Goodis
Scarface Armitage Trail
The Honeymoon Killers Paul Buck
Texas by the Tail Jim Thomson
Shock Corridor Michael Avallone
Straw Dogs Gordon M. Williams
The Big Enchilada L.A. Morse
Scorpion Reef Charles Williams

Forthcoming

The Users Brian Case
The Lying Ladies Robert Finnegan
Darkness at Dawn Cornell Woolrich

Further titles to be announced

Series Editor: Maxim Jakubowski

Born in the UK but educated in France, Maxim Jakubowski published his first book when he was only 19. After a career in industry he switched to book publishing, holding senior editorial positions with various British companies. An expert on and lover of sf, fantasy and crime fiction, he is also known for his books on movies and rock music, and has published over 25 titles in these fields. He has contributed to many definitive reference works, and to leading newspapers and magazines such as *The Observer*, *Time Out* and *Blitz*. He created the cult crime imprint Black Box Thrillers, which revolutionized the field in the early 1980s and was the forerunner of Blue Murder. He lives in London, where he divides his time between writing and his mystery bookshop, Murder One.

ODDS AGAINST TOMORROW

WILLIAM P. McGIVERN

Xanadu

blue murder

British Library Cataloguing in Publication Data
McGivern, William *1919–1982*
Odds against tomorrow.
I. Title
813.54[F]
ISBN 1-85480-048-5

First published 1957 in USA by Dodd, Mead & Company, Inc.

First published in the Blue Murder series in 1991 by
Xanadu Publications Limited, 19 Cornwall Road, London N4 4PH

Printed and bound in Great Britain by
Cox and Wyman Limited, Reading

To my brother Frank
with appreciation

ODDS AGAINST TOMORROW

CHAPTER ONE

For what seemed a long time he couldn't make himself cross the street and enter the hotel. He stopped in the middle of the sidewalk and frowned at the revolving doors and canopied entrance, indifferent to the nighttime crowd drifting past him, his tall body as immobile as a rock in a stream. People edged around him carefully, for there was a look of tension in the set of his shoulders, and in the appraising frown that shadowed his hard even features.

It was the finality of the thing that worried him, he realized, not the consequences. . . .

He knew the hotel, a middle-class commercial establishment close to the heart of the city, an old stone building that had been brightened up with a neon sign and shiny aluminum facings around a black and silver canopy. Lorraine had met him in the lobby once, he remembered; it wasn't far from her job. They'd had some beers before going home.

Finally he lighted a cigarette and flipped the match toward the sidewalk, hardly noticing the people strolling in front of him. In the end he didn't make up his mind at all; he simply started toward the hotel, urged forward by a pressure that seemed as inevitable as it was pointless. He sighed and thought: *Why not? Why the hell not?*

He stopped just inside the revolving doors and glanced alertly and cautiously around the lobby. Several groups of people stood talking near the newsstand, and a number of middle-aged businessmen sat about on hard, functional couches leafing through the evening papers. From a lounge off to his right, he heard the sound of loud juke-box music and the noisy laughter of men at the bar.

He skirted the groups of people and moved tentatively

toward the reception desk at the end of the lobby, his hands pushed deep into the pockets of his old overcoat, the faintly worried frown still darkening his face. At the desk he waited behind a woman with two children tugging at her skirt, controlling his exasperation as the room clerk told her how to reach a suburb of the city by streetcar.

"My brother would have met us, but he had to work," the woman said apologetically. "He's with the gas company, and they can call him out any time."

"You won't have any trouble, I'm sure."

"Yes—thanks a lot. Come on, children."

The clerk, a young man with thin blond hair, smiled up at him. "Yes?"

"I want to see Mr. Novak. Frank Novak. What room is he in?"

"Is Mr. Novak expecting you?"

The question irritated him, and he took his hands from his pockets and drummed his fingers on the counter. "Sure, he's expecting me. I wouldn't be here if he wasn't. What room's he in?"

"I'll ring him." The clerk smiled impersonally. "It's a house regulation. Whom shall I say is calling?"

His anger died quickly; he felt empty and foolish. "Sure, I see," he said, shrugging as if the matter meant nothing to him. "But he knows me. My name is Slater. Earl Slater—he might know me as Tex Slater. That's just a nickname. It stuck to me from the Army."

"I'll call Mr. Novak."

Earl Slater put his big bony hands back into his pockets. Running on like a fool, he thought: *Stuck to me from the Army.* So what? What difference did that make? His irritability twisted around inside him, sharpening as it searched for some release or outlet.

"Room Ten-six," the clerk said. "Mr. Novak would like you to come up."

"Well, thanks," Earl Slater said with a stiff little smile. He wanted to say something more, something that would readjust the exchange in his favor, but he couldn't think of anything that might help; words were like crutches to him, difficult, makeshift means to a limited end. The clerk was already talking to someone else in any case, so Earl turned from the counter and walked slowly toward the elevators. What was the room number? Ten-six. . . .

Facing the closed elevator door, he hesitated again, the frown deepening on his forehead. He lighted another cigarette quickly, and the tension in him charged his movements with a curious significance; he was like an animal in open country as he glanced nervously about the lobby, alert and graceful and wary.

Earl Slater was thirty-five years old, but he looked much younger; his complexion was the kind a woman might envy, clear, smoothly tanned, and he handled his rangy body like a well-conditioned machine, using it with a suggestion of careless precision and efficiency.

For all this, people weren't often attracted to him; they might be touched by the hunger in his eyes, or impressed by the power of his body, but the cold and delicate anger in his face usually kept them at a distance.

He dropped his cigarette into a sand-filled urn as the elevator door slid open. Straightening his shoulders, he stepped into the empty car and said "Ten-six" to the operator, a young Negro in a green uniform. "That the tenth floor?"

"Yes, sir," the colored boy said, snapping his fingers in a slow rhythm. "We're going right up. Right up." Turning, he smiled at Earl. "You hear the final score on the Eagles game?"

Earl Slater stared at him, his eyes shining and blank: he might not have been seeing him at all. "I don't care about football," he said gently.

"No?" The operator was still smiling. "What's your sport then?"

"Riding nice quiet elevators," Earl said, and let his soft Southern accent come down between them like a wall.

The colored boy's smile faded until it was no more than a little twist at the corner of his mouth. "I read you, Mister," he said, closing the door and throwing the starting lever with a lazy flick of his wrist. He hummed softly under his breath until the car came to a stop at the tenth floor. When the door opened, he inclined his head and said, "Don't mention it, Mister. Nothing at all."

Earl stared at him until the door closed, and then he let his breath out slowly, trying to check the frustrating anger pumping through his veins. A smart one, he thought. A real smart one. Turning he walked down the quiet corridor to Novak's room, forgetting everything for the moment but an exasperating dissatisfaction with himself; why hadn't he said something? That thought drummed in his mind. Why did he stand and take it like a block of wood?

Novak himself opened the door, grinning and extending a muscular hand. "Come on in. I'm Frank Novak," he said. "You're right on time, Slater." Novak was short, but put together compactly and powerfully, a dark-haired, dark-complexioned man with cold little eyes. "You're a big one," he said grinning at Earl, surveying him with eyes that remained cold and hard. "Come on in. I want you to meet a friend, Dave Burke. Dave, shake hands with Earl Slater."

Burke was standing in the middle of the room, a tall paunchy man with gray-blond hair and a complexion that had reddened by the rupturing of tiny blood vessels in his cheeks. He smiled and gave Earl an awkward little salute. "How're you?" he said. "Sit down and make yourself comfortable. You feel like a drink?"

"All right," Earl said. "Something light."

"How about a whisky and water? That sound okay?"

"Sounds great," Earl said. Burke laughed as if this were funny and turned to a dresser on which there were several bottles and a collection of glasses. "You use ice?" he said.

Earl didn't see any ice around, so he said, "No, never mind."

Burke laughed again, and Novak said, "Sit down, Earl. Take that chair. It's better than the others. You want a cigar?"

"No, thanks." Earl sat down with his overcoat in his lap, but Burke took it away from him and said, "Let's don't get this wrinkled up, Earl. I'll put it in the closet."

"It doesn't make a lot of difference. It's pretty beat-up."

Burke laughed at this too, and Earl realized he was a

bit tight; not drunk but loosened up to the point where everything was striking him as mildly funny.

The room was small and cheaply furnished but the view from the double windows gave an impression of space, with thousands of bright little lights blinking far below against a big darkness.

Novak sat on the edge of the bed, hands resting on his knees, and studied Earl with a faint smile. "It's not Buckingham Palace, is it?" he said.

"It's okay," Earl said, coloring faintly; he didn't feel at ease. "It's fine. I never stayed here, but I've stopped at the bar downstairs."

"And why not?" Burke said, laughing softly. He gave Earl a dark-brown whisky and water, and said, "Why not stop at the bar, eh?"

Novak said, "Sit down, Burke, and take a load off your mind." He was still smiling, but a thread of annoyance ran through his voice. "We might as well talk business."

"Sure thing," said Burke. This time he didn't laugh; he sat down carefully and rubbed a hand over his coarse, red features. "Sure thing."

Novak lighted a cigar, and when it was drawing smoothly he smiled through the smoke at Earl and said, "How old are you?"

"Thirty-five. Why?"

"Just curious. No offense." Novak leaned back on the bed and the overhead light touched the speculative glimmer in his little eyes. "It's a kind of a decisive age though. At thirty-five a guy should know whether or not he's going to make it." He grinned at Earl's puzzled frown, and then his eyes wandered casually over Earl's suit and shoes. "How do you figure you're doing? Got it made yet?"

"I don't know." Earl shifted his hands and feet, feeling harried and uncomfortable. "I never thought much about it. I'm not rich," he said, grinning awkwardly; but the admission irritated him, and a confusing anger grew in his breast. "I'm doing all right, I guess," he said, shifting his feet again, and looking down at his drink. "Right enough, anyway."

"You're not working, are you?"

"Well, not just now, no."

"When did you work last?"

"Couple of months back, I guess."

"That was the job at the Circle Garage, right?"

Earl smiled uncertainly. "How did you know that?"

"We've checked on you, kid," Novak said. "When I called you this morning you didn't know me from Adam. I mentioned a name to you, Lefty Bowers, a guy you were in jail with. That's all you know; that I'm a friend of somebody you knew in jail. Right?"

"I guess so," Earl said. He shrugged. "Yeah, that's all I know."

"I'm not trying to be mysterious," Novak said. "I just want you to understand a few things. First, Lefty told me you were a good guy, knew how to keep your mouth shut, could drive a car."

"Is that what you want? Somebody to drive a car?"

Burke laughed and Novak glanced at him with a little frown. He said, "Get me a drink, will you, Dave?"

"Yeah, sure thing," Burke said, heaving himself to his feet. "Sure thing."

"It's a little more than driving," Novak said. "That's why we checked on you. Burke used to be a cop, and one of his old buddies helped us out."

"A guy I knew for years," Burke said. "A great guy."

"It must be pretty big," Earl said. He tried to smile. "If you went to all that trouble it must be big."

"I hoped you'd understand that," Novak said quietly. "It's big enough, don't worry. But more important, it's safe." He tilted his head and studied Earl through the smoke curling up from his cigar. "I'd rather try for a hundred bucks and make it than get caught going for a million. I want you to understand that. I'm a serious guy, a businessman." He drew an envelope from his inside coat pocket and removed a thin sheaf of papers. After glancing through them for a few seconds, he said, "Well, here's what we found: Earl Slater, born in Texas, son of a farmer. Got into the Army at sixteen by lying about your age. Tried for the paratroopers but got transferred to the infantry after a training accident." Novak glanced at him. "Right so far?"

"I broke my leg jumping," Earl said, trying to be casual about it, to control his confusion and excitement; but the images Novak had recalled flashed through his mind like the flickering designs of a kaleidoscope. "One of my lines fouled and I came down too fast." He could remember the ground coming up at him, the corn stubble in the field sticking up like tiny red whiskers. They said he'd hit like an express train; the heels of his jump boots had been driven deep into the hard earth by the weight of his plunging body. He was sure he had heard the bone in his shin snap like a piece of dry kindling, but the medics told him that was just his imagination at work.

"You spent five years in the Army," Novak said. "Pretty rough deal, eh?"

"I guess so."

"Two years after the Army let you go you were arrested for stealing a car in Galveston. You served eight months of a two-year rap. Next time you were arrested it was for assault and battery in Mobile, Alabama, and that time—"

"Listen, I didn't steal that car," Earl said hotly. "I was drinking with the guy who owned it, and he told me to take it. But the bastard wouldn't say that in court because of his wife."

Burke laughed at this, his eyes almost disappearing in his fleshy red face, and even Novak smiled faintly. "Okay, you didn't steal the car," he said. "But after the three-month stretch in Mobile there was a rap for manslaughter. They hung four years on you that time."

"It was like the car," Earl said, with a weary, hopeless anger in his voice. "A guy in a bar came at me with a bottle. I clipped him good, and he busted his head on the bar railing. But his friends told the cop he didn't swing the bottle."

"Well, that was bad luck," Novak said. "I guess you've had your share of it, eh?"

"You're damned right I have," Earl said. He glanced from Novak to Burke, feeling the pressure tightening about his chest like an iron band. He hated having people pry into his past, classify him as this, that or the other thing because of the lies they found in old dusty records. "So what about it?" he said angrily. "I've done time, I'm out of a job. Are you guys any better off?" He stared at Burke. "You used to be a cop, eh? Well, what happened? They dump you for boozing?"

"Now hold it, sonny," Burke said. He didn't sound angry, but he began to rub his big fat-looking hands together slowly. "Just hold it, eh?"

"Well, what's the big deal?" Earl said, getting to his feet. "You're both sitting here with a patch on your pants in a four-dollar room. You think I give a damn what you found out about me?"

"Relax," Novak said sharply. "What we found out made us think you were right for a cut of this job. There's nothing personal about it. So don't go popping off."

"Well, okay," Earl said. He locked his hands together to control his trembling fingers. "What do you want with me?"

"It's a bank job," Novak said. "I'll tell you a little about it, then you say whether you want in or not. If you want in, I'll give you the whole deal by the numbers. If you want out—" He shrugged his big, powerful shoulders. "That's what you get—out."

"A bank job? You're sticking up a bank?"

Burke smiled, but he didn't laugh. He studied Earl speculatively, his eyes glinting in pockets of puffy flesh. "It's a small bank," he said dryly.

"Are you interested so far?" Novak said.

"I don't know. It's—well, I don't know."

"You want some details, sure." Novak stood and paced the floor in front of Earl, holding the cigar like a pointer in his big hand. "It's a small bank, like Burke says. A big one doesn't figure. First, you need too many guys." He shrugged. "Lots of guys, lots of talk, that's been my experience.

"Then the big banks are in the big cities. That means traffic. A car stalls in front of you, a fire truck blocks you off, an accident happens—bang! You're dead. Two, the big banks are ready for trouble. They got guards behind peepholes, they got alarms a teller can let off by touching his toe to a foot pedal, they got the local cops, the FBI, Brink's and Pinkerton all standing by to answer those alarms." Novak stopped and looked down at Earl. "I've done research. To take a big bank means men, cars, a hideout, guns, explosives—so the profit, if there is any, goes into overhead. You following this?"

Earl nodded slowly. "Yes, I guess so."

"With a friendly little bank in a country town, most of the problems disappear. That's what we're going after—a small, friendly bank that has one fat guard, and two middle-aged female tellers. The take should be good—around two hundred grand. There's four of us in the deal, and the split is four ways. How's your arithmetic, Earl?" Novak put the cigar in his mouth. "Can you divide four into two hundred thousand?"

"Fifty grand apiece?"

Novak patted his shoulder. "On the button."

"It seems like a lot of cash for a small bank," Earl said.

"It's there, don't worry," Novak said. "This is a wealthy community, with lots of classy people around. And it's got a business and industrial side to it—supermarkets, a canning factory, a couple of dozen wholesale mushroom houses. The bank stays open Friday nights from six to eight. Most of the factories pay their workers on Saturday, so the bank is loaded with payroll cash and the weekend deposits from the big stores and shops." Novak paused for effect. "When the bank closes there's close to two hundred thousand bucks in untraceable cash sitting in the tellers' cages. A half-dozen clerks stick around for another hour or so straightening out the books. One sleepy old guard is all that's standing between us and that dough. So what do you say? You want your share of it?"

Earl shifted in his chair. "Well, I don't know."

"I've spent weeks checking the area," Novak said. "I've figured out a foolproof plan—how to get into the bank, get the money, and get the hell away free and clear. There's no guesswork involved. It's a solid deal." He paused, frowning at Earl. "So?"

"It's your turn to talk," Burke said.

"Well—it's a big decision to make in a hurry," Earl said.

"Take your time," Novak said. "Burke, freshen up his drink."

"I've never been in on anything like this before," Earl said, trying to smile.

"Well, here's a chance to move up to the majors," Burke said. "Let me have your glass."

"Thanks." He was glad to have this immediate pressure taken off; he had always hated decisions. They worked up a tension in him, made him confused and angry and miserable. That was one nice thing about the Army, he thought, almost wistfully; someone else was paid to do the thinking. But now it was up to him to make the plans and give the orders. It had seemed simple this morning. Novak had a job for him—that was all. There might be something wrong with it, but what the hell? You couldn't pick and choose forever. Grab it, that had been his first cheerful reaction. Take any chance to get off the treadmill. . . .

That had seemed logical and inevitable. But now he wasn't sure of anything at all. . . .

"Well?" Novak said. "What's the verdict?"

"Damn, I don't know." Earl searched through his pockets for cigarettes, while Novak watched him with an irritable frown. "So what's worrying you?" he said.

"I don't know enough about the deal," Earl said, puffing nervously on his cigarette. With a surge of relief he remembered something; Burke had said it would be a four-way split. "Who's the other guy?" he said. "You said there's to be four in on it. I got to know something about the other guy."

"If you buy in, you'll meet him tomorrow," Novak said. "He's all right. He fits the job like a glove."

"Like a black suède glove," Burke said, laughing softly.

Earl felt that he was being hounded into a corner. "Can he keep his mouth shut? I mean, is he a dependable guy? I don't want to get mixed up with any clowns." He realized that he sounded frightened and foolish, and that brought a surge of color into his cheeks. "I can handle my end of things but I want to know who's backing me up. It's like the Army—you've got to be sure of every man in the platoon."

Novak said quietly, "I told you he's okay. That means he's okay. All you got to do is nod or shake your head. In or out. Understand?"

"Well, I can't make up my mind this fast," Earl said. He put out his cigarette, relieved to have postponed his decision; he wanted to get out of here now, get away from all this crowding, insistent pressure. "I'll call you tomorrow. Is that okay?"

"No, it's not okay," Burke said. He came to his feet, rubbing his big hands together slowly. "We want to know how you stand now. Not after you've talked it over with your girl and the parish priest."

Earl looked at him steadily for a moment. He wasn't conscious of coming to a decision but he suddenly knew what he was going to do: tell Novak to go to hell and knock this big rummy, Burke, flat on his tail. But before he could move, Novak put a hand on his shoulder and said easily, "Another day won't matter, Earl. It's okay. Call me first thing in the morning."

"Okay," Earl said. "Sure." The anger drained out of him and he nodded slowly. "I'll give you a call, don't worry." He felt grateful to Novak for making this concession to him; it made him feel important. "Thanks a lot."

After he had gone Novak and Burke regarded each other for a few seconds in a curious silence. Finally Burke smiled and began to make himself a drink. "Just what we need," he said. "A hillbilly full of temperament. To give the job a little tone."

"I think he'll do," Novak said. He picked up his glass and frowned at the bubbles on the surface of the liquor. "He's dumb as hell, but he'll do. Once he comes in, he'll stick."

"I don't know," Burke said. "He strikes me as trouble. I was a cop long enough to recognize the type. They're like ticking bombs." He shrugged his big, soft-looking shoulders and settled himself in a chair. "They go off in your face and you never know what hit you. I was a cop long enough to see it happen lots of times."

"You weren't a cop long enough to collect your pension," Novak said dryly.

"Okay, so I was canned," Burke said. "You want to say it, go ahead. That make you feel better?"

"I feel fine," Novak said, walking over to the window. For a few seconds he stared at the dark skyline and the sliver of moon that was emerging from behind the tall bulk of an office building.

"I'll bet he won't call you," Burke said. "Two to one he won't come in."

Novak shook his head. "I wouldn't take your money. He's hooked. Hooked solid."

CHAPTER TWO

AFTER LEAVING Novak's hotel Earl wandered aimlessly through the crowded streets for an hour or so, bored by his loneliness and irritated by the noise of the city, but reluctant to return to the empty apartment. Lorraine wouldn't be home for a couple of hours yet, and he was in no mood to sit around by himself and watch television. She might even be later tonight, he thought; now that he had some news for a change she'd probably get tied up for an extra hour or so. She ran the fountain and lunch counter in a large chain drugstore, and there were always details to keep her from getting away at anywhere near her normal quitting time. He understood this, of course; she had explained to him often enough. But it still irritated him. Particularly on a night when he had some news. . . .

She was good at her job, Earl knew. And it was a big one. The counter served a couple of thousand meals a day, along with the hour-by-hour Coke and coffee trade. The profit margin was small, and she had to watch everything like a hawk to keep the operation in the black. She always brought home figures and reports; the big thing, she'd explained several times, was to watch wholesale food prices and then put items on the menu that would return an extra penny or two in seasonal profits. That was the big trick. But there was more to her job than that; she also supervised six waitresses, a short-order cook, a couple of sandwich men and the girls on the cash register. She was quite a girl, he thought. Smarter than lots of men.

Finally he grew weary of his pointless drifting and turned off the avenue into a street that would take him back to his own neighborhood. He and Lorraine had a three-room furnished apartment in an old brownstone house. Lorraine had done the place to a turn, painting and waxing the floors, putting in her own furniture, and even rewiring some of the connections and replacing the fixtures in the bathroom. Earl had felt she was wasting her money, squandering it on something she didn't own; they'd clear out, he had told her, and the owners would have the benefit of her hard work and cash. But he had to admit she'd done a nice job; with the high ceilings and tall, old-fashioned windows, the place had a nice peaceful feeling to it.

At the entrance, he hesitated glancing at his watch—seven thirty. She wouldn't be home for another hour or so anyway, he thought, frowning at the dark windows of their apartment.

The wind was colder now and he could hear it twisting with a clawing sound through the black trees along the block. He pulled the collar of his coat up about his neck and shifted his weight from one foot to another, wondering what to do with himself until Lorraine got home. He didn't think about Novak's offer; he had unconsciously put that from his mind. It could wait. This was a trick of his with decisions; simply let them wait.

He started walking toward the red neon sign of the little tavern at the corner. Lorraine didn't like him to hang around there, but what the hell, he thought. It was a warm and friendly place and the regular customers were nice guys. Lorraine didn't mind a drink or two but she didn't like the idea of his sitting around bars in the daytime. She was right, of course; a guy his age should outgrow this sort of thing.

But there were times when a man needed a hangout, a place he could get away from things and feel at home. Like a noncoms club, he thought. Where you knew everybody and had your own chair and butt can. He felt expectant and cheerful as he hung his long overcoat on the post of a wooden booth, and took one of the stools at the bar. The bartender, a big, balding man named Mac, said "How goes it?" and "What'll it be?" with the same inflection and Earl asked him for a beer with a shot of rye on the side.

The barroom was warm and noisy, and the bright overhead lights were softened by layers of blue tobacco smoke drifting through the air. There were wooden booths along one wall, and an area in the rear with dart games and a couple of tables. Mac, the bartender, stood with his back to a wide mirror, which was flanked by orderly arrangements of whisky bottles standing on shiny aluminum shelves. Earl looked at himself in the mirror, studying his hard even features and the shadows drawn under his eyes by the lights above his head.

He felt warm and cheerful, with the beaded whisky glinting in the shot glass, and his cigarettes and change neatly arranged on the brown wooden bar. There were a number of cardboard signs pasted to the mirror, and he read them carefully, a little grin softening the hard line of his mouth. They were pretty damned good. *CREDIT IS DEAD—KILLED BY BAD DEBT*. You can say that again, he thought. And there was a new one that almost made him laugh out loud. It read: *PLEASE TELL US YOUR TROUBLES. WE'RE MAKING A LIST FOR THE CHAPLAIN.* That was all right, he decided, raising the shot glass to his lips. He hesitated an instant, the ritualistic pause of the straight-shot drinker, then emptied the cold liquor into his mouth with a quick flip of his fingers. He let out his breath slowly and pleasurably, feeling the heat of the whisky spreading out from his stomach and filling him with the promise of adventure and excitement. A sip of cold beer intensified the sensation and set up a dry, prickling demand in his throat.

"Do that again, eh, Mac?" he said, pushing the glass toward him with one finger. "Another nip, eh?"

"Sure thing," Mac said, taking the bottle of rye down from a shelf. He poured the drink, collected for it, and replaced the bottle. "Getting colder, I think," he said, glancing at the plate-glass window.

"You know, I was thinking that, too," Earl said. "I noticed it myself."

The men at the other end of the bar called for a round, and Mac went down to take their orders. Earl made a little circle on the bar with his shot glass, wondering how it was with some guys about names. Mac, for instance, he thought. Mac knew his name was Earl, but he never said, "Sure thing, Earl" or "What'll it be, Earl?" It was funny. It was probably because Mac knew him. As simple as that. No need to say "Sure thing, Earl" because they knew each other pretty well.

He glanced down toward the end of the bar, and caught the eye of a man he'd seen in here before.

"How's it going?" he said, raising his glass with a tentative little grin. "Long time no see, eh?"

"That's right," the man said.

"I've been pretty busy," Earl said, turning sideways on his stool. "But this afternoon seemed like a good time to hoist a few. You had the same idea, I guess."

"Yeah, that's right." The man nodded at him, smiling a bit blankly and then turned back to his friends.

One of them was a soldier, Earl saw, a stocky man with short-cropped blond hair and a healthy cheerful face. He had taken off his blouse and pulled down his tie, and Earl could see that he was the sort you'd want in a platoon, a sturdy, powerhouse of a youngster, with no sneakiness in his clear eyes and wide face. Looked like a krauthead, he thought; a good weapons man. Probably knew how to handle tools. Fix any damn thing that went on the blink. Wouldn't sit around wailing for a headquarters technician to come out and put things right.

The other three men were paying a lot of attention to him, buying the drinks and laughing at everything he said. Probably a nephew or a kid brother, he thought; in on furlough to show off his corporal's stripes.

Earl turned back to the bar and toyed with his second drink. The trouble with the Army, he thought, was that guys were just trained for one job. That was okay under ordinary circumstances, but in combat you couldn't wait for an HQ man. You had to be your own mechanic, your own map-maker, your own supply sergeant.

One night long ago a good idea had struck him; he had decided to write a memorandum to his old commanding officer and list all the things he had found wrong with the Army. Not just a gripe sheet but serious recommendations that might save a kid's life in combat. His old CO would see that they got up to where they could do some good—that had been Earl's idea. He had worked all night on it, he remembered, sitting in a little furnished room and covering page after page with things he wanted his old CO to know about; if men with experience didn't speak up, he had thought, how could you expect things to get any better? But after a long time he began to realize that he was missing the point; he knew what he wanted to say but he couldn't put it down right. It turned into a gripe list after all; a bunch of bitches for the chaplain.

He glanced at the sign on the mirror: *PLEASE TELL US YOUR TROUBLES. WE'RE MAKING A LIST FOR THE CHAPLAIN.* Earl smiled faintly but he felt depressed and weary; for some reason his mood of confident good humor had evaporated. What ever happened to the list, he wondered. It had kicked around in his things for quite a while, and then it must have got lost or thrown away.

The soldier boy and one of his friends were playing a wrestling game, he saw from the corner of his eye. They stood facing each other expectantly, hands swinging loosely at their sides. The other two men had taken their drinks from the bar and stepped out of their way.

"Now throw a punch at my head," the young soldier

said, smiling easily, his weight balanced on the balls of his feet. "Go ahead, let one fly."

The man facing him was smiling, too; he was inches taller than the soldier and thirty pounds heavier, a cheerful-looking man with big, bony hands hanging down from the sleeves of a well-worn suède jacket. "You're sure you got this stuff down pat now," he said. "I don't want to clout you by mistake."

"Don't worry about that," the soldier said. "We spent weeks on this in camp. It doesn't make any difference how big a guy is, really. It's just a question of leverage. Go ahead and swing. I'll show you how it works."

"With either hand?" the big man said.

"It doesn't make any difference," the soldier said, crouching slightly, and letting his arms swing out from his body. "Go ahead, Jerry."

"Okay," the man said doubtfully.

Earl had turned on his stool to watch them, a hand toying with the shot glass and a skeptical smile touching his lips.

The big man set himself and threw a clumsy, looping right at the soldier's head, but it didn't land; the soldier blocked it with his forearm, then twisted the man's arm quickly and forced him down to his knees. "You see?" he said, panting a little and holding the man on the floor. "See how it works?"

"That's damned good," one of the other men said, and the soldier flushed with pleasure. "Well, it's just leverage, like I told you." He released his grip, and the big man got to his feet, grinning and rubbing his arm.

"That's quite a trick," he said. "And it's worth a drink any day."

Earl finished his second drink and wiped his mouth with the back of his hand. "That stuff is nothing but a lot of crap," he said, smiling at the soldier. "Believe me, I know." He hadn't meant to say anything at all, but a frustrating and angry loneliness had forced him to speak; and now his words hung awkwardly in the silence, and the soldier, after a puzzled look at his friends, stared down the bar at him with a tense little frown on his face.

"You know a lot about it, eh?" he said. "Maybe you'd like to show me how much you know."

"Now let's just drink our drinks," the bartender said gently.

"Well, where does he get off at?" the soldier said. "Where does he get off saying it's a lot of crap?"

Earl managed a smile. He had just wanted to be part of the conversation, but it had all gone wrong. "I didn't mean any offense, kid," he said. "But that tricky stuff gets you thinking only about defense. You let the other guy lead. But you get a platoon thinking that way and they're in trouble. Know what I mean?"

The soldier laughed a little. "Do you?" he said.

"Sure, sure," Earl said quickly, eager for the chance to explain himself and set things right. "It's a defensive thing, that's what I mean. You lay back waiting to get hit. The payoff goes to the attack, get me?"

"So let's drink up," the bartender said. "Down the hatch, everybody."

"You're talking about something else," the soldier said, still staring at Earl. "Pentagon stuff, the big strategy. Me, I'm just a corporal."

"Well, maybe I sounded like a wise guy," Earl said. "That wasn't what I meant, kid."

"If you think this judo is phony, I can teach you otherwise," the soldier said. He was pushing it a little now, cocky and tough, savoring the respectful silence of his friends. "Come on down here a second," he said. "Come on, I won't hurt you."

"No, I got to get going," Earl said, trying to laugh it off.

"Hell, don't be in a hurry." The soldier grinned and held out his arms. "Come to Papa. Papa won't spank."

Earl's mood changed; he stared at the youngster for a few seconds, feeling a bitter, confusing anger ripping through him. Why didn't they teach these guys something before turning them loose, he thought. Here was something else the Army should know about. Young punks with two weeks of judo acting tough in barrooms. Getting the idea they were killers because they could show off a trick hold to their friends. Parlor commandos. . . . "Listen, kid," he said, standing and walking down the bar slowly. "Just listen, will you? I can tell you something for your own good if you'll listen. The punch your buddy threw wouldn't knock the hat off an eighty-year-old grandmother. Don't you realize that?"

"Well, you throw one," the soldier said; but some of the hardness left his face. He saw the power in the way Earl moved and he saw something in Earl's eyes that made his throat go dry and tight.

"Now relax, you guys," the bartender said. "What's the sense of getting yourselves all stirred up?"

"Let him throw one," the soldier said, swinging his arms out from his body and going down in a little crouch. "Go ahead, let him!"

A good kid, Earl thought; he didn't scare worth a damn. He felt suddenly warm and protective toward him; this one would be okay, he thought. He was worth teaching. . . . Grinning tightly, he said, "When you fight for real, you don't play by the Book—always remember that."

He dropped his left shoulder and snapped a hook at the boy's head. But he stopped the punch instantly, as the soldier moved to block it. For an instant Earl checked himself, seeing the sudden fear and comprehension in the boy's face. He was wide open and he knew it, suckered out of position by the feint. Earl didn't mean to hit him; a token tap would have proved his point. But the confusing anger shook him suddenly, and he pulled the trigger on the punch, snapping it into the boy's unguarded stomach with the power of a mule kick behind it.

The soldier went down, gasping in pain, his feet kicking spasmodically, his mouth opening and closing as he gulped for air.

"For Christ's sake," one of the men said hoarsely.

"He's not hurt," Earl said, wetting his lips. "He's just out of wind." His hands hung limply at his sides, and a hot shame ran through him; the three men were staring at him as if he were something dirty. "Look, he's all right," he said, as the soldier worked himself up to a sitting position. "Here, I'll give you a hand, kid. Just walk a little, that'll help."

But the man in the suède jacket pushed him away. "Never mind, you helped him enough."

"I didn't mean to hurt him."

"Okay, okay," the man said. "Why don't you go back and finish your drink?"

"I was just showing him something for his own good."

"Go finish your drink. Forget it."

The three men helped the boy into a booth. He put his head on his arms, and cried in a low, strangling voice, "Tell him not to go away, hear? Tell him, will you? I'll be okay in a second. I'll fix him."

"Sure," one of his friends said, rubbing his shoulders gently with the palm of his hand. "He caught you with a low one. Don't you worry, kid."

Earl walked slowly back to his stool, his whole body burning with shame. Why had he done it? Why had he hit him like that? He picked up his change with fingers that trembled helplessly, and then got into his old black overcoat. "I was just trying to show him something," he said to the bartender.

Mac looked at him steadily. "You showed him," he said.

"I just wanted to show him, that's all. It's something he should know, damn it."

"Sure," Mac nodded slowly. "He's nineteen years old. A big hero on his furlough. You showed him all right, Earl."

"Well, for Christ's sake," Earl said helplessly. "Tell him—tell him I'm sorry. Okay? Tell him, will you?"

"Sure, Earl. I'll tell him."

Outside Earl walked quickly through the darkness, the wind bitterly cold against his hot cheeks. Halfway down the block he stopped and looked back at the warm red neon sign that hung above the tavern. He stared at it for a few seconds, his arms limp at his sides, and then he rubbed the back of his hand roughly over his mouth and started for home.

CHAPTER THREE

In the apartment Earl snapped on the lights and the television set, and then walked up and down the floor for a while, rubbing his big hands together slowly. Well, to hell with it, he thought. That was all you could say sometimes—to hell with it. He didn't know why things went wrong with him, but worrying about it didn't help any; he knew that much at least.

Shrugging, he settled himself on the couch, lighted a cigarette and put his feet up on the coffee table. The apartment as usual was neat as a pin; Lorraine whipped everything into shape before she left for work. Against one wall stood a small white bar decorated with drink recipes in crooked black letters, and topped with cocktail glasses on wicker coasters. A coffee table and ottoman faced the television set during the day but at night these were moved aside to make room for their pull-out sofa. Lorraine had installed a small light over her side of the bed so that she could work nights on her figures and reports; this was a compromise for his benefit because he liked to watch the late TV shows in the drowsy semidarkness. They spent a lot of evenings that way, Lorraine working with cream shining on her face, and Earl smoking and watching the old movies flickering across the screen.

Now, as the set cleared, he sat up expectantly; he liked the children's shows that came on at this hour. The crazy antics of the little animated figures usually prodded him out of a depression that settled on him as night approached; for some reason he disliked the look of darkness pressing against the windows. The lights in nearby houses and the silhouettes of people against drawn curtains always filled him with a restless and bitter loneliness.

Usually the cartoons were an antidote against this mood. He had a warm feeling toward the announcer on the show, a brash and boyish-looking young man, who wore bow ties and chattered in a silly, funny way to his audience. His name was Danny Doodle, and he pretended to get mixed up during the commercials, saying things such as, "Use your doodle, and listen to your old friend, Danny Noodle, I mean Danny *Doodle,* and tell your nice moodle, I mean your nice *mother,* to use her doodle, her *noodle,* for Heaven's *sakes,* and buy some of those doodley delicious oatmeal wafers the first doodle in the morning . . ." Earl usually found the program good for a lot of laughs. But tonight was different; there was a black patch of anxiety in his mind that refused to be driven away by Danny Doodle's lighthearted nonsense. Finally he got up irritably and snapped off the set. As he watched blackness spread over the screen he realized that a similar thing was happening in his mind; the black patch of anxiety on the edge of his thoughts grew larger and larger until it finally flooded everything else from his consciousness. Novak, he thought, pacing the floor slowly, his body coiling and tense—that was the heart of the blackness. What to do about the offer? How to figure the deal. . . .

He couldn't pin down precisely what was bothering him; but this was a familiar frustration, this inability to isolate and analyze his problems. He was caught in a welter of vague, confusing fears, and the struggle to fight his way free tightened the bonds; his nerves strained and the pressure grew within him as he attempted to think himself toward a logical decision.

It wasn't the money. Fifty thousand dollars. It was an abstract, meaningless sum to him. He had no need for it. So why take a chance? He lived here for nothing. Everything taken care of. Clothes, food, even spending money, ten bucks on the dot every Monday morning. You never had it so good, he thought. You found a home. . . . The old Army taunts stung him. He had to get out; he'd always known that. He couldn't live here like a pet cat. It was time for him to do something for Lorraine. Marry her, get a regular job and make a regular home. But it wasn't just getting out of this deal. It was more than that. It was being important again. . . .

Why in the hell was he thinking about the Army so much, he wondered, his eyes flicking to the uniformed picture of himself that Lorraine had hung on the wall. The Army was no bargain. He frowned at the picture, a tinted, blownup snapshot a buddy of his had taken near Antwerp. Not much change over the years. Same weight, same shape. Lorraine liked the picture, he figured, or she wouldn't have spent eighteen dollars for a fancy silver frame. She was funny about money; she'd complain about a light bill or something, and then turn around and spend ten or twelve bucks for dinner and a few drinks at some fancy restaurant on Saturday night.

He wandered into the kitchen and looked at the clock. She should be along pretty soon. Unless something came up, of course. And trust Mr. Poole to think of something. Poole, the boss, treated the store as if it was some fabulous dame, hanging around as if he couldn't get enough of the place. Always stewing and worrying about it: why wasn't the tuna-fish sandwich special selling, and who forgot to put up the new display cards, and why the drug business was off . . . yakkity-yak, Earl thought, grinning a little as he thought of how Lorraine mimicked Poole sometimes.

On the chance that she'd be on time, he began to get dinner ready, taking three fat pork chops from the icebox, and then peeling a half-dozen potatoes and dropping them into a saucepan of salted water. She would bring the things for salad. Salad was her department. She was always quoting the stuff she got from promotion booklets sent to the store by food growers. "It's the best nourishment there is for your hair and skin," she told him frequently. To him it was just rabbit food.

After everything was set out for their dinner, he took a long shower, standing limp under the needle spray and letting the water drive against his shoulders and rush down his lean body. Drying himself he looked critically at his arms and waist; still in good shape, he thought, though his only exercise was trotting down to the corner delicatessen for late sandwiches and beer. He didn't look old—not much older than the young soldier at the bar, he decided. With water glinting in his coarse black hair, and his eyes dark against his tanned face, he could pass for a guy in his middle or late twenties maybe. An athlete, that's what you'd take him for. . . . His body was brown and hard, padded with springy and deceptively flat muscles. The bullet wound in his shoulder and the shrapnel scar on his leg had faded over the years; they had been angry-looking for a long time, but now they were almost lost in the surrounding flesh.

He put on faded khaki slacks and loafers, his mood cheerful and confident again; even counting delays, she'd be along any minute. With a drink and a cigarette he stretched out on the couch, savoring the cleanness of his bare arms and shoulders and the interacting pleasures of alcohol and nicotine. But as the minutes dragged on and on, he began to get restless; damn Poole, he thought furiously.

He got up and looked at the clock, trying to banish the fears and worries that picked at his composure. It was nine thirty then; but still she didn't come. It wasn't until after ten that he heard her key in the door, and by then his mood had sunk to a level of flat and bitter indifference.

When she came in he looked at her and said, "What the hell kept you? It's after ten, do you realize that?"

"I know, I know," she said a bit breathlessly. She gave him a quick hug, and then hurried into the kitchen without bothering to take off her coat. "It was a rat race all day long. Big shots from the home office snooping around, a row with Eddie over his wisecracking with customers, and then a session with Poole on the Friday menus." Her eyes flicked around the kitchen as she talked, checking the pork chops, the two neatly set trays, the saucepan full of peeled potatoes. "You must be starved, honey."

"I could eat," he said, as he freshened his drink at the bar. "I had a pretty busy day, too, you know."

She turned and looked at him for an instant in silence, her eyes wide and dark. "I'm sure you did," she said, speaking in a careful voice. "What did Mr. Novak want?"

"Novak?" Earl lifted his shoulders in a careless shrug. "He's got a job for me, that's all."

"What kind of a job?"

"Well, we just talked things over in general terms. Feeling each other out, I guess you'd call it."

She took a tentative step toward him, one hand moving to her throat. "Earl," she said, watching his face anxiously. "Novak—he's a friend of Lefty Bowers, isn't he?"

"I told you that this morning."

"And you knew Bowers in jail, didn't you?"

"Look, cut out the Mr. District Attorney routine," he said, smiling a little. "Yeah, I knew Bowers in jail. He told Novak about me. That's all." Earl shrugged and took a sip from his drink. "It's how things work sometimes. You know, contacts; a guy puts in a good word for a friend. It's the way the business world operates."

"What did Novak want with you? Why did he call you?"

"Lory, you're getting yourself worked up about nothing. I told you, he offered me a job. If I was taking it I'd tell you all about it, naturally. But I'm thinking it over. So there's nothing to talk about."

She turned away, sighing. "Would you fix me a drink?" she said.

"Come on. Cheer up. What do you want?"

"Something on the rocks. With a little water." She sighed again but this time she smiled faintly. "It's nice to be home, anyway. I'll freshen up a bit while you fix the drinks. We can talk about everything after dinner."

"Sure, that's the ticket."

She hurried off, but called back from the bathroom, "Earl! Did you pick up my gray dress from the cleaners? I left you a note about it on the television."

He glanced at the set; there was a note there all right, propped up against a cigarette box. "I didn't see it," he said. "Sorry."

"Oh, damn! Well, there'll be time in the morning." The bathroom closed on the last of the sentence, and the shower began to run. Earl shrugged and went about making her drink. She always needed something to worry about, he thought. There was a sense of urgency about everything she did, a kind of high physical tension that charged her with mettlesome excitement. That had been the thing that attracted him at first, the reason he had made himself start a conversation with her at the drug store. . . . When was that? A year or so ago, anyway. She was just average-looking, with a wide, pale face and black shoulder-length hair, but her high-strung, responsive-looking body had been a real challenge; he had wanted to know her tensions directly and intimately, to calm her down, and gentle her with his own hard needs.

He had been prepared for an explosion; that was the way she looked, desperate for some kind of release. But he learned that she never hit very high peaks of emotion; the sense of quivering excitement wasn't an act, but it was fed by any damned thing that came along. A world war or a World Series, it wouldn't make any difference to Lorraine, he thought, grinning a little.

When she came out of the bathroom she frowned at her drink and said, "This looks pretty strong. Did you put any water in it?"

"A little."

"It looks strong. Do we need any whisky, by the way? I saw some bourbon today that looked like a real buy. Six years old, four dollars and nine cents a fifth. That's pretty good, isn't it?"

"You can't go wrong at that price."

"I'll get a couple of bottles tomorrow." She had put on slacks and a blue cashmere sweater, and tied her long hair back in a pony tail; in the soft and flattering light she might have passed for a young girl. "Do you want some cheese and crackers?" she said. "It's going to take some time for the potatoes to cook."

"No, I'm fine."

She talked to him as she puttered in the kitchen. "Did you see the story about those high-school boys in the auto wreck? I can't imagine why they give driving licenses to lunatics like that. Two of them were killed—one of the boys' fathers is president of the Atlas Packing Company. I don't suppose his money is any comfort to him tonight."

"I guess not," Earl said.

He stretched out on the sofa, as Lory flitted irrelevantly

from topic to topic, her voice holding no more significance for him than the clink of utensils and the crackling of the heating frying pan. Finally she came in with her drink and sat beside him on the sofa. He was staring at the ceiling, thinking of his own problems; he was hardly conscious of the light weight of her hips against his side.

She rubbed the palm of her hand slowly over his bare chest. "What's the matter with you?" she asked him.

"Nothing. I'm okay."

"How's your drink?"

"It's okay. Everything's fine, Lory." He saw that she was all tightened up; a pulse was pounding in her throat, and her hands were unsteady as she lighted a cigarette. "Tell me what Novak wanted," she demanded suddenly. "Please tell me, Earl. Please. It isn't fair to make me worry like this."

"There's nothing to tell," he said, his voice sharpening with irritation. "He offered me a job. I don't know whether I want any part of it. So relax, for God's sake."

"It's something crooked, isn't it? You wouldn't be acting like this if it weren't." She shook her head quickly, her eyes bright and cold with fear. "Don't do this to me, Earl. Please. I feel you're heading for trouble. It's like a weight crushing me so I can't breathe. I can't think of anything else."

"Except Friday's menu and Eddie's wisecracking with customers," he said impatiently. "Stop working yourself up, Lory. This thing can't hurt you, no matter which way it goes. You got nothing to worry about."

She looked at him for a moment in silence, and then stood and went quietly into the kitchen. He heard her take the frying pan from the stove and switch off the burner. When she returned and turned out the lights in the living room he knew from the sound of her footsteps that she had slipped off her loafers. "How could you say that?" she said; her voice was trembling, and when she snuggled down beside him he felt her tears on his bare shoulders. "I'd die if anything happened to you—don't you know that?"

"Sure, Lory," he said, sighing. "Sure."

"We don't need anything from anybody," she said. "We've got all we need, a home for just you and me. Don't do what

Novak wants, Earl. Promise me that, honey!" She was whispering the words against his chest, but a thread of fierce and desperate determination ran through her soft voice. "Will you promise me, Earl?"

He felt a faint desire for her; the darkness and the whisky, and the soft fragrance of her body wrapped themselves around him warmly and excitingly, tempting him to forget Novak, to forget everything but the easy, convenient pleasure she was offering him. But his need wasn't enough to counterbalance his irritation; he knew she was just using her body as part of the locks and bars of her quilted little prison. Forget Novak, forget everything and sink back into oblivion with her—that's all she wanted. But he couldn't work up any anger, either; he understood her needs, and there was pity mixed with his exasperation.

"I guess I'll fix up my drink," he said.

Her fingers stopped moving on his chest. For a moment or so she was silent, breathing slowly and quietly. Then she said, "Will you make me one, too?"

Earl sat up and lifted himself over her, feeling guilty but relieved to be away from the insistent demands of her body. He made two drinks, then snapped on the lamp at the foot of the sofa and began looking for cigarettes. There was a pack in his pocket, but he needed an excuse for turning on the lights.

"There's some on the coffee table," she said.

"Oh, yeah. Thanks."

She had stretched out with her arms above her head. The position flattened her stomach and lifted her breasts into sharp little cones beneath the blue sweater. She smiled at him, her eyes soft and quiet. "That light's awfully bright," she said.

Earl sat down on the ottoman in front of the television set and lighted a cigarette. He didn't want her, and he wished to God she'd cut out the sales pitch. He hadn't wanted her for a long time, he thought with a stir of anger. He was just a damned stud, just doing a job.

"I'm getting hungry," he said. "Don't you think we'd better get dinner started?"

"All right." She went into the kitchen and snapped on the light. He tried to think of something to say that might take her mind off her hurt feelings. "Those pork chops all right? I told Meyers what you said about the ones he gave me last week."

"They're just beautiful." The enthusiasm in her voice was genuine; she was inspecting the chops with critical pleasure. "Just enough fat on them and they're thick enough for a change." She put the frying pan back on the stove with a brisk clatter. "You'll see the difference."

He shook his head and sipped his drink. Lorraine turned on the burner, then stepped into her loafers and came into the living room with her drink. For a few seconds she stood looking down at him, analyzing the worried frown on his face. "Honey, listen to me," she said. "Will you listen to me without getting mad or upset?"

"Sure, sure," he said. "I'm not some wild dog you have to tiptoe around. I can listen. What do you want to say?"

She knelt beside him and pressed one of his hands tightly against her breast. "You know I love you, Earl. Don't you know that?"

"Sure, honey." He felt smothered and trapped, but the yielding, supplicant position of her body brought a strange constriction to his throat; he touched her smooth hair awkwardly. "Yes, Lory, I know that. It's—it's important to me."

"You know that I wouldn't lie to you—that I wouldn't tell you anything that wasn't for your own good. Don't you know that?"

"Sure," he said. "I know that."

She tightened her grip on his hand, staring at him with wide, anxious eyes. "If you do something crooked, everything we mean to each other will be ruined. Because you'll keep going crooked once you start. And sooner or later they'll catch you."

"Not with Novak running things," he said, feeling a sudden loyalty toward Novak swelling in his body. "He's smart, Lory. All I got to do is follow orders. And this job is so big I'll never need anything else."

"What is it?" she said, whimpering the words in a trembling little voice. "For God's sake, what does he want you to do, Earl? Why did he pick on you? Why couldn't he leave you alone?"

"Look, he's giving me a chance, if you'd only see it that way. He could have picked a dozen other guys. He's a big operator, Lory. But he picked me." Earl jabbed a thumb at his chest. "Me, a nothing, a guy without even a job. And he's giving me a chance. While all you do is whine about yourself. Why don't you think about me for a change? I'm nothing, don't you understand?" The words came out in a thick, bitter rush and he jerked his hand away from her and began to pace the floor, his anger and frustration swelling and pounding for release. "I grew up in a shack on three dirt acres. Does that tell you anything? We lived like niggers. We lived right beside 'em, in the same kind of a shack, eating the same stinking food, and wearing the same rotten clothes. And my old man tied me up and beat me like a dog for playing with them when I was a kid and didn't know any better." He shook his fists in her white scared face, furious with the need to make her understand. "Can't you see? Can't you get it? There was nothing, no toilet, no furniture, nothing at all. That's what I came from, Lory." He rubbed his forehead, feeling the dry, bitter taste of shame in his mouth. "That's what I was, Lory. Let me tell you something. Once I saw a picture of a harmonica in a catalogue. It cost ninety-five cents. I decided I was going to own that harmonica. Nothing would stop me. I saved two years. And you know the closest I ever came? Fifty-two cents. That was the closest I ever got, Lory." He let his big hands fall to his sides. "Fifty-two cents. I didn't make it, Lory."

"But lots of people have it hard starting out," she said uncertainly; she was confused by the intensity of his outburst. "I didn't even get to finish high school, you know."

"Sure, you had it tough," he said wearily. "Everybody did, I guess. But maybe I had it tough in a special kind of way. I lied about my age to get into the Army—well, I would have lied to get into hell. Anything was better than that shack."

"That's all past now. If you'd settle down to a job—you could be anything you wanted."

"With my record? Bosses love that. They start sweating if they see you within six feet of the cash register." He pounded a fist into his palm. "Two jail stretches for nothing. If I go up again it's going to be for something, I promise you."

"Lots of companies would give you a chance. You won't let them, that's all."

"Yeah, yeah," he said, mocking her with his tone; his anger dissolved into a sullen futility as he realized that he couldn't make her understand. "Why in hell should I let them pry into me? Would you like some fat bastard wrinkling his nose at you while you say, 'Yes, sir, I've been a bad boy, but they taught me my lesson and you can kick me in the tail if I get out of line.'" He chopped impatiently at the air with his hand. "No, Lory, no! I can't take that stuff."

"You're just thinking about yourself," she said, beginning to cry. "You're not thinking about me."

"Oh, for God's sake," he muttered, rubbing both hands through his hair. "Let's forget it. Let's forget it, in the name of sweet Jesus Christ."

She got quickly to her feet, brushing at her tears with the backs of her hands. "We can't forget it, Earl. Listen to me—please listen to me for just one more minute." She put her arms around him, and when he stiffened against the pressure of her body she only clung to him more fiercely. "Let's go away, Earl," she said, in a desperate whisper. "I've got time coming at the store. Two full weeks. You remember the lodge we went to last spring? We could drive up tomorrow. You loved it there, didn't you, Earl? You loved it. I know you did."

"Yeah, it was nice," he said slowly. It had been a fine time; clean air and walks through the woods, a good, healthy time.

"We could get the same cabin," she said smiling quickly as she felt the tension easing in his body. "We could broil steaks and sit around the fire at night. Remember Tony, the fellow at the hotel you used to chop wood with? Well, you could see him again. Please, please, Earl. Let's go away."

"Well, it seems kind of childish," he said rubbing a hand over his short black hair. "I mean, just pulling out without any plans or anything."

"Let's do it that way, Earl. Please, please. Let's just pack and leave."

"I don't know," he said. "Poole won't like it."

"I don't care, I don't care about him. Don't say any more about it. You're starved, and it's my fault. You need food." She laughed and hugged him tightly. "You're too big for your own good, that's your trouble."

As she turned toward the kitchen the front doorbell rang, and she hesitated, glancing at Earl with a frown. "Now who could that be?"

"Well, you'd better see."

Lory dabbed at her eyes as she hurried across the room. "What a time to bother people," she murmured under her breath. "It's probably something that would wait until tomorrow morning as likely as not." When she opened the door Earl saw Margie McMillin's blond head shining in the dim hallway light. He sighed and lighted a cigarette. Margie lived upstairs. Lorraine got along with her fine but he could only take her in small doses; she meant well enough, but her incessant chatter ground on his nerves like a file. She came in saying, "This is a ghastly time to bother anybody, but I know you two are a pair of night owls. I knew you'd be up. Hi, Earl. How's my favorite boy friend?" She peeked into the kitchen, and clapped a hand to her forehead. "You haven't had dinner yet!"

"I got home a bit late," Lory said.

Margie grinned at Earl. "Boy, if I'd just known you were down here all alone."

"Lory was about to fix dinner," he said, hoping she'd take the hint.

"That sounds cozy," she said. "I wish Frank would get home late some nights. So we could have a real late dinner. Like the French." She struck a pose to show off her body, ripe and compact in slacks and a white silk blouse. *"Oui? Non?* How's my French, Earl? Pretty sharp?"

He was trying to control his exasperation. "What's on your mind, Margie?"

"Seriously, *very* seriously, we want to ask you to do us a big favor."

"Me?" Earl said.

"I haven't talked to Earl about it yet," Lorraine said sharply. "I'll call you in the morning, Margie."

"I'll ask him myself then," Margie said. "Don't go shaking your head at me, Lorraine. After all, it's my anniversary."

"Look, what's this all about?" Earl said.

"Just this, lambie pie." She came toward him with tiny steps, and smiled demurely into his eyes. "Frank's talked his boss into letting him have Thursday and Friday off—because it's our anniversary. Well," Margie held up her hand and counted on her fingers, "with Thursday and Friday and a little cheating on Monday, that's five full days almost."

"It sounds great," Earl said, watching her with a little frown. "You going away?"

"To Florida," she said, pretending to swoon. "Swimming, lying in the sand, dancing all night—I can't even bear thinking about it."

"Let me talk to Earl later," Lorraine said. "We haven't had dinner yet."

"I'll hurry, I promise," Margie cried. "There's one hitch, Earl. Frank's mother was coming down from Scranton to watch the baby but she wired us yesterday that she can't get here until Saturday morning. I told Lorraine about it, and she suggested—" Margie put the tip of her forefinger against his chest. "She suggested that you could help out until Frank's mother arrived."

"What do you mean?" Earl said. He looked at Lorraine. "Do you know what she's talking about?"

"I just told her I'd ask you," Lorraine said, wetting her lips. "It's no real work. The baby sleeps all day and I'd take over at night."

Margie hugged herself. "And Frank and I will take over nights in Florida," she said. "Say yes, Earl—please."

Earl smiled uncertainly. He looked at Lorraine then and the smile faded, and a little frown settled between his eyes. "You figured I could baby-sit for them, eh? Is that it?"

"I told her I'd ask you about it. They're really stuck—" She smiled anxiously. "It wouldn't hurt you, really it wouldn't. Tommy's an angelic child."

"Yes, you wouldn't know he's there half the time," Margie said. "I could show you about the formula and everything. . . ." She glanced quickly at Lorraine. "Well, I'll let you talk it over. Maybe I should have let Lory prepare you for the shock. Frank says—" The look on Earl's face brought an uneasy smile to her lips. "He says I'm always rushing in where angels fear to tread."

"That's a fresh way of putting it," Earl said. "What's he driving a truck for when he can think of sharp things like that? Why doesn't he get a job writing on television?"

"Well," Margie said, with color moving up in her cheeks, "well, that's nice, I must say."

"Now stop it, both of you," Lorraine said.

"So what's wrong with driving a truck?" Margie said. "It's a lot better than sitting around doing nothing, if you ask me."

"You're right," Earl said slowly. "Dead right."

"I'm sorry, Earl. I didn't mean to be catty. I'm sorry." She backed toward the door, trying to smile into the anger in his face. "I just thought I'd ask—because we're stuck, like Lorraine said. I've got to get back upstairs. Frank was just pouring me a beer. Good night all."

When the door closed, Lorraine said quickly, "There's nothing to be upset about—they're friends of ours. You can't blame them for asking a favor."

He stood watching her with cold, furious eyes. "That's how you figure me, eh? A baby sitter?"

"No, Earl, no. But they're neighbors, after all, and they feel— Where are you going?"

He went to the closet and pulled a sweater over his bare shoulders, then got into his black overcoat. "I've got a job, in case you're interested. I'm not available for baby-sitting."

"No, Earl, I won't let you."

He turned to her, his anger a steady, powerful support to the decision he had made. "Get yourself another bus boy," he said. He picked up the note from the top of the television set and threw it at her feet. "You want your gray dress from Berger's? Well, goddamit, go get it." His voice shook with emotion. "You want the potatoes peeled, you peel 'em. You want to baby-sit with McMillin's brat, go right ahead. But count me out, Lory." He was so angry his voice broke like that of a child trying not to cry. "What do you want of me? That's what I want to know. You want me wandering around the streets without even a bar I can go into? A bar where I'd be welcome like other guys? You want me to smile at that little whore upstairs, and change her kid's diapers while she's off in Florida with that stupid jerk of a husband of hers? Is that what you want?" His voice rose in a fury. "Is that it, Lory? Do you want to beat me into nothing? Nothing at all?"

"I just want you to stay with me," she said, shaking her head in anguish. "That's all, Earl. I swear it."

"You don't know what you want," he said, breathing heavily. "You don't know yourself, Lory. But I'm different. I know what I've got to do."

He slammed the door after him when he left, and the crash of it echoed and reverberated up and down the drafty stairways of the old house. Lorraine stood in the middle of the room with her hands pressed tightly across her mouth, staring with wide, frightened eyes at the closed door. Finally she let her arms fall to her sides. After a while she went slowly into the kitchen and put one pork chop into the smoking skillet.

CHAPTER FOUR

SHORTLY AFTER NINE the following morning, John Ingram sauntered into the lobby of Novak's hotel. He was a small and slender man in his middle thirties, neatly turned out in a pearl-gray overcoat, glossy black shoes and a light-gray, snap-brim fedora which he wore slanted at a debonair angle across his forehead. There was a dancer's rhythm in his light, sure footsteps and in the easy, balanced movements of his body. He walked as if he were listening to the strains of a military band, head back, shoulders straight and his hard leather heels clicking out a neat tempo against the tiled floor of the hotel lobby.

Ingram was a Negro; his eyes were dark brown, alert but

somewhat cautious and his skin was the color of well-creamed coffee. There was a foxy look about his small face, and a neat mustache added to the suggestion of dapper, big-city sharpness; but the over-all projection of his personality was neither shrewd nor arrogant; he seemed merry rather than clever, as if he were dressed for a masquerade party and realized his costume was an outrageous contradiction of his true station in life.

He walked briskly across the lobby and entered an empty elevator. The operator, a colored man, glanced curiously at him but said nothing. When a stout, middle-aged white woman stepped in, Ingram moved to the rear of the car and removed his hat with a punctilious flourish.

The woman pretended to ignore the gesture. She stared through Ingram and said "Seven, please" to the operator in a cool, detached voice.

Ingram, smiling broadly and obsequiously, said, "I'd lak to go to flo' ten, if you please, boy." His manner was a parody of shuffling conciliation; a defensive chuckle rippled the butter-smooth surface of his voice and the inflection of the sentence rose and fell in an apologetic croon.

The operator glanced sharply at him, a warning glint in his eyes. "What's that? Ten?"

"Thass right. Ol' ten." Ingram bobbed his head, smiling unctuously at the white woman. "Ol' big dick, thass how the gambling men call it. Ol' big dick." He laughed shrilly, slapping his hat against his thigh.

The woman stared stonily at a spot of flaking paint on the door of the car. She seemed ill at ease; spots of color had risen in her cheeks, and her lips compressed in a thin, exasperated line. When the door opened at the seventh floor she stepped out quickly, the swing of her wide hips suggesting an emotional reaction dead center between confusion and indignation.

The operator closed the door and looked around at Ingram, making no move to start the car. "Now who do you know on the tenth floor?" he asked quietly.

"Friends of my father's," Ingram said, giving him a slow, mysterious wink. "Old golfing buddies. Pappy was quite a character. Belonged to all the good clubs. Shell-Share-The-Road Club, William's-After-Shave Club—" Ingram laughed softly. "He was practically a charter member. So elevate us, man, elevate us."

The operator grinned at Ingram, then laughed indulgently and threw over the starting lever. "You're quite a character, too, I guess. But you watch yourself around here. That woman was minding her own business. This isn't a place to be acting like a cane-field darky and making folks embarrassed."

When the car stopped at the tenth floor, Ingram patted him on the shoulder and said, "Don't flout the law, man! Integrate!"

In the empty corridor Ingram started briskly for Novak's room, but after a half-dozen strides he slowed down in an effort to get his nerves in shape; his air of alert confidence was evaporating, burning away in the corrosive fear that ran through his body. He took a handkerchief from his breast pocket, and dabbed at the blisters of sweat that had broken out on his forehead. Just relax, he thought, rather desperately; laugh and talk, play it by ear. See how much he knows. . . .

Straightening his shoulders he replaced the handkerchief in his pocket and adjusted the points carefully against his good blue suit. As he approached Novak's door he fashioned a discreet and self-effacing smile for his lips; this was armor of a sort, a conciliating politeness that usually protected him against slights or condescensions. The pose was also a weapon; he could exaggerate it if necessary, broadening the smile and accentuating the obsequious head-bobbings, until his manner became a derisive burlesque of terrified humility. This upset white people, for some reason; it usually prodded them into foolish and pretentious reactions, making them unwitting partners to his sardonic charade. There was some satisfaction in that; not much, but some.

With his hat in hand, he rapped softly on Novak's door. When he heard footsteps inside the room the fear began to go through him in cold little shocks. Easy, easy, he thought, fixing the smile on his lips.

Novak's greeting told him nothing at all. They shook hands, and Novak led him inside and introduced him to a big, red-faced man named Burke, who looked as if he might have been a heavyweight fighter who had gone soft on drink. Burke said, "Nice to know you, Johnny," and put out a big, meaty hand.

Ingram felt some of his tension easing; things seemed to be all right, nice and casual. "Sit down, and make yourself comfortable," Novak said, lighting a cigar. He wore a white silk sports shirt and the heavy black hair on his chest showed like a smudge under the transparent material. "How're things going?"

"Just fine, Mr. Novak." Ingram sat on the edge of a chair, smiling carefully. Burke picked up his hat and said, "Well, I'm going down for the papers. See you around, Johnny."

Ingram stood quickly. "I hope so, Mr. Burke."

"So do I," Burke said, with a little grin at Novak.

When the door closed behind him, Novak sat on the edge of the bed and leaned back a bit, locking his hands around one of his knees, and working the cigar over to the corner of his mouth. He stared at Ingram for a few seconds in his silence, with no expression at all on his dark, broad face.

"Well, you know why I'm here," Ingram said, making a helpless little movement of his hands. "Might as well get down to business, eh, Mr. Novak?"

"You want money. Six thousand dollars' worth of it. That's a lot, Johnny."

"But you know I'm good for it. I'll give you any kind of interest you want, Mr. Novak." Ingram took the handkerchief from his pocket and patted his damp chin and forehead. "You know I'm good for it. I can't go to regular loan outfits, that's the trouble. They don't consider a gambler as being steadily employed."

"But I'm not in the loan business, Johnny."

"Yes, sir, I know that." Ingram smiled quickly. "But we've known each other a good spell, and you know I'm good for it. You name the terms, anything you say will be fine. Twenty per cent, thirty, I don't care." His voice was becoming shrill, he realized; rising like a frightened girl's. With an effort he got himself under control. "Well, how about it, Mr. Novak? Can you help me out?"

"What do you need the money for?"

"A pile of debts and bills two big Indians couldn't shake hands over," Ingram said. The lie came out easily, accompanied by the embarrassed little chuckle; the foolish, improvident darky, that was the best approach to use, he had decided. "I never could keep taxes and checkbooks and things like that straight. And after my mother died, I had a lot of bad debts. Folks are hounding me a little, and I'd like to get 'em off my back. You know I'm good for it, Mr. Novak. And I got a lot of things you could take as part security. A camera, a good hi-fi set, and—"

Novak shook his head. "I don't want that stuff, Johnny. I'm no pawnbroker."

"Will you take my note then? Will you, Mr. Novak?"

"That depends. First of all, let's start leveling with each other, okay?" Novak stood and began to make himself a drink at the dresser, and Ingram twisted on the chair to watch him with wide, frightened eyes. "What do you mean, Mr. Novak?" he said, in a soft, husky voice. "I'm telling you the truth, I swear it."

"Save it, save it," Novak said irritably. He sat down again and stared at Ingram in a heavy silence. "You're in trouble," he said at last. "So let's cut out the crap."

"I swear to God—"

"You're in trouble with Tenzell," Novak said, his voice falling coldly across Ingram's feeble protest. "You gave an undated IOU to Billy Turk for six thousand dollars. And he sold it to Tenzell at a twenty-five per-cent discount. Now Tenzell wants the money, doesn't he? Now—tonight."

Ingram wet his lips. "Who told you, Mr. Novak? Is it all over town?"

"Never mind who told me. It's true, isn't it?"

"Yeah, it's true," Ingram said, shaking his head wearily. "I shouldn't have tried to con you. I'm in bad trouble, Mr. Novak. If I don't get that dough, I don't know what's going to happen to me."

Novak smiled faintly. "I can tell you, Johnny. You'll get the hell beat out of you by some of Tenzell's boys. Not just once or twice, either. That's the best that can happen, I guess you know. If Tenzell gets really mad, you're through. Kaput."

Now that the charade was over, Ingram felt a bone-deep lassitude settling over him. "Can you help me out, Mr. Novak? I'll pay you back. You know that."

Novak stood and walked slowly over to the windows, holding the cigar in his teeth, and rolling the glass between his big hands. "Maybe," he said. "But it's a lot of cash."

"I know—I'll give you any kind of a deal you want."

Novak frowned out the window at the bright sunlight that was glinting on the sides of the city's buildings and falling in long patterns into the streets. In the blue sky a four-engined plane gleamed like a tiny silver cross. "This is going to be operation backscratch," he said, turning and looking at Ingram. "Understand? I'll lend you the dough. But I need some help from you. That sound all right?"

"Why, sure," Ingram said, smiling anxiously. "I'm grateful to you, Mr. Novak. I'll do anything if you just pull me out of this hole. You know that."

"Okay," Novak said, returning to sit on the edge of the bed. "I'm planning a job, Johnny. A bank job. And I need a colored guy to make it work. A colored guy is the shoehorn that gets us into the bank. That's you, Johnny. A nice shiny shoehorn."

Ingram was trying to smile, but it was a shaky effort; he felt empty and weightless, his insides consumed by fear. "You're kidding, Mr. Novak. You're kidding me."

Novak's eyes were cold. "I don't kid around, Johnny. Neither does Tenzell. Think it over."

"But I've never done anything like that, Mr. Novak. I—I don't have the guts for it."

"Guts you don't need. I've got other guys for that end of the job. It's your skin I'm buying, nothing else."

"Mr. Novak, you're making a mistake." Ingram shook his head desperately. "I'm a card player, just a plain ordinary citizen. You don't want me on a job like this."

"Is that your answer?"

"Wait, please wait! I'm scared—I'm scared, Mr. Novak."

"Of Tenzell? Of me?"

"Let me just think a minute. Please, Mr. Novak."

"Sure, take your time. It's a big, solid job, if you're interested in details. And you'll get a quarter of the take. Think it over. It's better than winding up in an alley looking like somebody stuck your head in a mix-master."

Ingram smiled nervously and lighted a cigarette, sucking the smoke deeply into his lungs. "Yeah, sure," he said. If his mother were alive it would be different, he thought despairingly; not easier, but different. For a long while taking care of her was all that mattered. He had made all his decisions with her in mind; keeping her comfortable, playing cards with her, seeing that there was plenty of food in the house and all the bills paid—those were his first considerations. He wanted her to be comfortable and quiet in her last years, free to entertain her old friends, to go to church and live the kind of respectable life she enjoyed so much. The Tenzell business would be different if she were alive. He wouldn't let that hurt her, even if it meant stealing the money. If she were living now, he'd grab Novak's offer without a second thought. One thought would be enough—her comfort and peace. But now there was just himself, and it was easier to be afraid. But why should he be? What am I scared of? The questions scurried like rats through his mind. He could get away from Tenzell, blow out of town. But they'd catch him some day. It wouldn't be a bullet, that's what made him sick with terror. They'd come into his room on a dark night or catch him in an alley, and there was no telling what they'd do to him—enjoying it, laughing at him. He had a terror of being beaten; it was an old fear; it had been with him all his life.

The door opened and Burke came in carrying the morning papers under his arm. He looked questioningly at Novak, and Novak said, "Well, how about it, Johnny? Time's a-wasting. You want me to take Tenzell off your back?"

Ingram tried to smile but the effort only stretched the skin tightly over his sharp cheekbones. "I'm your shoehorn, Mr. Novak."

"What's that?" Burke said, laughing; his face was flushed and his eyes bright with a stupid good humor. "What's the shoehorn bit, Johnny?"

Novak glanced irritably at him. "It means Johnny's in. That's the deal, four of us. Now we get down to work."

"Well, let's have a drink and celebrate," Burke said. "What's yours, Johnny?"

"Make 'em light," Novak said. "We've got work to do."

"Sure, sure," Burke said in a big, genial voice. As he turned toward the dresser the phone rang, and Novak lifted the receiver and said, "Yeah? Oh, sure. Come on up, Tex. We're ready to roll."

"Tex?" Ingram raised his eyebrows and smiled faintly. "Sounds like I'm moving in high society."

"He's okay," Novak said. "Don't worry."

CHAPTER FIVE

EARL'S MOOD was one of relaxed and uncomplicated contentment as he stepped into the elevator; the pressure within him seemed to have been dissipated by his decision to accept Novak's offer. Now he was sustained by a solid and unfamiliar sense of importance; he knew he was on the inside of something big and that put a lift in his stride. You made your breaks, he thought, as the elevator began to rise.

He wasn't worried about failure, because he didn't have the imagination to picture disaster in vivid and personal terms; it was this lack that made him a good soldier. The whole thing might go wrong, of course; there was always that chance. That much he understood; but he couldn't conjure up the colors and textures and details of failure—sirens, for instance, or the smash of bullets into his body or the potential horror of waiting to die in a gas chamber or electric chair.

He didn't think of these things. Unconsciously he had shifted the responsibility for what he was about to do onto Novak's shoulders. Novak was running things. It was a little like the Army, he thought comfortably; you did what you were told, even if the orders were stupid and dangerous. That didn't matter; if things went wrong it wasn't your fault.

Last night after leaving Lorraine he had called Novak.

Then he had strolled through the quiet streets for several hours, his anger at Lorraine fading away as he savored the peace that had come with his decision.

Lorraine was all right, he was thinking, as he went down the corridor to Novak's room. A good kid; nervous and clinging, but what woman wasn't if she liked a guy? When this was over he'd take her away and they'd settle down somewhere and enjoy life. He had told her that this morning; she had needed cheering up and he had done everything he could do to get her into a better mood. Everything, he thought, grinning a little.

Novak opened the door and said, "Come on in. You know Burke. This is Johnny Ingram. Johnny, Earl Slater."

Earl stepped into the room, giving Burke a smile, but when he turned and put out his hand to the other man a little shock of confusion and hostility went through him; the man was colored; a sharply dressed colored man with a drink and a cigarette in his hand. Earl let his arm fall slowly to his side. "What's this?" he said, feeling puzzled; was it some kind of a joke, he wondered.

But Novak wasn't treating it as a joke; he sat on the edge of the bed and said casually, "Johnny's in this deal, Tex. He's the guy who makes my plan work. You understand?" He glanced up then, and his voice sharpened as he saw the confusion and anger in Earl's face. "You understand?"

"Yeah, sure," Earl said slowly, watching the Negro with bright, blank eyes.

"Okay, take a seat. We're ready to get down to business."

"Drink, Tex?" Burke said, nodding at the bottle on the dresser.

"Yeah, give me a little something," Earl said. "I got a kind of funny taste in my mouth."

Burke poured whisky over ice and handed the glass to Earl. Then he freshened his own drink and sat down on the window sill. Ingram crossed his legs carefully, his glass resting on his knee and an expression of sly amusement on his small foxy features. He chuckled amiably and said, "I'll bet you got a dark brown taste in your mouth, Mr. Slater. That's the worst kind, that's the truth."

Earl realized he was being baited, but Ingram's conciliating smile threaded his anger with a frustrating confusion. He felt hot and prickly all over, as he tried to sort out his feelings. "Yeah," he said at last, "yeah, that's right. You're pretty smart, I guess." But the words struck him as foolish and pointless.

"Well, thank you," Ingram said, bobbing his head.

"Sit down, Earl," Novak said. "Might as well be comfortable."

There was only one seat left in the room, an overstuffed armchair beside Ingram. Earl looked at it for an instant, then smiled faintly and said, "I guess I'll stand."

He leaned against the door, and pushed his hat back on his head.

"Okay," Novak said quietly. "The bank we're taking is in a sleepy little town in southeastern Pennsylvania. It's called Crossroads. Maybe you've never heard of it. But after this job, you'll know it like the palm of your hand."

As he described the features of the town, and the roads and highways leading into it, Earl drew on his cigarette and watched the Negro from the corner of his eye. The sense of relaxed well-being he had enjoyed was gone; now his chest was tight with pressure and a relentless little pain was throbbing in the middle of his forehead. Why had they brought a colored guy into it, he thought, with a heavy anger.

"About the split," Novak said, "I'm laying out dough for this job. I'll take that out first. Afterwards we split what's left four ways—right down to the penny."

"Maybe you'd better explain to them about the expenses," Burke said.

"I was coming to that." Novak took a sheet of paper from his back pocket, and studied it for a moment or so. "It's all itemized; you guys can go over it if you want to. First, there's two cars. One's a station wagon you'll use on the job. It's nothing to look at but the engine is souped-up and she'll go like a bat. The other car is an ordinary black sedan we'll use for the getaway."

"We switch cars after the job," Burke said. "That throws

off anybody tailing us." He sipped his drink and grinned. "The whole deal is smooth as oil."

"Both cars have phony plates and phony papers," Novak went on. "The cops will trace them back to a couple of guys named Joe. The papers and plates came a little high, but they're worth it. Now there's a few other items. A waiter's outfit for Ingram here, and chauffeur's jacket and cap. And some other stuff for him that I'll come to later on. The tariff is around sixty-five hundred bucks. I take that out of the loot before we split it up. Is that clear?"

"Sure," Earl said. "Afterward even-steven. Everybody equal."

"That's right," Novak said, nodding slowly. "Let me tell you something; most jobs go wrong after the hard work is done. Brink's is an example. That Merchants Bank job in Detroit last summer is another. Beautiful jobs, planned by experts. Everything smooth as silk." Novak stared around the room. "But all these experts are in jail today. You know why? Because they shaded somebody on the payoff. That's where the trouble starts. You got a sorehead who can always blow a whistle on you. He took the same risks as everybody else, but he didn't get the same kind of payoff. When he's broke and has a few drinks, it all boils over and he talks. That's how the experts get their big smart tails kicked into jail. But it won't happen to us. Everybody in this deal is up the same frigging creek if something goes wrong—so everybody is going to get the same share of the loot." Novak stood and put his empty glass on the dresser. "I've spent time and dough looking for this particular bank, and I don't want any trouble—now or later. In the next three weeks I'm going to make robots out of you. Every step you take is on a split-second timetable. I've done the thinking; all you guys have to do is follow orders. Now here's how it starts. . . ."

Ingram lighted another cigarette as Novak began to explain the details of the job, outlining each man's particular role and responsibility. Ingram was preserving his look of poised interest with a physical effort; it took all his control just to sit quietly and listen to Novak's hard, efficient voice. The Texan's cold, contemptuous smile made it impossible for him to concentrate on what Novak was saying; the words simply broke into meaningless fragments in his mind.

Ingram was no stranger to hatred; he was a realistic man and he had heard and seen enough in life to convince him that hatred was as tangible a thing as the hard city sidewalks under his feet. But he had lived in the North all his life, in the colored neighborhoods of large cities, and he had kept out of trouble by sticking with his own people and minding his own business. He had no patience with Negroes who made an issue out of being served in white restaurants and bars; why get stared at or pushed around over a sandwich or a glass of beer? That was his feeling.

In his own neighborhood he felt safe and secure, a man of some standing; people listened to him with respect. Even with white persons he got along all right; he knew lots of cops, bondsmen and bookmakers, and within a business framework, they treated him decently. He chatted with them about sports and politics in bonding offices and police stations, but he never pushed against the boundaries of these associations. If their talk turned to social or personal matters, he effaced himself effortlessly, his manner becoming one of courteous disinterest. It was an unadmitted truce, he knew; they avoided certain words and topics when he was present, and he reciprocated by keeping out of their conversations when he knew his comments wouldn't be welcome.

The arrangement suited him fine; he had no complaints. He was a big toad in a small black puddle, and that's where he was going to stay. He had no need to make a splash in the big white puddle. But in spite of these tolerances and adjustments, a fear lurked within him that was as ineradicable as a child's fear of darkness or strangers.

Occasionally while riding in a subway or strolling in a crowded street, he would realize that someone was staring at him; the knowledge always caused an uneasy stir in him, made him feel nervous and vulnerable. Usually he would try not to look around; he would try to forget about it, fixing his eyes on something neutral, the ads in the subway or the displays in a shop window. But finally, alerted and uneasy, he would make a cautious examination of the people near him, knowing with dread that he would find someone staring at him with revulsion and hatred. It could be a man or woman, old or young, even a child; but the look was usually the same, a mixture of disgust and contempt and anger.

That was how the Texan was looking at him, and it made Ingram feel frightened and helpless. But worst of all it made him feel guilty and ashamed of himself, as if he deserved to be looked at that way. That was what cut like a whip. . . .

Once he hadn't been too bothered by such things; other colored people scorned them, laughed about them, and he had taken confidence in their collective derision. "Let 'em look, let 'em stare—ain't they never seen anything brown before? No never?" Joke about it. . . .

But then something happened which added an ominous significance to those occasional glances of disgust or hatred. His mother had become ill while visiting her sister in Mobile, Alabama, and he had gone to bring her back home. He was just out of the Army at the time, but he left his sharp clothes up North and took care to walk softly and mind his own business. Somewhat to his surprise he was treated with an almost ritualistic civility by Southern people; there was a gap between them, marked and unbridgeable, but in all permissible contacts he was aware of courtesy and even tact.

It was on the train coming back North that the incident occurred. They had made an unscheduled stop in the town of Anniston. No one knew why, but rumors flitted about, and a contagion of excitement began to spread through the day coaches. A doctor was needed; something had happened up in one of the sleepers. People stirred and lighted cigarettes, their matches flaring like beacons in the darkness. Outside yellow lamps gleamed on the small wooden station. Rain was falling and the streets were like gold in the soft illumination.

News filtered into their car; a white woman had become hysterical, and a doctor was needed to administer a sedative. Once in a silence they heard her sobbing. Ingram huddled down inside his coat and tried to go back to sleep. Across the aisle his mother snored peacefully, her gold-rimmed spectacles glinting in the half darkness, her big soft body filling like a balloon with her easy breathing. She was resting easily but he couldn't; the other people in the car were chattering and moving about restively, and he couldn't isolate himself from these distractions.

Finally he went out to the vestibule and there, in a flurry of nervous talk with one of the colored bus boys, he got an account of what happened—the woman claimed that she had been molested by her Pullman porter. He had tried to open the curtains of her berth—or something. She was too hysterical to supply any details. The porter was a regular on the run, the bus boy had known him for years, and he insisted the woman was crazy. Probably imagined the whole thing.

They talked in low voices, strangely furtive with each other, and then Ingram had gone back to his seat and pulled his collar up about his face, making himself a shapeless, inconspicuous bundle in the darkness.

But a little later he became aware that a crowd of men was gathering under the station shed. They stood watching the train, talking in low voices, their faces long and pale in the yellow light. Occasionally a match would flare at the top of a cigarette, and Ingram could see the flash of alert, speculative eyes.

It was an orderly, almost passive group; but Ingram sensed an urgency about them, a heavy and significant intensity. They pressed together in a cohesive knot, bound together by a silent understanding and purpose.

Someone snapped on the lights in the car, and the men saw Ingram in the window. One of them pointed at him, and the rest drifted closer, staring up at him with eyes that were beginning to brighten with excitement.

It was excitement and curiosity at first; Ingram felt like a freak or an animal in a cage. But their emotion changed quickly to something else, to something oddly joyous and fierce. One of the men shouted at him, and another laughed and bared his teeth in the darkness. Ringed by their bright, menacing eyes, Ingram felt the hatred of the group like the heat from a blast furnace.

Someone shook his shoulder. He turned quickly and looked up into the big meaty face of a man in a policeman's uniform.

The officer said quietly, "Better get in one of the toilets, boy. And lock the door after you. You understand?"

"Yes, sir," Ingram said.

"You'll be all right," the officer said. "Don't worry. But it upsets them looking at you. Better not to rile 'em." The man's voice was casual and soft, almost friendly; he was not berating Ingram, he was simply stating a fact. *It upsets them looking at you. . . .*

"Yes, sir, I understand," Ingram said. "Thank you, sir." Like something scalded he went down the aisle to the cold little toilet at the end of the car. Crouching in there on the seat, with the acrid stench from the rusty pipes in his nostrils, Ingram felt no sense of anger or outrage; instead he felt small and mean. That's what the men saw, he thought.

Finally, like an answer to a prayer, the car jerked and the train began to roll. . . .

Ingram never found out what happened to the porter. He watched the papers for a week or two, but he never saw anything about the incident. They'd probably put the man on another run, he had decided; that would be the best thing to do.

Novak slapped his hands together briskly, and the sound made Ingram sit up so abruptly that he almost spilled what was left of his drink.

"Well, that's it," Novak said, looking at them with a hard, pleased smile. "Three weeks from Friday. That's D day. We'll spend the next three weeks drilling on the timetable, the getaway, everything."

Burke collected the glasses and began making a second round of drinks. "We need a little something to celebrate the deal."

Ingram stood up, his hands cold and shaky; he wanted to get away from here, away from the look on the Texan's face. "I'd better run along, Mr. Novak. I got some plans to make."

"I'll get in touch with you tomorrow, then. And I'll get in touch with Tenzell today."

"That's fine, Mr. Novak."

"Hell, what's the hurry?" Burke said, passing drinks to Earl and Novak. "One for luck, eh?"

Novak smiled at his glass. "Here's to happy days. With maybe fifty thousand bucks in our wallets the future can be mighty bright."

Earl stared at his drink, a little frown shadowing his eyes. He hadn't followed Novak's explanation; his attempt to concentrate had been frustrated by the pressure building inside him. There was no target or direction for his feeling; he was caught up hopelessly and impotently between confusion and anger. It was always that way, he thought, still frowning at his glass. Nothing was ever easy and clear for him.

Burke said, "Here's luck," and drank deeply, letting the liquor flow down his throat in a smooth rush.

Novak looked at Earl. "Well, what're you waiting for? Something wrong with the whisky?"

"No, the whisky's all right," Earl said, frowning thoughtfully at his glass. He turned it around for a few seconds in his big fingers, unaware of the uneasy little silence settling over the room.

"What's eating you?" Burke said at last.

"I'm wondering about the glass, that's all," Earl said. "You sure it's mine?"

"You got your hand on it, right? That's my rule—if I got my hands on a glass, it's mine."

Earl looked speculatively at the glass. "You might have got 'em mixed up."

"How the hell do I know? You didn't have your initials on it, did you?"

"What's wrong with you?" Novak said, watching Earl with narrowing eyes.

"Just this," Earl said, casually. "I'll work with Sambo if I have to, but I'm not about to drink out of the same glass with him." There was no anger in his voice; he was simply stating a fact, articulating a principle that was too ingrained in him to require qualification or discussion. The pressure within him had eased; he was sure of his ground now, no longer racked by conflicting tensions. Shaking his head slowly, he let the glass fall from his hand. The liquor splashed on the beige carpeting, and the ice cubes rolled and bounced on the floor like a pair of oversized dice. "I don't take chances in a case like this," he said.

"Man, the odds are with you," Ingram said, but no one was listening to him, or looking at him; Novak and Burke were watching Earl, their faces thoughtful and slightly uneasy.

"All right, you made your point," Novak said. "Knock it off now."

Ingram was grateful they didn't look at him; his cheeks felt hot and feverish, stinging as if he'd been slapped across the face. He was nervous and afraid, but a reckless anger made him say, "Well, I'll take four-to-one odds any time." He sipped a little whisky, and then placed the glass carefully on the dresser. Smiling coolly at Earl he said, "Pappy would say I was foolish, though. Even with those odds. Don't use a dipper after the poor white trash—that's what he always told us."

Saying that meant trouble, Ingram knew; it was like waving a red flag at a bull. He was on the balls of his feet, ready to move fast, ready for anything. But he didn't know Earl Slater; he wasn't prepared for the speed of his reflexes, the power in his body. One instant Slater stood six feet from him, relaxed and indolent, a thumb hooked over his belt, and a faint little smile on his lips; the next instant he was on Ingram like an animal, slamming him back against the wall with a spine-numbing crash.

"Don't ever say that to me!" he shouted. He slapped Ingram savagely with his open hand then, and the impact of the blow was like a pistol shot in the room. "You hear me?" he cried, his voice trembling with a fury that swept away all his reason and control.

"Cut it out!" Novak shouted. "Both of you, goddamit." He and Burke caught Earl's arms, but it took all of their weight and strength to pull him away, to force him back across the room.

"You fool, you crazy fool," Novak said in a hot, raging voice. "The color I care about is green. You hear that? Green!" He stared at Earl, his big chest rising and falling rapidly. "You want a part of this deal, you keep your hands and mouth to yourself. Otherwise, clear the hell out. I need Johnny, understand? You got that straight?"

Earl pulled his arm away from Burke, and straightened the collar of his coat. The instant of action had purged him of anger; he was able to smile at Novak. "There won't be any more trouble." He glanced at Ingram, the smile still playing about his lips. "That's right, ain't it, Sambo? We understand each other now, don't we?"

Ingram touched his bruised lips gently. "I read you," he said in a soft, empty voice.

Earl nodded at Novak. "See? There won't be any more trouble. It's like training a dog. You need a stick and a little time. That's all."

"I don't want any more of this," Novak said. "Pound that into your head."

Earl shrugged as he turned toward the door. "It's all over, don't worry."

Ingram stared at his back, still holding a hand against his stinging lips. Maybe it's all over, he thought, and maybe it's just starting. Just starting, big man. . . .

CHAPTER SIX

In the middle of October the signs of a hard winter were evident throughout Hunting Valley, the broad natural depression sheltering the small village of Crossroads; stiff winds had swept away the brilliant fall leaves from maples and buttonwoods, and the trees stood now like rows of stark, gloomy sentinels alongside the hard expanses of farmland. The crops had been harvested, and the fields were bare and lonely; in the thin sunlight ice gleamed on the corn stubble, and brazen crows picked over the ground within easy gunshot of outbuildings and farmhouses.

Earl had seen all this as he drove down the valley into Crossroads, and it struck a cold, weakening blow at his spirits; for some reason he had been plunged into gloom by the dying season, by the sights of birds wheeling against dull gray skies and bright leaves spinning helplessly down to the inhospitable ground.

After checking into the hotel he went about unpacking with deliberate speed and care, trying to shake off his depression. He put his shirts and socks away, hung his overcoat in the closet and made a neat arrangement of his toilet articles in the mirrored medicine cabinet above the handbasin. After that he glanced around the room, unconsciously taking an inventory: bed, two chairs, clean white plaster on the walls and ceilings. This was a habit from the Army; he didn't feel comfortable in a new place until he had come to some sort of a conclusion about it. The room impressed him favorably; it was neat and substantial. He could imagine a salesman working on his accounts here or relaxing on the bed after a long day's drive. Anybody might put up here for the night, a businessman, a honeymooning couple or a plain tourist.

The permanent feel of the place comforted him and helped dispel his gloom. He strolled to the windows and stared down at the Crossroads bank, an old-fashioned, two-story brick building with barred windows and large, brass-handled doors. The room had been chosen for this view; Novak had reserved it by phone two weeks ago. The bank was just like Novak had said, he thought; a friendly old place you could take apart with a can opener.

The street below him was busy with traffic—panel trucks, station wagons and occasional sports cars darting along like squat bugs. He liked the look of Crossroads; the buildings on the main street were only two- or three-stories high, and most of them were done in red brick with white-trimmed windows and doorways. In a hardware store he saw a display of beautiful shotguns, stocks gleaming with designs worked in dull silver. The town had class, he thought; the people looked like money.

Tweed jackets, sports cars with muddy fenders, cashmere polo coats over breeches and riding boots. Everything easy and casual. At the intersection, a bunch of teen-agers were chattering on the sidewalk, laughing in the bright sunshine. The girls were pert and well-scrubbed in jeans and pony tails, and the boys were turned out in flannels and tweed jackets. There was a drugstore behind them, and Earl smiled faintly as he looked at it; that was where things would start tomorrow night. At a few minutes after eight. . . . Then they followed the timetable, each man swinging into action on a split-second schedule.

Earl left his room and went down a flight of steps to a hallway with two exits; one opened on the lobby, the other led directly to the street. This fact was essential to their plan; it would be necessary to leave the hotel tomorrow night without going through the lobby.

Earl stepped out onto the sidewalk and entered the restaurant beside the hotel, taking a seat at the counter and ordering ham and eggs and coffee from a buxom pink-cheeked waitress. It was a quarter to ten, and there were only two other customers in the restaurant; a truck driver working hungrily at breakfast, and a middle-aged man looking through a newspaper and sipping a cup of coffee. Burke would be along soon, Earl thought, checking his watch. He was stopping at a motel about a mile away, and after this morning's contact would keep out of Crossroads. The colored man, Ingram, wasn't due until tomorrow afternoon.

It was ten o'clock when Burke shouldered his way through the door, hands jammed in the pockets of his overcoat, and his big face whipped to the color of raw beef by the stinging wind. He took the stool beside Earl and pushed his hat up on his forehead. "Some weather, eh?" he said. "At six this morning I wouldn't have bet against snow."

"I guess it's coming all right," Earl said.

"You can say that again." Burke grinned at the big, pink-cheeked waitress. "How about something substantial? Bacon and eggs, with some hashed browns on the side, okay?"

When she walked back to the kitchen Burke glanced at Earl. "I like this weather," he said. There was a smell of whisky about him, mingling with the fragrance of a sweet after-shave lotion. "It's good weather to work in. Makes you want to tackle anything."

"Yeah, that's right," Earl said.

They sat in silence until the other two customers buttoned

up their coats and went out into the street. The restaurant was warm and comfortable, a haven against the cold, with the aroma of coffee and sugared buns mixing pleasantly in the air. From where Earl and Burke sat they had a view of the bank building and half a block of Crossroad's main street.

"Pretty little town," Burke said again.

The waitress brought his breakfast, and he sighed expansively and picked up a knife and fork. "That looks great," he said.

"You want more coffee?" the waitress said to Earl.

"No, this is fine."

"I'll be back in the kitchen if you need anything else."

"Sure."

Burke buttered a piece of toast and stirred it around in egg yolk. "Yes, it's a pretty little town," he said.

"What did you want to see me about?"

"Oh." Burke glanced toward the kitchen, then turned to Earl. "Novak stopped in the bank yesterday—a final check. And there's been a change. They've got a Red Cross drive on, and the collecting table is in front of the gate that leads back to where the bank officers have their desks. You get the picture? You got to go around that table."

"You made a trip just to tell me that?"

"A little thing out of place might upset you. You know what I mean? You're expecting it to look one way, and bang!—it's different. That could rattle a guy."

"I'll try to keep calm," Earl said dryly. "Judas priest, I think Novak's the guy getting rattled."

"He just coppers all the bets. Don't you worry about him." Burke glanced out the window and something made him smile. "If you want to worry, worry about that guy. He's the competition."

In front of the entrance to the bank stood a tall, middle-aged man in a slate-gray police uniform and black leather puttees. The forty-five at his hip was buckled to a glossy Sam Browne belt, and despite the freezing weather his raw, big-knuckled hands were bare; leather gauntlets were tucked under the diagonal strap of the Sam Browne, neatly in place beside a book of traffic tickets, and a leather-encased pen-

and-pencil set. He wore a trooper's hat with a black chin strap, the wide brim shadowing his long angular face.

He was pretty big, Earl thought; better than six feet, with wide shoulders pushing at the seams of his whipcord jacket. Now as he turned to glance down the street, Earl saw deep-set serious eyes and a solid width of hard jaw line. He didn't look smart, Earl thought; there was nothing quick or alert in his face, only a kind of stubborn watchfulness. The hair at his temples was streaked with gray, and his skin was brown and coarse, like leather that had been seasoned and toughened by exposure to all kinds of weather.

"There he is," Burke said. "The law."

"Well, so what?" The solid authority in the sheriff's manner irritated and angered him. Staring up and down with his hands on his hips, like somebody's tough old man. . . . "He's just a hick-town cop," Earl said.

"Maybe," Burke said, but his eyes narrowed as he watched the sheriff strolling down the block. "I'll bet not a cat or dog dies in this town that he doesn't know about it. He looks like a hunter, and that's what makes a smart cop."

"I hunted a lot," Earl said. "It didn't make me smart."

"Did you like hunting?"

"It was something to do, that's all."

"Well, that's not enough. This guy loves to hunt. Watch him."

They saw the sheriff pause under the marquee of the movie theater, and then stroll into the lobby, bending over a bit, his eyes scanning the tiled flooring.

"What's he looking for?" Earl said.

"Cigarettes, probably."

Earl grinned. "Don't they pay him enough to buy his own?"

"There's a law in this state against smoking in movie theaters," Burke said patiently. "If he finds butts, he'll know somebody's breaking the law."

"Isn't that brilliant," Earl said.

"You're missing the point. Tonight he'll probably have a talk with the manager. He'll stop trouble before it starts. That's smart." Burke sighed and looked down at the backs of his wide, puffy hands. "I was a cop for quite a while, you know. Almost eight years.

"Did you like it?"

"I liked the gun and badge. That's why kids want to be cops, I guess." Burke glanced at Earl, a sheepish little smile on his lips. "You know something? I used to hang around gin-mills when I was off duty just hoping trouble would start. You know, punks getting fresh with a waitress or drunks noisy and looking for a fight." He sighed again, but the little smile lingered on his lips. "I loved to watch their faces when I'd pull my coat back and let 'em see the gun."

"If you liked being a cop, why didn't you stick with it?"

"I liked good clothes and good liquor, too," Burke said dryly. "I could get a new suit just by doing a guy a favor. It was easy." He shrugged his soft shoulders. "The lieutenant gave me a break the first time I got caught. Next time he didn't." Burke wadded up his greasy paper napkin and dropped it on the plate. "That's the whole story."

"Well, here comes your hero again," Earl said, looking out the window.

The sheriff was crossing the street at an angle, covering the ground with long efficient strides, but his manner was deliberate and there was no suggestion of haste or urgency in his movements.

Burke touched Earl's elbow. "Now watch this," he said.

The window framed the scene—the traffic, the bank building, and the tall sheriff angling swiftly across the street.

"Watch what?" Earl said.

"The kids at the corner," Burke said.

Earl saw three teen-aged boys lounging at the intersection, fresh-faced youngsters in jeans and black leather jackets. They were grinning expectantly, staring at a young woman who was strolling casually toward them along the sidewalk. She hadn't noticed them; she was minding her own business, occasionally pausing at shop windows, an attractive young woman in tweeds and brown leather loafers. She was quite obviously pregnant; this was what had caught the youngsters' interest. One of them rubbed his stomach significantly; and his two companions began to laugh.

"Smart little punks," Earl said. He didn't like this sort of thing; it made him feel cheap. Burke put a hand on his arm as he started to rise. "Never mind," he said, "you don't want to get yourself noticed. You're too late anyway."

The sheriff had come up beside the young woman, smiling down at her and touching the brim of his hat in a soft salute. She grinned and said something to him, still unaware of the teen-agers staring speculatively at her from the corner.

The sheriff shortened his stride to hers, and they strolled past the boys, chatting easily until they came to the stop light. There the sheriff said good-by and smiled after her as she crossed the street and entered the next block. Only when she was out of sight did he turn and stare at the three boys, his big raw hands resting on his hips.

It was apparent that he didn't need to say anything; the boys avoided his eyes, looking foolishly up and down the street. Finally, in concert, they turned and hurried off, their heels clicking out a quick and nervous rhythm on the sidewalk.

"Why didn't he do something?" Earl said.

"He did," Burke said, getting to his feet. "He stopped trouble. Nothing big, just something that might have embarrassed the woman and got the kids in a jam. A little neighborhood hassle, some bad feeling all round. That's what he stopped. That's how he earns his dough." He took a few toothpicks from a porcelain cup on the counter. "Don't worry about him, kid. He won't get in our way."

"Hell, who's worried?" Earl said. He still felt a cold antagonism toward the big cop; there was something familiar about him, he thought, although he knew he'd never seen him before in his life.

"You take care of the check," Burke said. "I'll pay you back tomorrow night." He grinned and patted Earl on the shoulder. "I'm expecting some dough by then. . . ."

Ten minutes later Earl drove out of Crossroads on the main highway, making a careful note of all intersections and landmarks. He was an expert at this kind of thing; his directional instincts were uncannily accurate and he had an excellent memory for terrain. In the Army he had been able to lead his platoon for miles without straying more than a degree or two off course. He was like a good bird dog, with a compass inside him to keep his nose to the scent.

Earl spent two hours following the network of narrow dirt roads that twisted through the rolling farmlands around the village of Crossroads. To the general information he had received from Novak, he added details for his private intelligence; detours, bypasses, short cuts and dead ends—he pinpointed and measured them, storing them away for possible future use. Twice he drove back to Crossroads and started out fresh from the corner of the bank building, plotting alternative escape routes to fit any conceivable emergency. He even checked the alleys of the village, knowing he would need them if they were trapped by a traffic jam or roadblock.

The work filled him with importance; it seemed a solid and serious thing to be doing.

At two o'clock he stopped for gas at a station on the main highway a few miles from Crossroads. He told the boy to fill it up and got out to look at the weather. The sun had gone under the clouds, and the sky was dark and heavy in the west. A thin cold rain had begun to fall, and a wind stirred the bare trees. But now the gloom of the countryside didn't depress him. The black fields and the great V-shaped flocks of geese pointing high and south against the gray skies—for some reason they seemed to make his own loneliness significant and bearable.

The gas attendant whistled and said, "Boy, this is a real sleeper. She don't look like much, but she'll go, I bet."

Earl turned and saw that the boy had raised the hood and was staring admiringly at the engine. "I told you I just wanted gas," Earl said, his anger putting a bite to the words. "Put that damned hood down. I'm in a hurry."

"Well, sure, I didn't know—" The boy was in his late teens, open-faced and confident, but the anger in Earl's voice brought a flush to his cheeks. "I was just going to check the oil and water. It's part of our regular service."

"Never mind the regular service," Earl said. He realized that he was behaving stupidly, marking the incident in the boy's memory. It was a small thing but it could be serious; Novak had told him expressly not to gas up near Crossroads. "Sorry I snapped at you," he said, trying to smile. "But I'm in a hurry."

"I should have asked you, I guess. But she's a beautiful job." The boy's smile came back. "High-compression head, special carburetors—I'll bet she travels."

"I'm on the road a lot," Earl said. He took his change and tipped the boy a quarter. "Saving time means saving money."

The boy grinned and patted the hood. "I'll bet she'll take those foreign sports jobs without much trouble."

"She can move all right," Earl said. He waved good-by to the boy and started back for Crossroads. It wasn't too serious, he thought. Lots of salesmen drove stepped-up cars. And his explanation had been quick and neat. *Saving time means saving money*. That would make sense to the kid. That wouldn't give him anything to gossip about. . . .

Earl drew up alongside the bank in Crossroads and checked his watch. Two thirty, but he wasn't hungry. He decided to drive over the escape route before stopping for lunch. Pulling out slowly from the curb he tried to imagine how it would be tomorrow night; dark to start with, the colored man and Burke in the seat behind him, and the car plowing away under full power. He drove down the tree-lined side street and turned left at the second intersection. After a half-dozen blocks he came to a slum area, rows of shabby houses with muddy front yards and colored people moving along the sidewalks. Another half mile and he was out in the country, traveling on a hard-surface road that ran between meadows and stands of poplar trees. This was where he would use all the power he could ram out of the souped-up car—on this six-mile stretch. Earl touched the accelerator and the speedometer needle swung smoothly to fifty, then to sixty and on toward seventy, the engine whining softly with the tremendous surge of power. Earl laughed as the cold rain stung his face through the open window, and he sensed the black trees whipping past him.

Tomorrow night he would barrel along here at almost twice this speed, with every second he could save adding a precious margin of safety to their escape. This was part of Novak's plan; the powerful car and the straight, hard getaway road, a combination that would hurl them beyond any roadblocks that could be thrown up by the state cops.

Earl slowed down when he came to a big, rain-blackened barn on the right of the road. Here Novak would be waiting for them in the sedan. Changing cars would just take a few seconds. The station wagon would go into the empty barn, rammed inside an old corn crib; it might not be discovered for days. They would roll off in the sedan, the colored man at the wheel in a chauffeur's jacket and visored cap, Earl and Burke wearing overcoats and fedoras that Novak had bought in Philadelphia. They would hit the main highway about two minutes after leaving the bank in Crossroads. In another few minutes they would be gone for good, rolling smoothly toward Baltimore, miles outside the roadblock area.

Earl drove on past the barn and turned into a road that led away from the highway, twisting deeper into the back country. He relaxed and lighted a cigarette, enjoying the smooth power of the car under his instinctively efficient hands. After a while he came to raw country, neglected and run-down; the pasturage there was overgrown with heavy-headed thistle, and the fence posts hung rotten and useless on rusted strands of barbed wire.

Earl stopped and climbed out onto the muddy road, staring around with a faint smile on his face. He liked the rough, abandoned look of this area; there was work to be done here, good hard work. A heavy silence settled around him, broken only by the rain and the occasional lonely cry of birds in a stand of trees rising like black smudge on the horizon. He pulled his muffler tight about his throat, and strolled down the road, enjoying the fresh, damp air on his face. It was getting dark, he realized, and it was just a little after three. Only a few silver patches gleamed in the gray sky, and the birds sounded as if they were settling down for the night.

But he didn't mind the cold and lonely approach of evening; he was in a relaxed and cheerful frame of mind. He was thinking about Lorraine. It occurred to him that their trouble was living in the city, cooped up in a little box with nothing to look at but lots of other little boxes. Depending on dozens of strangers for their food and drink and clothing. Grocers, delivery boys, plumbers—people you were helpless without.

At the top of a rise, he stared over a meadow that rolled away from him like a sea, hazy and insubstantial under soft, pearl-colored layers of fog. There was a stone house in the meadow, almost hidden by big black maples and oaks. Except for a wisp of smoke curling out the chimney, the place looked deserted; there were no dogs around, and the doors of the old barn swayed crookedly in the gusting wind.

Earl lighted a cigarette and flipped the match into the water runneling coldly in the ditch beside the road. Then he stood quietly and looked at the house. He felt his splintered thoughts merging into a confident, unified idea; after this job he and Lorraine could clear out of the city and find an old place with some good land around it. He would go into farming. Somewhere he had read that the government passed out all sorts of books and pamphlets on soil erosion and crop rotation, things like that. He could learn the whole deal, he thought. Why not? He was no dummy. He could use an ax, and he was handy with tools. And Lorraine's know-how about food would come in handy. She could put up enough fruit and vegetables from a garden to last them through the winter.

They'd live alone, free as the air, with no demands on them from anybody. They could spend their evenings with a drink or two in front of a wood fire, laughing at the snow and wind blowing by their windows. No more worrying about Mr. Poole and the drugstore. No worries at all.

As he walked back to the car an old hound dog scrambled under the fence and trotted along inquisitively at his heels. Earl stopped and patted the big, knobby head, grinning at his wagging tail and excited, squirming body. All alone out here, he thought. Probably covered twenty miles today, chasing after rabbits and squirrels like a fool. The dog followed him eagerly to the car, and Earl remembered he had half a bologna sandwich in the glove compartment. He laughed and said, "Got something for you, boy," and the dog's tail swung to the excitement in his voice. He fed the dog, and then shook the big, knobby head with his two hands. "Pretty good, eh? Good as a rabbit if you're hungry."

They would have dogs in the country, he thought. Bird dogs, smart and hard-working, not house pets under Lorraine's feet all the time. "So long," he said, giving the dog's head a last rough shake. "Better get home now and get your supper."

But the dog didn't want him to go; he crowded against Earl's legs and tried to climb into the car when he opened the door. Finally Earl picked up a lump of dirt and raised his arm threateningly. "Beat it! Beat it!" he shouted, and the dog backed away from him, his tail dragging between his legs. He wheeled and trotted off, occasionally looking warily and mournfully over his shoulder at Earl. No spirit, Earl thought, watching the dog slink away along the muddy road. Somebody must have beat it out of him or tied him up and starved him; that would do it. That really broke a dog for good.

Earl brushed the crumbs of the sandwich from his hands and got into the car. He felt irritable for some reason; probably just hungry, he thought.

Half an hour later he was back in Crossroads. He went into the restaurant beside his hotel and ordered coffee and a roast beef sandwich. The place was warm and comfortable with the bright overhead lights pressing against the rainy gloom beyond the plate-glass windows.

The same pink-cheeked waitress was on duty. She smiled at his damp overcoat and said, "You got wet, didn't you?"

"I couldn't help it," he said.

"The coffee will fix you up. How do you like your roast beef? Rare?"

"That's it. Rare."

Earl lighted a cigarette and glanced out the rain-streaked window at the bank. The lights were on and he saw a woman working in the teller's cage that faced the front doors. It would be like that tomorrow night, he thought. Tellers and clerks tidying up their accounts for the weekend. Not worrying about anything but a missing dime here and there.

Earl was interested in a detached way at the condition of

his nerves. He had been afraid the waiting would be the worst part of the job; with time hanging on his hands he usually became restless and impatient. But he felt just fine, relaxed and easy, savoring the hot coffee and the warm, peaceful quiet of the restaurant. Tomorrow he'd stick close to the hotel room, keeping an eye on the bank and waiting for the colored man to show up. Then the waiting would be over.

He heard the door open behind him and felt a draft of cold air on his neck. Turning he saw the tall sheriff standing just inside the door, shaking water from his broad-brimmed hat. The sheriff's hair was short and black, shot with silver at the temples, and his gray, whipcord jacket smelled cleanly of the cold and rain. As he walked to the counter, Earl felt the impact of the man. There was a solid, ingrained assurance about him, an effortless confidence that Earl had seen in certain officers; authority was a habit with those men, a self-endowed right which they exercised without the slightest doubt or fear. They didn't expect to be obeyed; they knew they would be. . . .

The waitress smiled and said, "Hi, Sheriff. Where did all this rain come from?" She poured a cup of coffee. "Would you like pie or something?"

"No, just the coffee, Millie."

The waitress chattered on about the weather while the sheriff sipped the hot coffee. There was no suggestion of indifference in his silence but he gave Earl the impression that small talk was not one of his enthusiasms.

Earl watched him from the corner of his eyes. The sheriff sat steady as a rock, elbows on the counter, the coffee cup hidden in his two big hands, listening to the waitress' theories about the weather with an expression of polite attention on his long face. The sharp overhead light glinted on the black piping at the sleeves of his jacket, and splintered on the butt plate of the forty-five at his hip. He was bigger than Earl had thought, solid and tall, with a powerful-looking body and hands that seemed made for any kind of work or trouble. The local hawkshaw, Earl thought, with a pointless bitterness, not talking, full of two-bit secrets. Turning slightly, he studied the sheriff's unrevealing profile, seeing the way the brown skin stretched across his face like the leather on a well-worn shield. He felt confused and irritable as he stared at the sheriff; he doesn't scare me, he thought, trying to rekindle his previous hard confidence. Not one damned bit. . . .

The fact that the man didn't even glance at him was exasperating; and he felt a strange, illogical need to force himself on his attention. He could nod or say hello, he thought. That wouldn't kill him . . . But in spite of this feeling he also had a perverse notion that the sheriff was aware of him after all, and was drawing certain silent conclusions about him.

Maybe he had noticed him driving in and out of Crossroads today, tooling around without any apparent purpose. Or maybe he had seen Burke sitting with him this morning, the two of them eying the bank. . . .

He wondered what to do; it wouldn't be smart to attract the sheriff's attention, but it could be just as stupid to sit here and let him go on speculating about him. The problem tightened his nerves. Why hadn't Novak thought of this? Brains were his department. But underneath Earl's confusion and worry was a half-understood need to be something in the sheriff's eyes. The man's stolid indifference bothered him more than anything else.

Earl caught the waitress' eye and said, "Let me have another coffee, okay?"

When she refilled his cup, he smiled and said, "This is pretty country around here."

"Well, it is when the weather's nice."

"I was out looking at farm land, and I got soaked. You can't get a real idea of property from a car."

"You're interested in farming?"

Earl laughed and said, "Well, I don't know. But I came into a little cash lately, and I figured I should put it into something solid. I'm tired of the big-city life, anyway."

"I don't blame you. I go over to Philly shopping sometimes, but a few hours of it is enough for me."

"That's how I feel." Earl was smiling at her but watching the sheriff from the corner of his eye—this would put an end to his speculations, he thought. "So I thought I'd make a switch. You can always get into the city for a while if you want to."

"What kind of farming are you going to try?"

"Well, stock maybe. Sheep or steers. Maybe a dairy herd, if I can find just what I want."

"You should talk to Dan Worthington; he's the biggest real-estate man around here."

"I'll do that—but first I like to get my own idea about things."

"That seems a good idea. Most people jump into things too fast, if you ask me."

Earl was glad she had said that; it would give the sheriff the picture of a solid and thoughtful guy. Nobody's fool.

The sheriff put a dime on the counter and got to his feet. "So long, Millie," he said. Without glancing at Earl he adjusted the chin strap of his hat and left the restaurant.

Earl looked after him, the cigarette halfway to his lips. "He's the big deal around here, eh?" he said.

The waitress smiled and shook her head. "Nobody ever thinks of Sheriff Burns that way. He's just—" She paused and shrugged, a little confused by the anger in Earl's eyes. "Well, anybody in trouble thinks of him first, put it that way."

"A nice guy, eh?"

The warmth in her voice irritated him. Staring out at the bright yellow lights of the bank, he began to drum his fingers restlessly on the counter. He was suddenly glad they were going to hang the job on this sheriff's placid little town.

CHAPTER SEVEN

AT FIVE O'CLOCK the following afternoon John Ingram was playing poker in a small, noisy barroom in Crossroads. He had arrived by bus an hour or so before, wearing an old overcoat and carrying a worn, scuffed overnight bag. The bar was on the main street at the southern end of town, one of a row of shops catering exclusively to Negroes.

When he left the bus, Ingram chatted with several men lounging in the doorway of the barroom, asking them about the area and inquiring about job possibilities. Giving information had made them feel important, and they all talked at once, providing loud and frequently contradictory answers to his questions.

Ingram listened politely to their jumbled array of facts and opinions, laughing and shaking his head when anyone interspersed the account with irony or humor. They were laborers for the most part, amiable and courteous, well-intentioned men, and Ingram knew they would resent any display of big-city cockiness from him; the arrogant Negro, he had learned, was always a potential source of trouble for other Negroes. In addition, he was almost always a bore; righteous and looking for slights, quick to criticize other colored people for being mannerly and minding their own business. . . .

While chatting with them Ingram had spotted Earl Slater, the Texan, strolling along the opposite side of the street. They had stared at each other blankly for an instant or so, their faces empty and unrevealing; but in the gathering darkness Ingram had seen the sudden tension in Earl's deliberate strides, and he knew the sight of him was responsible for this. Just seeing me is enough to steam him up, he realized. The thought brought a quick flush of shame to his cheeks. It would be long before he forgot the scene in Novak's room, forgot the weight of the Texan's hand across his face. . . .

One of the colored laborers suggested they go inside for a drink. Ingram spent half an hour coasting along on a beer, and then someone at the poker table in the rear called for a player. Ingram was the only person available; he had tried to beg off, but they coaxed and cajoled him until he realized he was calling attention to himself by refusing to play.

And now, after fifteen minutes play, he knew the game was crooked.

It wasn't risking money in a crooked game that bothered him; he could beat the man who was cheating with his eyes closed, and the stakes weren't high enough to matter one way or another. They were just playing for quarters, keeping their bets on paper so there wouldn't be any money in sight in case the sheriff looked in. But crooked games usually ended in rows, Ingram had learned; and he couldn't afford to be part of any kind of row.

The cheater was sitting on Ingram's right, a tall, yellow-skinned man named Adam. He had prominent teeth, a head like an artillery projectile, and noisy, demonstrative manners; he laughed and talked constantly, imploring fortune for cards and moaning in mock anguish when they fell to other players. The trick he had been using was simple but risky; in a smart game he would have been caught in the first couple of hands.

Adam was using a daub to mark the high cards; to his left ear was taped a thin tube of gummy paint, and after touching this with his finger tip, he could place minute identifying dots on the backs of face cards and aces. He knew what he had to beat in every hand, and he was taking greedy advantage of his information, winning pot after pot and laughing shrilly at his good luck. If he'd just take it easy, Ingram thought despairingly.

Ingram was ahead out of sheer indifferent luck; he was simply calling bets and putting down his hand, eager to find a tactful way to get out of the game.

"Your deal," the man sitting across from him said quietly. "Let's see something beside numbers for a change, okay?" The man was called Rufe and the other players addressed him with respect; he was solemn and cautious in his play, but there was a flash of alert intelligence in his heavy-lidded eyes.

"I'll try to oblige," Ingram said.

The mood of the table was changing, Ingram knew; that was as palpable to him as the noise from the bar, and the layers of blue smoke swirling in the air. The losers had become confused and angered by their bad luck. They were watching him suspiciously, the bright overhead light drawing deep shadows in their solemn, brown faces.

Ingram dealt quickly, not looking at the cards.

Why was he here? Why had he got into this? He was desperately afraid of what lay ahead of him tonight—if he were caught the police could do what they wanted with him, beat him senseless, send him to jail to rot, strap him into the electric chair to die. Any of that; he'd deserve it all.

His spirits sank to a gloomy depth. The air around him smelled warmly of cigarette smoke and beer, and men stood drinking along the short wooden bar, their happy, shouting voices rising sporadically above the music blaring from the huge juke box. It was a haven against the unfriendly darkness; it had begun to snow outside, and Ingram saw the soft flakes drifting past the windows in a fragile silence, flashing in a white splendor as they spun into the yellow glare of the street lights. But the sight of this made him feel small and lonely and helpless; he became aware then that Rufe was staring silently at him and the muscles of his stomach began to ache with a cold fear.

"There's something funny with this deck," Rufe said slowly. "I ain't accusing anybody, I'm just saying what I think."

"They aren't my cards," Ingram said. "You were playing with 'em before I came in the game."

There was a murmur of support from men who had crowded around the table.

"Look, he's pretty fast to defend himself," Adam said. "Nobody's accused him of nothing."

"We'll look at the cards," Rufe said quietly.

The odds were rigged against him, Ingram knew; when the marks were discovered there would be an explosion at the table but by then Adam would have got rid of the paint tube behind his ear. In the excitement that would be easy enough; he could drop it on the floor, then institute a search for it. When the tube was found, he would insist it belonged to Ingram.

"Now listen to me a minute," Ingram said. "I'm no card cheat. But I know something about gambling." He stared desperately around at the other players, realizing in an agony of fear that his attempt at composure was feeble and unconvincing; his forehead was damp with sweat and the tension inside him made his whole body tremble. "I'll show you who's cheating," he cried, leaping to his feet. "Give me those cards."

"Don't listen to him," Adam said. "He's trying to talk his way out of it."

"Everybody get his hands on the table," Ingram said. "Come on! Only the guy who's cheating won't like this—palms down and keep 'em there."

Rufe was looking at Ingram with interest. Finally he nodded and said, "I'm willing."

Only Adam objected. "This is crazy. What's all this hocus-pocus about?"

Rufe stared at him in silence. Finally he said coldly, "I'm willing to give him a chance. Why ain't you?"

"He's going to trick us, that's all," Adam said, but after another glance from Rufe he put his hands down tentatively and unhappily, as if he feared the surface of the table might be red-hot to the touch.

Ingram said, "All right, I'll show you what's been going on now." His body was trembling with relief, but he shuffled the deck with an authority and speed that brought an appreciative chuckle from the men ringing the table. He flipped four cards to Rufe. "Worth opening with?"

Rufe turned over the cards: four aces gleamed under the naked bulb over their heads. "And here come the K-boys," Ingram said, tossing out the kings. "And behind them the ladies, and the jacks. They're real informative cards—read 'em from either side if you know where to look. See that little red dot up in the corner of the ace? Look good, you can't miss it."

As the other players leaned forward to study the cards, Adam raised a hand casually, but Ingram was waiting for this; he caught Adam's wrist and pushed his hand back to the table. "Which ear you got it behind?" he said quietly.

"What's this?" Rufe said, his heavy-lidded eyes glancing up at Adam. "What's all this?"

"I read about it in a book," Adam cried in a shrill, stammering voice. "A trick book—you know the kind. How to prank your friends. They sent me a little tube of paint to put behind your ear—it's a joke, that's all." He wet his lips. "That's the funniest part of the whole thing, ain't it? That you'd think I was really cheating you. Ain't that the funniest thing about it?"

"Why, you son of a bitch," Rufe said, shaking his head almost thoughtfully. Then he hurled himself across the table, his hands grabbing at Adam's throat, and his weight driving the man down to the ground.

The table had gone over with a crash. Everyone began shouting counsels and exhortations as the two men rolled across the cigarette-littered floor. The bartender pulled down the shades on the front windows and someone turned up the juke box to drown out the sounds of the fight.

Ingram was trapped helplessly; twice he tried to push his way free, but he couldn't dent the mass of bodies crowding him up against the wall. He had no clear idea of how long he was pinned there; his thoughts were confused and frightened, and they drained away all his spirit and strength.

The noise died abruptly; a white man in a steel-gray uniform had pushed his way through the crowd, and his tall presence cut the heart of the men's excitement. They backed away from him, smiling sheepishly, and he stared around with an expression of exasperated impatience on his hard face. "Get up, you two," he said, glancing at Adam and Rufe. "What's this all about?"

Several men began talking at once, awkwardly and evasively; they were like school kids caught misbehaving by a popular teacher, Ingram thought. The sheriff digested their jumbled accounts without any particular change in his expression. Then he looked thoughtfully at Adam. "You'll get unhealthy hanging around barrooms, Adam. I think you'd better stick to the outdoors for a good while. And, Rufe, next time you want to hit somebody, think twice and don't. You understand me?" The sheriff turned then and stared at Ingram. "I want to talk to you," he said. "Mind coming along to my office?"

"I didn't do anything," Ingram said, wetting his lips. But he knew the protest wouldn't help a bit; the sheriff was more interested in him than he was in Adam or Rufe—Ingram had sensed that right away. "I was just minding my own business," he said, making a fluttering little gesture with his hand. "I didn't do anything."

"I just want to talk to you. Come on along."

Ingram sighed and picked up his grip; there was nothing else he could do. Outside in the snow and darkness they walked side by side down the street, the sheriff's big hand light on Ingram's elbow. The snow was melting as it touched the ground, and the streets and sidewalks were black and shining in the splash of light from shop windows. The people hurrying by nodded to the sheriff, and he returned their greetings with a touch of his fingers to the broad brim of his hat.

"Sheriff, I didn't do anything," Ingram said, as they waited at the intersection for a traffic light to change. "The man was cheating—I just pointed it out, that's all."

"That isn't what I want to talk to you about," the sheriff said. "Come on."

The shops they passed were crowded; this was Friday night, Ingram thought in panic. In just two hours the job was supposed to start. . . .

Then Ingram saw something that sent a shock of alarm through his body.

The Texan had appeared on the sidewalk ahead of them, stepping out from a hotel doorway and pausing in the stream of pedestrians to light the cigarette hanging from his lips. He blew out a long stream of smoke as he turned and sauntered along the sidewalk, his eyes idly checking over the colorful displays in the shop windows.

He hadn't seen them, Ingram realized, pulling his neck down into the collar of his coat. Maybe they could slip by him. . . .

But it didn't work that way.

Earl stopped for no apparent reason and stared directly at Ingram. For an instant he didn't seem to recognize him; then his mouth fell open slowly and an almost comical expression of confusion and anger spread over his face. The cigarette he had been raising stopped short a few inches from his lips, and his whole body became tense and rigid; he stood facing them like a figure carved from stone, his eyes flicking warily from Ingram to the sheriff.

The fool, Ingram thought despairingly. Why didn't he drift along, pretend not to notice them. . . .

The sheriff was staring straight ahead, moving with measured, deliberate strides, seemingly unaware of Earl's intent appraisal; but Ingram felt the man's fingers tighten around his arm, clamping there like bands of iron.

As they passed, Earl turned and looked after them, his body motionless in the busy traffic, the cigarette burning unnoticed in his dry lips.

CHAPTER EIGHT

EARL STARTED after them until they turned left at the next intersection; and then he swore softly and flipped his cigarette into the street. The colored guy had got himself into some kind of trouble, ruined all their careful planning; now they were all in trouble.

Earl knew he must find out what had happened, and then decide what to do next; there was no time to contact Novak. But the responsibility didn't worry him; his fury at Ingram crowded everything else from his mind. He walked toward the intersection, sustained and nourished by anger. A hard smile touched his mouth as he moved through the nighttime shoppers, his hands shoved deep in the pockets of his overcoat.

The sheriff's office was located in a one-story red-brick building a half block from the main street of Crossroads. A graveled driveway bordered by evergreens led up to the doorway, and encircled a small park in front of the building. In the quiet lobby Earl removed his hat and smoothed down his hair. The place was more like a respectable office than a jail, he thought, glancing around curiously. Carpeted floors, hunting prints on the walls, a rubber plant in a little reception room by the front windows. On a cork-surfaced bulletin board there was a notice of a Boy Scout meeting, and a large colored poster announcing a clothing drive by the School Improvement Society.

The look and feel of the place reassured him; this was village law and order, he thought, polite and dumb, everybody half asleep as they went around looking for chicken thieves or out-of-season gunners. To his left was an office separated from the lobby by a wooden counter. He saw a trooper working there in an atmosphere of filing cabinets, bulletin boards and telephones, the clear bright illumination shining on his serious face. The trooper sat with his back to the closed door of another office, frowning intently at a sheaf of papers on his desk.

Earl had no plan. But he had to find out what had happened to Ingram. The other office belonged to the sheriff, he guessed. Ingram was in there with him now; he could hear a murmur of voices beyond the thin partition, and he recognized the colored man's anxious, diffident accents.

The trooper glanced up from his reports. "What can I do for you?"

Earl smiled and put his big hands on the counter. "I'm wondering if you could tell me the best way over to New York."

"Sure thing." The trooper took a map folder from the drawer of his desk and came over to the counter. "Take the main street out of Crossroads. Follow the signs to the Delaware Memorial Bridge." He spread the map out on the counter, and indicated the route with a pencil. "Here we are in Crossroads. You just follow those bridge signs, and they'll take you straight to the Jersey Turnpike. There's no way to miss it."

"It looks simple enough. Thanks a lot." Earl smiled at the young trooper. "You the sheriff or constable here?"

"No, just a deputy."

"You got a nice little town. Nice and quiet."

"We try to keep it that way."

Earl's smile became insinuating. "I saw lots of colored people around. Don't they keep you busy?"

The trooper didn't return his smile. "Most of them were

born and raised right here. There's no reason for them to cause trouble."

"Well, I saw a trooper bringing one in just ahead of me. I thought it was a regular thing."

"There's no charge against him," the trooper said shortly. "He's new in town and the sheriff just wants to talk with him."

"Oh, I see," Earl said, still smiling faintly. "Well, that's a pretty good idea. Have a little talk with them right at the start. That makes sense."

The trooper folded the map decisively. "Anything else, mister?"

"No, nothing at all," Earl said. "Thanks very much."

In the shelter of the doorway, Earl lighted a cigarette and pulled his collar up about his throat. The snow had turned into a hard, purposeful rain that pounded on the wet, black streets with a sound like that of distant machine-gun fire. He glanced at his watch, and saw that it was nearly seven o'clock. Just one hour left. . . .

Pulling down his hat brim, he strode across the street and stepped into a doorway that provided some shelter from the gusting wind and rain. He threw away his sodden cigarette and shoved his hands into his pockets. In the wet, cold darkness he settled down to wait for Ingram. . . .

Twenty minutes passed before the colored man came hurrying down the graveled path, his collar turned up against the rain and a lumpy suitcase swinging from his hand.

Earl moved out of the doorway and angled swiftly across the shining street, cutting away the distance between them with long, powerful strides. The rain muffled his footsteps as he came up behind Ingram and said sharply, "Don't turn around, Sambo. Keep moving."

The side street was dimly lighted and the occasional pedestrians paid no attention to them, hurrying past with eyes on the ground, and chins hidden under turned-up coat collars.

"What did he want?" Earl said. He was half a stride behind Ingram, close enough to see the rain on his brown cheek, and the nerve twitching at the corner of his mouth. "What did he want? Start talking."

"How long I planned to stay in town, what I worked at—that's all." Ingram's voice was shrill with fear. "But he got my name. I had to give him my name. You hear? He got my name."

"I'll be waiting for you up in my hotel room."

"I can't—didn't you hear? He knows me."

"You do what I tell you, Sambo. God help you if you don't."

Earl quickened his strides, passing Ingram without bothering to wait for an answer. On the main street he headed for his hotel, dodging occasionally to avoid the umbrellas wielded by women bumping and burrowing along like moles through the wet crowds. Without looking to see if Ingram was following him, he turned into his hotel and went quickly up to his room. He snapped on the lights and put his wet overcoat on the back of a chair. If he doesn't show, Earl thought, if he rats out on us. . . . The .38 Novak had given him was comfortable weight in the pocket of his suit coat. Just let him try, he thought, taking out the gun and hefting it in his big hand.

He put the gun away when he heard footsteps on the landing. Smiling faintly he pulled open the door. Ingram stood staring at him with wide, frightened eyes, his small body looking drenched and miserable in the drafty hallway.

"Come on in," Earl said. "Move, damn it."

Ingram stepped quickly inside and put his suitcase on the floor. "It's wet, man, really wet." His teeth were chattering and his voice sounded high and foolish in his ears. "Never saw anything like this before." He shifted his weight from one foot to the other, staring about the room with quick, nervous eyes. "Really crazy, eh?"

"Yeah, it's wet," Earl said. He sat on the edge of the bed and stared at Ingram. "It's wet because it's raining, Sambo. Do you understand that?"

"I understand," Ingram said. "You're coming in nice and clear."

"All right. We can skip the weather. How did you get mixed up with the law?"

"I was in a card game that ended in a fight. The sheriff

came along and took me in." Ingram wet his lips, remembering the powerful feel of the sheriff's hand on his arm. "He wanted to know what kind of job I was looking for, where I was going to live, stuff like that." Ingram hesitated. "He treated me all right," he said, prodded by Earl's watchful silence. "He gave me the name of the hiring boss out at the mushroom farms, and told me where I could find a room. With a woman named Baker, I think he said."

"Well, isn't that nice?" Earl said dryly. "What else did he want to know?"

"He asked me where I learned about cards, and I told him I just picked it up here and there."

"Why was he interested in that?"

"There was somebody cheating in the game. I had to call him out to save my own hide."

"Judas priest!" Earl said explosively. "You were supposed to come into town and stay nice and quiet. Instead you hit here like a circus parade. Get in a fight, get yourself arrested. Is that your idea of staying nice and quiet?"

Ingram smiled nervously, knowing he couldn't explain any of it to the Texan. The man's mind was made up against him, sealed tight. "It just happened," he said. "I couldn't help it."

"Okay, get the stuff out of your suitcase," Earl said, glancing at his watch. "It's seven thirty. We start moving in a half hour."

"Listen, I can't do it," Ingram cried. "Don't you understand? He's got my name."

"Why didn't you give him a phony?"

"I was too scared. He'd have known if I lied to him. He's like that. And if he got suspicious he might have went through my suitcase and found all that stuff."

"That's tough, Sambo," Earl said, shaking his head thoughtfully. "Real tough. You get in a fight, get yourself picked up by the cops, but you don't have enough brains to give 'em a phony name. That's real tough for you."

Ingram smiled shakily. "You got to get somebody else."

"There isn't time, Sambo."

"Well, we got to put the job off for a couple of weeks."

"We're ready to roll tonight, Sambo." He spoke in a flat,

empty voice, completely without emotion or inflection. "Burke and Novak are on their way by now. It's too late to change anything. Get the stuff out of your suitcase."

"You aren't listening to me," Ingram said frantically. "They got my name, don't you understand? They'll send it to every cop in the country. They'll stake out my friends, my family, so I won't have a prayer. You might as well put a gun to my head and pull the trigger. You got to get somebody else."

Earl stood and took the .38 from his pocket. He hefted it slowly in his hand, watching Ingram's reaction with a cold smile. "Novak gave us a job to do," he said finally. "So get this, Sambo: we're going to do it. Just like we planned." Earl spoke quietly, but his voice was beginning to tremble with emotion. "You understand me? You're going to do what you came here to do. Otherwise I'll blow a hole right between your eyes. You believe that, Sambo?"

"You wouldn't mind doing it, I bet," Ingram said softly. "It wouldn't bother you, would it?"

"I didn't want you on this job, remember. I knew you'd rat out if you got a chance. But you'll stick—because I'm holding a gun at your head. Now open that suitcase and save your whining for your friends."

"Well, maybe that's best," Ingram said, sighing heavily. "No point depressing strangers with my troubles." He glanced at Earl's hard features. "Laugh, clown, laugh—that's my motto. That's your philosophy, too, I guess. The smiling Texan—that's you, man."

"Don't bother being cute. Open the suitcase."

Ingram sighed again and swung the overnight bag onto the bed. He released the catches, raised the lid and removed a folding tray and eight cardboard containers. Earl arranged the containers in rows on the tray, then opened a drawer and lifted out a thermos and a half-dozen cellophane-wrapped sandwiches which he had bought that morning in a town a dozen miles down the highway. While he filled the containers with coffee Ingram put on a waiter's cap and stiffly starched jacket which he had taken from the suitcase. He adjusted the cap at a rakish angle, and buttoned the gleaming white jacket tightly about his throat.

"At yo' service," he said, clicking his heels together, and bowing obsequiously to Earl. "We aim to please around this heah place."

"You look fine," Earl said shortly. "You're just right for a monkey suit."

"Thank you kindly," Ingram murmured, smoothing down the front of the jacket.

The change in the Negro's manner infuriated Earl, but it also made him feel awkward and uncomfortable; the man was laughing at him, he knew, but what the hell for? That's what he couldn't figure out: what was funny about this deal?

"Man, that coffee smells good," Ingram said, smacking his lips with comical relish. "We got enough to spare a cup for ourselves?"

Earl saw then that Ingram was smiling with an effort; his lips were trembling with fear or cold or something. He turned away, angered and embarrassed by the sight. "If you want some, take it, for God's sake," he said. "You might as well get warm."

He walked to the bay windows and pulled the curtains back with a finger. There was a crowd in the brightly lighted bank, and quite a few shoppers still hurrying up and down the sidewalks. The rain had almost stopped but it looked to him as if the weather was turning colder; he began to wonder about ice forming on the hard-surfaced roads and highways. Well, it would be there for anybody who followed him. . . .

Earl stared down the street at the drugstore. The red neon sign above the doorway threw a circle of crimson light on the blackly shining sidewalk. He glanced at his watch. Just about twenty-five minutes more . . .

A footstep sounded behind him, and he wheeled quickly and pulled the gun from his pocket. Ingram said, "Hey, man!" in a soft, terrified voice as Earl jammed the gun into his side, almost knocking the container of hot coffee from his hand.

"You just relax," Earl said, staring at Ingram's frightened face. "You hear? Just take it nice and easy."

"Man, you better do the same," Ingram said, shaking his head slowly. "I was just bringing you some coffee."

"Never mind about me," Earl muttered, turning back to the window. "Just stand here and keep your eyes open. When you see Burke, you get ready to move. . . ."

CHAPTER NINE

SHERIFF BURNS BUTTONED UP his long black slicker as he stepped from his small private office. Morgan, his deputy, smiled at him and said, "Good night to be on the way home, if you ask me. It's pretty miserable, eh?"

Burns looked out the window. The rain was still lashing the sycamores behind his office, although it sounded as if it might be easing off a bit. Adjusting the chin strap of his hat, he glanced at the radio phones that kept Crossroads in direct, round-the-clock contact with the State Police substation five miles down the highway. He didn't bother answering Morgan's comment about the weather; Burns didn't consider the weather a very significant topic just now. He had no prejudice against irrelevant chatter except when it wasted time; most people enjoyed wrapping themselves in cocoons of idle conversation, and he suffered this without really understanding it, victimized somewhat by his essential good humor and tolerance. Still staring at the radio phones, he said, "Who was that in here while I was talking to that colored fellow?"

"Oh—a fellow asking for directions."

"What did he look like?"

"Let's see: pretty big, tall and rangy. Black hair, tanned face. Kind of hard-looking."

"Was he wearing a black overcoat and a brown felt hat?"

"Yeah, that's right." Morgan knew something was bothering the sheriff. He waited patiently, his expression deliberately impassive; as a six-month rookie he had learned to keep his hero worship under wraps. Burns was just another man, he realized, although there were still times when he felt this judgment was ridiculously inadequate. Like saying Everest was just another mountain.

"Did he talk about anything else?" the sheriff said.

Morgan hesitated, reassembling every detail of the conversation. The sheriff always wanted details; nothing was irrelevant in his opinion until it had been proven so. But the conclusions he drew from details frequently bewildered Morgan.

"I got the feeling he didn't like colored people." Morgan was encouraged by the sheriff's thoughtful nod. "He asked if the colored folks here gave us a lot of trouble—just like he'd ask if two and two made four. You know what I mean?"

"Did he happen to mention the colored man in my office?"

"Why, yes he did!" Morgan was excited and surprised. "He saw you bringing him in and he asked if he was in trouble."

"So?"

"Well—" Morgan hesitated. "I said there was no charge against him."

"That wasn't necessary, was it?"

"No—but he got me kind of annoyed." Morgan punched the space bar of the typewriter in exasperation. "I should have kept my mouth shut."

The sheriff pulled on his gauntlets and said, "Keep your ear close to that speaker tonight. If anything takes the State Police cars away from this area, I want to know about it. Right away. Understand?"

"Yes, sir."

At the doorway the sheriff paused and glanced at Morgan with a slight smile. "Don't blame yourself for being annoyed at that character. I'm getting annoyed with him, too."

At the corner of Main Street the sheriff paused and glanced up and down the blocks of busy shops, his figure tall and black in the shining slicker. Everything seemed nice and quiet; people hurrying along the wet sidewalks, couples strolling into the movie, merchants making their weekend deposits in the brightly lighted bank, the traffic whizzing through the town in orderly lanes. Crossing on the green light, he stopped beside the bank and stared for a few seconds at the battered blue station wagon that was parked on the side street. It looked like a candidate for a junkyard, but the sheriff knew all about the powerful engine under its hood. Tommy Bailey at the Atlas station had told his boss about it, and the news had drifted casually back to the sheriff. He hadn't thought much about it at the time. Lots of people liked to soup-up old cars. Nothing unusual about that. But then the colored man had come to town, a big-city Negro with soft hands and considerable know-how with a deck of cards. And when he'd taken him in for a little talk the tall, dark-haired man who owned that station wagon had popped right in to pump Morgan about it.

So what did it add up to? Two strangers . . . a big-city card shark and a man who had spent a day poking about the area in an old crate that could move like a streak of lightning. A man who said he wanted to go into farming but sounded as if he didn't know a damned thing about it. *Hadn't made up his mind whether to try sheep or steers or a dairy herd. . . .* That's what he said, just as if there weren't a hundred different problems in land and money involved in such a choice. . . .

The sheriff glanced at his watch: twenty to eight. For an instant he hesitated, staring at the car, and then letting his eyes sweep down the shining street. It didn't add up to anything yet. That's what nagged at him—that little word *yet.*

There was the fragrance of a good dinner in the warm hallway of the sheriff's comfortable home on the outskirts of Crossroads. He hung up his hat and slicker, smoothed his hair down and went into the living room to warm his big hands at the fireplace. Everything in the worn and faded room was part of the life he had lived before his wife died; the family pictures on the mantel, the crocheted mats on the backs of the big chairs, the shelves of familiar books beside the hearth. He liked things as they had been in those happier days, and he had resisted the sporadic attempts of his daughter to brighten up the place.

Filling a stubby black pipe, he called, "Nancy? You home?"

"Yes, Dad. In the kitchen."

"That sounds hopeful." He strolled down the hallway, unbuttoning his uniform jacket. "What's for dinner?"

"Roast beef, hashed brown potatoes, et cetera, et cetera. You'll manage."

"An army could manage on that."

"Do you want a drink? There's time." She stood at the stove with an apron over the dark skirt she had worn to the office, a tall girl with blond hair and something of her father's strength in the planes of her face.

He didn't want anything to drink because he might have to go out again, but he said, "Sure, let's celebrate, honey. Want me to do the honors?"

"No, I'll take care of it." When she turned from the stove he put a hand on her arm. "Hard day?" He studied the clean, familiar lines of her face with a smile. "All tuckered out in the interests of Slade and Nelson, attorneys at law?"

"Just the usual—nothing out of the ordinary."

He patted her shoulders. "Well, it's a nice night to put your feet up and relax."

She glanced at him briefly and said, "How very true." Then she slipped past him and went into the pantry for glasses and the bottle of whisky.

The sheriff sat down at the kitchen table and took his time applying an even light to the tobacco in his pipe. Rain pattered against the sides of the house, streaming down the dark windowpanes in slow, level waves. A good night to put your feet up and relax, he thought. An innocent comment, but it annoyed her. But how was he to know that?

She made his drink, whisky with a touch of water, and put it beside him on the table. "How about you?" he asked her.

"I don't feel like anything."

"Means I drink alone then. Most pretty girls would save a man from that."

She pushed a strand of blond hair from her forehead. "How was your day?" she said.

"Like yours, I guess, just the usual routine." He couldn't tell whether she was really interested or not; she was stirring the gravy and her voice had matched the mechanical rhythm of her turning hand. "I had a speeder this morning, an idiot salesman with a schedule he couldn't have kept with a jet plane. He had to be in Wilmington by ten, but had three calls to make in Crossroads first."

She went into the pantry, and the sheriff sipped his drink slowly, relishing the warmth spreading through his body.

When his daughter returned he tried to think of something else to talk about, but this was always a difficult chore for him; he had no taste for tidbits of conversation and his occasional jokes never seemed to strike her funny bone. And his thoughts were turning on his own problems. The two strangers. . . . He wondered what they were doing. He had given the Negro the address of Mrs. Baker's boardinghouse. He should be there by now. If he really wanted a room.

"Well, what happened to your speeder?"

"Oh, him. Well, I had to throw the book at him. His commissions aren't worth a child's life." Finishing his drink, he said, "Excuse me a second, hon. I've got to make a phone call."

He went into the hall and dialed Mrs. Baker's boardinghouse. When she answered he said, "Sheriff Burns, Mrs. Baker. Hope I didn't take you away from supper."

She laughed. "If you did I wouldn't mind none. What is it, Sheriff?"

"I sent a man over to your place a while ago. I just wondered if he'd shown up yet."

"No, not yet. What was his name?"

"John Ingram."

"I'll watch for him. I'll keep something hot for him. And I'm much obliged to you, Sheriff, for recommending my home."

"Don't mention it. Good night, Mrs. Baker."

When he put the receiver down the sheriff realized that his vague uneasiness was hardening into suspicion. He knew his town well and he trusted his feelings about it; when something felt wrong he became cautious. His picture of the village was made up of conscious and unconscious impressions, tactile, emotional, intuitive. The place had a right-and-wrong impact on him and when something was wrong he couldn't relax until he had pinned it down. But when everything felt right the town seemed whole and perfect; the smell of burning leaves or factory smoke, the sounds of traffic and the activities of dogs, cats and small boys, all of these merged into reassuring patterns of harmony and sense.

Now something was wrong; the pattern was blurred and little storm signals flew in his mind.

"Hon, I've got to get back to the office for a while," he said, buttoning his jacket.

"Right now? Before dinner?"

"I'm afraid so, hon." He saw the quick disappointment in her eyes and it puzzled and hurt him; why couldn't he ever figure out this girl of his? He had felt she was bored, and would just as soon be alone. But no. She wanted to have dinner with him, and had gone to a lot of trouble to make a little occasion of it. Instead of chops or an omelet, there was roast beef with all the trimmings. That meant she must have shopped on her lunch hour, probably had driven all the way to Pierce's for the roast. . . .

"I may not be long," he said rather awkwardly. "Could you hold things up for half an hour?"

"It doesn't matter. I might as well go ahead."

Every kid in town brought him his problems, he thought, somewhat bitterly; they trusted him, listened hopefully to his injunctions or suggestions. Grownups, too. Men with business worries or family mix-ups talked them out with him, knowing his judgments were usually tempered with humor and common sense. He was not an educated man but he had a knack of seeing straight to the core of a situation without being distracted by emotional irrelevancies.

Everybody in town leaned on him—everybody except this girl of his.

It was a failure that had rebuked him since his wife's death a dozen years ago. When Nancy was just a child he had been ruefully amused by his inability to understand her completely; sometimes she would snuggle in his arms for hours at a stretch, but on other occasions he couldn't even coax a smile to her lips. When his wife was alive it hadn't seemed too serious. His wife used to say: "She's a real live girl, not a little toy. Just let her be, let her grow. Open your arms and let her go—she'll come back, don't worry."

But with his wife gone he had felt his inadequacies much more keenly. He had been eager for Nancy to marry, feeling that might solve most of it. He had dreamed of gunning trips with her imaginary husband, family dinners on Sunday, and grandchildren to teach all the things he knew about the woods and fields around Crossroads. It wasn't a selfish dream; he wanted it for her, not himself. The right kind of man would fuse all of her contradictory moods into his own strength and needs, and children would challenge her quick intelligence and release the springs of compassion he knew were locked beneath the cool surface of her personality.

If they could only talk things over, he thought. Sit down with a cup of coffee and be free and easy with each other. He didn't want to run her life, but he longed to be a useful part of it. When she wanted to take a job in New York a couple of years ago he had sent her off with a smile—even though he knew the house would be a tomb without her. But he had opened his arms and let her go, as he'd promised his wife he would. She seemed happy in New York. Her letters bubbled with excitement. New job, new friends, all kinds of fun. He had visited her several times, wearing a good suit and determined not to play the hayseed in front of her friends. She shared an apartment with a saucy, bright-eyed girl who did something with women's clothes in a department store. The walls were covered with odd-looking pictures and bullfight posters. They sat on little stools about eight inches high and ate dishes made with sour cream and wine.

He had adopted an approving manner for her sake. Her friends chattered like birds, but he didn't expect her to share his preference for men who could hunt together for a week without using more than a few dozen words the whole time. One young man had asked him how many bandits he'd killed, but he was too old to fall into traps like that. He had got along fine. Nancy hadn't been ashamed of him; if she had been he couldn't have stood it. Not for himself, but for her.

And then, without any warning, she had returned to Crossroads. He knew something was wrong, but there was no way to bridge the awkward gulf between them; they had both tried but the attempts had been frustrated, and finally lost in a waste of banalities.

It was such a damned loss, he thought now, feeling the stiffness and hurt in her silence. She was a lovely, moody child in his eyes, but she had the hips and breasts of a woman, and her limbs were slim and graceful and strong; she was more than ready for the pain and joy of a home and children, but here she was keeping house for a father who couldn't even guess at the thoughts running through her head. In spite of her maturity, she was still the little girl who had baffled him with her reserve and her secrets; she had to carry her troubles by herself because she wasn't able to ask him for help. And that was his fault, not hers.

It was a hell of a thing to fail in, he thought wearily. "I'll shove along," he said, touching her shoulder. "I'm sorry, hon. Dinner smells wonderful."

"I'll leave yours on the stove," she said.

"Sure. Thanks." He hesitated an instant, smiling at her smooth cheeks, then turned and walked into the front hallway. The rain had stopped, but he put on his slicker anyway; at this time of year you couldn't tell. He adjusted the chin strap of his hat, checked his gun out of long habit, and stepped out into the night.

CHAPTER TEN

AT EIGHT O'CLOCK the last customers were ushered from the bank. The stout, elderly guard called a smiling good night to each of them before he stepped back inside and pulled the big double doors shut against the windy darkness.

The lights in the shops along Main Street went out one

by one and the stream of shoppers evaporated quickly from the shining sidewalks. The rain had stopped but a wind lashed the sides of the buildings, reverberating against the metal trash cans and stirring currents and whirlpools in the dark waters rushing along the gutter.

It was one minute after eight.

Earl and Ingram stood at the windows of the hotel room staring down at the closed doors of the bank. Their faces were pressed close to the curtains, and their eyes shone softly in the dimly lighted room. Earl glanced down the block to the drugstore. "I'll be right behind you," he said, whispering the words into Ingram's ear. "I'll be watching you."

"You keep watching me and that guard's gonna blow your head off," Ingram said dryly. Fear hadn't left him, but some of it had been dissolved in an exasperated anger; he didn't care about Earl's contempt for him, but he couldn't be indifferent to Earl's stupidity—the man was ready to get them all killed through his dumb suspicions and hatred. Instead of concentrating on what was coming, he was indulging his prejudice like a spoiled child. "You watch yourself," he muttered softly. "You're acting like you never pulled anything but a toilet chain in your whole life."

But Earl didn't hear him; he was staring at the doors of the drugstore, his fingers tightening on Ingram's arm. "Here it goes," he said, his voice hard with tension.

The doors of the drugstore had been pushed open by a white-jacketed Negro balancing a tray of sandwiches and coffee in his right hand. As he stepped into the pool of light from the neon sign, a big man in a dark overcoat moved toward him from the shadows of the side street. The Negro started for the curb, but before he could take two steps the man in the overcoat stumbled heavily against him, jarring him with his bulk, and knocking the tray of coffee and sandwiches from his hand.

It appeared to have been a simple, unavoidable accident. No one who watched the sequence of events could have thought otherwise . . .

"Get set," Earl said sharply.

Burke was adding to the confusion now, he saw, apologizing profusely to the delivery boy, and then stooping in an awkward attempt to retrieve the soggy sandwiches and the split-open cartons of coffee. The boy was staring in dismay at the mess of food on the sidewalk. Burke patted his shoulder consolingly, and took a wallet from his hip pocket. The boy shook his head quickly at that, then picked up his tray and hurried back into the drugstore. An elderly couple stopped and smiled sympathetically at Burke before going on their way. It was a small incident, forgotten as quickly as it happened . . . Burke shrugged and walked across the street, strolling toward the bank building, his black, bulky figure almost lost in the shifting shadows of the night. Earl checked his watch for the last time. They had about eight minutes to work in; it would take the counterman at the drugstore that long to make up a fresh order for the bank.

"All right," he said to Ingram. "Grab that tray."

There was no need to take anything else from the room. Earl's things were in the station wagon, and Ingram's overcoat and fedora could be safely left behind; they were standard-brand, secondhand clothes and the police would learn nothing from them.

Earl went quickly down the stairs and opened the door that led directly to the street. He stepped out, pulling his overcoat collar up around his throat, and glanced casually up and down the sidewalk. This was the one chance moment in Novak's plan; a pedestrian pausing in front of the hotel might have delayed them. And their schedule allowed precious little tolerance for delays. But the sidewalks were deserted, shining and empty under the street lamps. Earl waved Ingram on. "Get going," he said.

The injunction was unnecessary; Ingram was already on his way, the tray balanced professionally in his right hand as he angled across the street toward the bank building.

Earl watched Ingram's white-jacketed figure move into the semidarkness, before drifting across the street to intercept Burke, who was sauntering casually toward the intersection. Everything was working perfectly; the sidewalks were empty and the town was quiet as they fell in step with their hands deep in the pockets of their overcoats and their faces shadowed by the turned-down brims of their hats. They didn't speak or look at one another, but Earl could sense the excitement in Burke; his breath was coming sharply and rapidly, whistling faintly through his flattened nose.

Twenty yards ahead of them Ingram trotted up the steps of the bank and rapped sharply on the glass panel of the big, brass-handled door. The sound carried clearly along the street, sharp and distinct in the silence. They had the town to themselves, Earl thought, glancing over his shoulder. Only an occasional car or truck came through the town, yellow fog lights gleaming, and tires spinning with a liquid sound on the wet asphalt.

Ingram rapped a second time, and then turned to look down the street at them, his eyes white and scared in the darkness.

"Goddamit," Burke said. His voice was a high, sharp whisper. "What's the matter?"

"Slow down," Earl said. They were closing the distance too rapidly. He put a hand on Burke's arm, forcing him to match his own measured strides.

They heard the metallic click of a sliding bolt, and then light flashed over Ingram as the door swung open. A voice said, "You're late, Charlie. Come on, these people can't work on empty stomachs." It was an old man's voice, high and strident, but charged with a folksy good humor.

Ingram murmured something under his breath, holding the tray in front of his face. The guard moved aside to let him enter, hands resting negligently on his hips.

Ingram heard Burke and Earl coming up behind him, their heels striking the sidewalk with an urgent emphasis. He stepped quickly into the warm and bright interior of the bank, seeing the women in the tellers' cages directly ahead of him and several men working at desks behind a low wooden railing. No one paid any attention to him; the men at the desks didn't look up, the tellers were busy with their accounts.

He stood in the glare of bright lights with warm air on his face and a feeling of busy, serious work going on around him—that was all he knew, that and the fear being driven through his body by the desperate pounding of his heart.

Ingram heard the guard say, "Sorry, gentlemen, we're closed for—" But then his voice broke off in a sharp grunt of pain.

The door closed with a soft click, and Earl passed swiftly in front of Ingram, looking big and dangerous as he stepped over the wooden railing and pointed a gun at the startled men at the desks. "Everybody keep quiet," he said, without raising his voice. "Just stay nice and quiet." The girl at the switchboard near the side door stared at him in terror, her face twisting in a spasm of hysteria. "Get those earphones off," Earl yelled sharply. "Stand up and keep quiet. You scream and I'll start shooting." The girl came quickly to her feet then, clamping both hands across her trembling mouth. "That's right; don't be a hero," Earl said, his gun swinging easily over the four men at the desks. "Everybody take it nice and quiet. Nobody's going to get hurt."

Burke had pushed the guard ahead of him toward the tellers' cages, prodding him in the back with his gun. "Okay, girls, I want it all," he said quietly. "You get cute and Dad here gets it right in the spine. Got that clear?"

A man at one of the desks said, "Do as he tells you, Jennie. You too, Ann." He stared at Earl's gun, his eyes big and frightened behind rimless glasses. "We're all going to do just what you want. There's no reason for you to hurt anybody."

"Fine," Earl said. "That's just fine. Now keep quiet."

Burke had taken the guard's gun and pushed the old man into a corner. Now he was stuffing bundles of cash into a long linen bag he had pulled from the pocket of his overcoat.

"How much longer?" Earl said, risking a glance at the front door.

"Rush it up, sister," Burke said, stepping to the second cage.

Ingram swallowed the dryness in his throat, forcing the bitter taste of fear deep into his stomach. It was going to work, it was going to work—the thought sounded in his mind like a breathless prayer.

"All right," Burke said, backing toward the front door. "Let's go."

Without taking his eyes from the men at the desks, Earl stepped over the wooden railing and joined Burke. He said, "Okay, everybody stay put for a while. Just think how lucky you are." He nodded at Ingram, as Burke pulled open the door and went quickly down the steps of the bank to the dark sidewalk. Earl started after him, but before Ingram could move, a powerful voice shouted an order.

"Hold it there! Get your hands up!" The command came from behind a car that was parked across the street about fifty feet from the entrance to the bank.

Burke swore in bitter, despairing confusion and dropped to his knees, the gun in his hand swinging up toward the parked car. As he fired, one of the women tellers began to scream softly and terribly, her voice breaking into convulsive, senseless tremors. Ingram couldn't force himself to move; he stared out the door, helpless with fear, the tray trembling giddily in his hand. Burke was sighting along the barrel of his gun when an orange flame seared the darkness behind the parked car. The report of the shot went banging down the street as Burke rolled over backwards, shouting senseless words in a high, raging voice. Earl tried to lift him to his feet, but Burke struggled to a sitting position and fired three wild shots into the shadows behind the parked car. Another orange flash appeared against the darkness. Earl staggered as if he had been struck by a two-by-four; his knees buckled when he stumbled into the side of the building and his head rolled on his shoulders in pain. Burke sat cross-legged on the wet sidewalk, a sagging, heaving buddha, one hand supporting his weight, and the other pointing his gun in an awkward, straight-armed gesture at the parked car.

It was only then that Ingram's paralysis broke; he screamed convulsively and threw the tray of coffee and sandwiches to the floor.

The men who had been at the desk were lying on the

floor. One of them raised his head and shouted at him, "Get down, you fool! You want to be killed!"

"No, no," Ingram cried wildly. He leaped over the wooden railing and ran to the rear of the bank, fighting down a hysterical compulsion to laugh. . . . They didn't know he was part of the job. They still thought he was the delivery boy.

The switchboard operator was backed against a wall with her hands over her mouth. Another shot sounded outside and she jerked as if an electric shock had gone through her body. She began to moan in fear, staring at Ingram with wild, frantic eyes.

"Lie down flat," he shouted at her. "You're all right."

She didn't seem to hear him; she stood trembling against the wall, a shrill, keening moan forcing itself through her compulsively locked hands.

Ingram ran to the side door and twisted the key in the lock. Pulling open the door he plunged into the darkness, fear like a mad animal at his heels. The sound of another shot brought him to a skidding stop. He had to get away from the firing, he thought wildly. To his right was a haven of darkness, the side street stretching away to safety. To his left was Main Street, its wet pavement gleaming colorfully under the light from the traffic signal at the intersection. Rain was coming down again, driven like hard pellets through the swaying black trees. He needed an overcoat; they'd catch him trying to run away in the waiter's jacket. And he needed something hot to drink. His thoughts were broken into crazy splinters by fear. Forget about something to drink . . . run and hide. That was the only thing that mattered. Find a place to hide.

A few people were coming down Main Street toward the bank, but their progress was slow and cautious; the sound of the last shot had driven them all into alleys and doorways.

Something moved in the darkness near the curb, and a gasp of terror tightened his throat. He turned to run into the safety of the side street, but then he heard a metallic clicking coming from one of the parked cars. Ingram crept forward slowly, stepping off the sidewalk onto the sodden plot of grass that bordered the street.

"Earl?" he whispered frantically. "Earl? You there, Earl?" It had to be Earl; he must have stumbled around here after getting shot. . . .

"Goddam!" The voice was just a few feet from him, tight with pain and fury.

Another shot exploded in front of the bank, and a man shouted an order in a huge, powerful voice.

"Ingram?" Earl cried softly. "Ingram! Come here."

"Where?"

"Here, you fool."

Ingram crept swiftly toward the angry whisper and found Earl kneeling in the gutter, supporting his weight against the side of the car and pulling impotently at the door handle with his good hand. "Go around the other side," he whispered, the words coming in painful little gasps. "You got to drive. I'm hit. Move, damn you."

Ingram crouched low and ran to the driver's side, prodded by the anger in Earl's voice. He wasn't thinking any more; his mind was a vacuum, empty of everything, empty even of fear.

Sliding into the car he opened the opposite door and hauled Earl in beside him, tugging frantically at his awkward, pain-cramped body. Earl cursed weakly and Ingram saw the sweat standing out on lips and forehead.

"I didn't mean to hurt you," he said foolishly.

"Shut up! Shut up!" Earl bent forward and shoved the key into the ignition. "The starter's on the left. Let's go." Ingram fumbled around beside the steering post and Earl said, "On the floor! On the floor!"

The motor caught with a swelling throb of power. Ingram tramped on the gas, and the car shot out from the curb like something blown from a cannon.

"Easy, damn it," Earl yelled at him. Ingram was fighting the spinning wheel, trying desperately to keep the car in the street. "Feed it slow." Earl twisted around, breathing harshly and stared out the rear window. "Make the first left. Then give it everything." In spite of the pain and weakness, his voice cracked like a whip. "You want to live, Sambo, you make this crate move."

"What happened? What went wrong?"

"Never mind that now. You just drive. Left here—left, you fool." Ingram hurled the car into the turn without checking his speed; the tires screamed hideously as they clawed into the wet pavement, and Earl grabbed the yawing wheel with his good hand. "Hit the gas now," he yelled. "Give it everything."

The rain was coming harder now, flailing at the side of the car and driving through the fog lights in thick crystal streaks. They swept through a slum area, and up a swerving incline that brought them onto a straight stretch of road.

"Let her out," Earl cried. "Pound it. We got to get to Novak."

"I can't drive any faster. I'm doing sixty now."

"Faster, I'm telling you."

"I can't."

"You afraid of getting a ticket?" Earl's foot came down hard on Ingram's, pushing the accelerator flat against the floorboards. The car leaped ahead like an angry animal into the walls of rainwater, the motor snarling under the full load of power.

"You're crazy!" Ingram shouted the words over the roar of the engine. The car swayed wildly as the tires spun and hissed on the slick surface of the road. "We'll kill ourselves."

"So will the sheriff if he catches us," Earl said. "Drive, damn you. We got to get to Novak." He leaned forward and rubbed the mist from the windshield with the sleeve of his coat. "I'll tell you when to stop," he said. There was no pain in his shoulder. He was weak from shock and loss of blood, but the pain wouldn't start for a while yet. . . . Why hadn't he dropped the sheriff, he wondered. He had seen his tall black figure behind the parked car. One shot would have settled him for good. But he hadn't even tried. And he hadn't tried to pick up the money. It was lying right next to Burke's hand, thousands and thousands of dollars stuffed into a long linen bag. Why hadn't he grabbed it?

He shouted suddenly, "Slow down. Here he is."

As Ingram drove his foot against the brake he saw the red taillights of a car shining ahead of them through the rain and darkness. He was thrown forward by the skidding, wrenching stop, but the steering wheel kept him from smashing into the windshield. Earl had nothing to hold onto and only his instinctively outflung arm saved him from a split skull; his forehead struck his wrist instead of the dashboard, and the blow merely stunned him for an instant. He straightened slowly, feeling that he might be sick; the pain in his shoulder was starting now, spreading nauseatingly into his stomach and loins. A bullet never hurt much at first. That was the only good thing about getting shot up. His thoughts drifted. It was funny, damned funny . . .

"Get out," he said to Ingram. "Tell him the job went wrong. Then come back here and give me a hand." He found a reserve of strength and said harshly, "Go on, move."

Ingram climbed out and ran through the driving rain to Novak's car, his feet slipping on the treacherous surface of the road. Novak cranked the window down and stared at him, his wide, hard features softened by the faint light from the dashboard.

"What's the matter?" he yelled over the drumming rain; he could see the haggard fear in Ingram's face.

"We got caught," Ingram said, gripping the door with desperate, grateful fingers. "Burke's shot and killed. And Earl's got a bullet in him. He's hurt bad. We got to get out of here. They're coming after us."

"How about the money, for Christ's sake?"

"We didn't get nothing. It all went wrong. We're lucky to be alive. I'll get Earl. He can't make it alone."

"Yeah," Novak said, staring at him with narrowing eyes. "You do that."

Ingram ran back to the station wagon and jerked open Earl's door. "Come on," he said. "We got to hurry."

"Pull me toward you," Earl said. He ground his teeth together, and his voice came out thin and cold and hard. "Pull me, Sambo. I got to get my feet under me. I can walk okay."

"Sure, sure," Ingram said. "Try your damnedest. We got to make it fast."

But as he took hold of Earl's lapels, the sudden accelerating roar of Novak's car sounded through the rain-drumming silence. The noise froze him; he stared at Earl's sweat-blistered face, unable to move or think, conscious of nothing but the giddy fear flowing through his body. Earl twisted away from him, cursing as he rubbed the steam from the windshield. Ingram ran down the road shouting, "Wait, please wait, Mr. Novak," in a shrill, imploring voice. But finally he stopped, his breath coming in long, shuddering sobs.

The taillights of Novak's car became smaller and smaller, until they were tiny crimson dots that bobbed up and down on the horizon and then disappeared altogether into the darkness.

Ingram felt the cold rain driving into his face, and the wind molding the waiter's jacket tight against his wet body. He began to shiver; he was chilled to the bone, and the wind cut his cheeks like a whip made of ice.

He went slowly back to the car, hugging his body with his arms. Earl stared at him, his eyes flat and expressionless.

"He ran out on us," Ingram said helplessly. "Left us here."

They stared at each other through the rain and darkness, enveloped in a silence that was as lonely and menacing as the night itself.

"All right, get in," Earl said in a weary, bitter voice. "We got to keep moving. Just you and me, Sambo. Just you and me now."

CHAPTER ELEVEN

THEY DROVE STEADILY for half an hour, burrowing deeper and deeper into a black countryside, following the narrow muddy roads that twisted like the coils of a net through the woods and meadows of the broad valley. Earl told Ingram where and when to turn without qualifying or explaining his orders. Outside of these clipped instructions, he paid no attention to him; he had rolled his window down, and was watching for the landmarks that were occasionally revealed by the crazily bouncing headlights of the car. He had remembered the lonely farmhouse he had seen while driving around these back roads, and he was trying to find his way back to it. Someone lived there, he knew; there had been smoke coming from the chimney. But they weren't young people. Otherwise there would probably be a look of paint and fresh curtains about the place, and the doors of the barn would have been rehung and closed against the weather. Old people, probably waiting to die on their worn-out patch of land. Or just an old man all by himself. . . .

It was what he needed for tonight, a place to go to ground. The rain would wash away the tracks of the car, and he would have a breathing spell in which to think and make his plans. They wouldn't catch him tonight. . . .

He wasn't afraid, and he wasn't even angry any more; he would pay off Novak someday, but dwelling on the ways and means was a luxury he couldn't afford now. Everything had gone smash, and he accepted this calmly; they just hadn't figured on the sheriff . . . Now his job was to stay alive, to stay free. He had been wounded and hunted before, and he had made out all right; he'd lick this, too.

To survive had become his goal, to live from minute to minute, hour to hour. His needs were basic and simple, a doctor, money, another car. I'll get them, he thought, as he stared at the wet, black countryside. I'll lick this thing. Get back to Lory. He was sustained by the essential simplicity of his problem. In other defeats he had been confused and infuriated by the complexity of his needs, and the anonymity of his enemies. He never knew what he wanted or who stood in his way of getting it. But now everything was coldly, transparently clear.

"Turn left here," he cried; there was an exultant lift to his voice as he saw the crossroad. This was where he had met the old hound dog.

"Where we heading?" Ingram said, fighting the bouncing, sliding car.

"Just another hundred yards or so," Earl said. "It's a place we can stay for the night."

Ingram drove on until the headlights picked out a rotting

wooden gate that hung crookedly on rusty hinges. The entrance was partially blocked by a tall ragged hedge of lilac that grew along the fence line, but he saw a lane twisting back to an old stone farmhouse, and a single yellow light shining palely from a first-floor window.

Ingram pulled the gate open, drove the car beyond it and climbed out again to push the gate back into place.

"I got to get out of these clothes," he muttered, as they approached the farmhouse, with the car plunging and plowing through the thick mud plastering the lane. "I got to get warm."

Earl saw his lips were trembling. Couldn't take a little cold . . . none of them could . . . "Without this rain we wouldn't have a chance, Sambo. Remember that."

"I just said I got to get warm."

"I heard you. Now listen; you go up and knock on the door. Tell whoever answers that we need a place to sleep for the night. I'll be right behind you, don't forget."

Ingram braked to a sliding stop in the muddy yard in front of the farmhouse. When he cut off the motor the sound of the rain became intensified; they could hear it hammering metallically on the roof of the car, and pounding with a muted but heavier effect on the soft, sodden earth. "Don't forget one other thing," Ingram said, looking at Earl. "We're both in the same mess. I got a right to decide how to get out of it. Just remember that."

Earl shifted his position, and removed the gun from the pocket of his overcoat. "You see this?" he said, watching Ingram steadily. "It means you don't have any rights at all. Get this straight now; we aren't partners in this deal. We don't vote on things. You got a chance just as long as you jump when I tell you. You got that, Sambo?"

Ingram saw the dashboard light flickering along the blue barrel of the gun. "I got it," he said, looking up into Earl's dangerous eyes. "Yeah, I got it."

"Start moving."

Ingram climbed out and went quickly up a flight of sagging wooden steps to the porch of the farmhouse. Earl came around the car holding the gun in his overcoat pocket, and stepping carefully to avoid the deep cold puddles of water in the yard.

There was no sound for a few seconds after Ingram knocked but then they heard a shuffle of footsteps within the house. The door opened very slowly and a bar of widening yellow light fell across the rotting boards of the porch. A frail, gray-haired woman in a black shawl peered up at them, her birdlike eyes shining behind small, rimless glasses. One hand held the shawl tightly about her throat, while the other brushed ineffectually at erratic wisps of gray hair that fluttered in the cold wind. She wore black rubber boots, and a number of old shapeless sweaters, but the meagerness of her body seemed to be accentuated rather than concealed by the layers of bulky clothing. She took a step forward, peering up into Ingram's face with an air of excitement and surprise. "You've come back, eh? Crawling back with your tail between your legs, like I said you would." She began to laugh then, tilting her head to one side in a gesture of flirtatious derision; her manner was scornful and complacent at once, as if she were rebuking a child who had ignored her advice and gotten himself into trouble. "And who's your friend? Who's your fine friend?"

"He's sick, I mean he's hurt, ma'am," Ingram said.

"Oh yes, indeed," she said in a thin, self-satisfied voice. "You need things—oh, yes. They weren't kind to you in the cities, were they? But I warned you, didn't I?"

Earl realized she was half crazy. "We're cold and tired," he said, trying to manage a smile for her piercing little eyes. "Could we come in and get warm?"

"Papa will want to talk to you, of course," she said. "I should send you around to the back door, but never mind. It's blew down, I think. Come in, and mind you wipe your boots."

They followed her into a drafty living room where an old man lay against the wall in a double bed. He worked himself up on one elbow as they came in, glaring at them with alert, suspicious eyes. It was impossible to guess at his height or weight; the shape of his body was lost under the mound of dirty quilts that covered his bed. But it was very obvious that he was aged; his wispy white hair floated grotesquely in the draft, and his whiskers gleamed like silvery moss on his sunken cheeks and throat.

"He's come crawling back," the old woman announced in a perky voice. "Like I told you all along."

"Close the door after you, can't you even remember?" the old man said irritably. "You'll freeze us all, Crazybone. Go on. Get."

"Oh, all right," she said, shrugging indifferently. "I'll nail it up tight." She pushed aimlessly at the strands of gray hair. "Seems like it should be fixed once and for all." But she didn't move; she stood staring at the tips of her boots without any expression at all on her face.

"Go close the door," he said quietly. "Close it, you hear?"

She turned and stalked from the room, her rubber boots squeaking dryly on the cold floor boards. The man sighed and put his head on the pillow. "You fellows been in an accident?"

"Yeah, that's right," Ingram said.

"Bad night to be outside. Only a rich man or a fool goes out in weather like this." He chuckled softly, flicking glances at them with suspicious little eyes.

The old woman returned and opened a door on the opposite side of the room. She smiled back at Ingram, her glasses flashing in the gloomy light. "I told you you'd come back," she said.

"Don't pay her no mind," the old man said, as she slipped through the doorway. "Crazybone's a little daft. She's my wife. Crazybone's just a name I gave her. Real name is Martha, like George Washington's wife. We used to keep a dozen colored hands a long while back. When the farming went bad they drifted off to the city mostly. Crazybone's always looking for 'em to come back. What kind of accident was you in?"

"There's just the two of you here?" Earl said.

"Don't need nobody else. Seems like we get along better every year. Eat less all the time." He chuckled again, but his eyes were switching back and forth between them like vigilant little swords. "Pretty soon we'll stop eating altogether. That'll be a good trick, won't it?"

"You got any whisky around?" Earl asked him. He felt very weak; the strength seemed to be draining out of him from the wound in his shoulder. It wasn't bleeding much; but that could be bad or good, he wasn't sure which. A small heap of wood burned in the great stone fireplace, but no warmth penetrated the thick cold dampness of the room.

"No whisky, no gin, no beer," the old man said, shaking his head with finality.

"How about coffee?"

"Told you we eat less all the time. Same goes for drinking." He seemed proud of their abstemiousness; his eyes twinkled with sadistic merriment. "A man can get along without lots of things. You learn that when you're old as I am. What happened to you? You sick, mister?"

"Where did your wife go?"

"Hard to tell about Crazybones. She keeps a man studying, I can tell you."

"Go take a look," Earl said to Ingram. "See what she's up to."

"Oh, don't worry about her," the old man said.

"You got a phone here?"

"Don't need one."

"How about neighbors? Any people likely to stop by tonight?"

"Nearest house is a mile down the road. No call for anybody to come by. What's worrying you anyway?"

Earl glanced around and saw a radio on a table beside a sagging sofa. "That work?" he said to the old man.

"Wouldn't have it around if it didn't."

Earl went slowly across the room, limping to favor the pain in his side, and sat down on the sofa. He turned on the set and a light gleamed faintly behind the rheostat. Finally the strains of a dance band overcame the static and flooded the cold air with incongruously cheerful rhythms. Earl rested weakly against the arm of the sofa. The pain in his shoulder beat slowly but solidly, pounding against his nerves with sledge-hammer blows.

He glanced around, taking an automatic inventory of the room. There was little furniture, just the bed, sofa and a couple of straight-backed chairs. The mantelpiece above the massive field-stone fireplace was crowded with junk; dirt-rimmed bottles, yellowing newspapers, a few chipped cups, several faded photographs in wooden frames. The floor boards were of uneven widths, buckled with cold and age, but they were like iron under his feet. It was a house built to last a dozen lifetimes, he thought, looking at the stone walls and hand-hewn beams that ran along the ceiling.

The dampness cut into his bones like a knife, but in spite of the cold there was a sharp odor of decay in the room, a sour-sweet putrescence like the stench from a heap of rotting vegetables. And there was something else, Earl realized, a medical smell, an acid stink that bit sharply through the humid chill of the room.

"What kind of trouble you fellows in?" the old man said slyly.

"Don't worry about us," Earl said. "Do what you're told, and you won't get hurt."

"I can't answer for Crazybones. She don't pay much mind to anybody." He stared at Earl with bright, excited eyes. "What'd you do? Kill somebody?"

"No," Earl said shortly.

"You steal something then? Break into a store?"

The old man's prying eyes made him uneasy; there was something fierce and sick about him, like the sweaty reek of a lynch mob. Their trouble had stirred him up, Earl realized, pumped his frail old body full of invigorating excitement.

"You're hurt, ain't ye?" he said, peering closely at Earl. "Got a bullet in ye, I can tell."

"That's right. And I got six in my gun. Think about them, Pop."

"You got no call to hurt us. We're old people, mister."

Ingram came back into the room and said, "She's all right. She's fixing up some food."

"You better get the car out of sight," Earl said.

"Nobody coming by here in this cloudburst."

Earl looked at the old man. "Any place in back he can hide it?"

"The barn is dry enough but somebody might see it there."

"You said nobody ever came by this way."

"Well, that was before you stopped in, mister." He chuckled at this and glanced slyly at Ingram for approval. "You fellows might make the place popular. Anyway, we got some coon hunters in the country at night and fox hunters in the day. They're a sight. All dressed up in red coats and shiny black boots. Women, too. Sometimes a fox goes to ground in a barn or woodshed, and then the hunt piles up while they poke around trying to start him running again. They might stumble on your car, yes sir. I wouldn't put it in no barn if I was you."

"Where would you put it, Pop?" Earl realized the old man didn't want them to be caught right away; he wanted to prolong the excitement, to lie in bed and watch them squirm and sweat.

"There's a little road runs from the back of the house into the woods," the old man said. "They used to mine mica there years back, and one of the old quarries would be a nice place for the car. Nobody would ever see it there."

"Can he get the car down that road?"

"Oh, sure. It's a fine little road." The old man winked conspiratorially. "And tomorrow the tracks will all be washed away. Got to think of that too, you know."

"All right, Sambo," Earl said. "Get started."

"Damn it, you hear that rain? Let's wait till the flood stops."

"I hear it," Earl said quietly. In the silence the sound of the rain was like an angry flail beating against the sides and roof of the house. He stared at Ingram, and said, "How much money you got, Sambo?"

"I don't know. Forty, forty-five dollars."

"Put it on that chair."

"What's the matter with you? You think there's something to buy around here?"

"Do like I say, Sambo. Put the money on the chair." Earl

took the gun from his pocket and shifted forward onto the edge of the sofa. The effort brought a sudden sheen of perspiration to his face, but the gun in his hand was relentlessly steady. His voice rose suddenly, trembling with a savage anger. "Then get out of your clothes. Jacket, shirt, pants. You hear, Sambo?"

"Have you gone crazy?"

"I'm just making sure you don't run out on me. I can't guess what's going on inside that woolly head of yours, so I'm not taking any chances. You might decide this is a good time to skip." Earl's eyes glinted with bitter humor. "I'm the anchor in this deal. I'm hurt, I can't travel. You—"

"You're crazy," Ingram said frantically. "We've got to stick together. We don't have a chance any other way."

"You got money, you got the car," Earl said. "You could make it to the highway and be on your way. Leave me stuck here with a bullet in my shoulder."

"It's what's in your head," Ingram cried. "It's your idea, not mine."

Earl's eyes narrowed with tension. "Start field-stripping, Sambo. You can rat out if you want, but you won't get far in your birthday suit. You can't stop for gas, you can't buy a mouthful of food. If you don't come back here, you'll freeze. So you'll come back. Not for me, but to save your hide."

"I'm not thinking that way, I swear it." Ingram despised his fear, but he couldn't control it; his voice trembled like that of a frightened child. "It's freezing outside. I'll die out there."

"Start stripping," Earl said harshly, and at that the old man began to laugh in shuddering little gasps. "Don't let him wheedle you," he cried, watching Ingram with hot, expectant eyes. "Make 'em toe the mark and cut the buck, I say."

"Shut up!" Earl said. "You hear? Shut up!"

Ingram took the money from his pocket and dropped it on the chair. There was no point arguing any more; Earl was crazy enough to shoot him. Then he'd be all alone, hurt and helpless, but he couldn't see that far ahead. Ingram pulled off the soaking jacket, then his shirt and trousers, making a soggy pile of them on top of the money. The cold bit deep into his bones, making them ache with a heavy sort of pain, and he could feel goose pimples crawling along his bare arms and legs. His teeth began to chatter, and when he picked up the car keys they stung his fingers like pieces of ice.

The old man tittered softly, squirming under his great mound of dirty quilts and blankets. "Only a fool or a rich man would go outside on a night like this," he said.

The music from the radio was warm and bright and intimate, pointlessly gay in the bitterness of the room, incredible and incongruous as hummingbirds fluttering through a winter storm. Ingram flushed with shame as the old man chuckled and stared at him with brutal, clinical curiosity. Earl looked away from Ingram's thin body, the movement of his head abrupt and angry. "All right, get going," he said in a thick, hard voice. "Don't stand there."

He didn't look up until he felt the blast of cold wind sweep into the room and heard the front door pulled shut with an obvious effort against the storming night. Then he stared at the pile of wet clothes on the chair and let out his breath slowly and wearily. The pain was all through him now, sick and turbulent and demanding, but it didn't seem to have anything to do with the wound in his shoulder. It won't take him long to get rid of the car, he thought. It's just a quick ride . . .

The dance music broke off in the middle of a phrase, and a smooth impersonal voice said, "We are interrupting this program to bring you a special bulletin from the State Police. In an unsuccessful attempt to hold up the National Bank in Crossroads, one man was killed and another wounded shortly after eight o'clock tonight."

The old man got up on his elbow, breathing heavily with excitement, and Earl shifted closer to the radio.

". . . as yet the dead bandit has not been identified by police. Sheriff Thomas Burns of the Borough of Crossroads surprised the holdup men as they were leaving the bank. He ordered them to halt, but they opened fire. In a gun battle which took place on the main street of the village, one robber was shot to death and his accomplice seriously wounded. The wounded man escaped in a blue Pontiac station wagon, bearing California license plates QX 1897—I will repeat that license number—QX 1897—traveling southwest from Crossroads. He is wounded and believed to be armed. He is six feet tall, weighing about one hundred and seventy to one hundred and eighty pounds, with black hair and dark blue eyes. He was last seen wearing a black overcoat and brown felt, snap-brim fedora. Roadblocks have been established by State Police, and motorists are urged to report any suspicious calls for assistance to State Police immediately. Mr. Charles Martin, President of the Crossroads bank, has reported that all funds taken in the holdup have been recovered. Stay tuned to this station for. . . ."

Earl snapped off the irritatingly impersonal voice, and stared bitterly at the gun hanging in his hand. No mention of Ingram at all. Just him. Wounded, dangerous, needing a doctor. That was him, all right. Like some animal in a cage. *Don't get too close, folks, he's mean and he bites.* But nothing about Ingram. It was just like Novak said it would be. Nobody noticed colored people.

"So they killed one of your fellows," the old man said. "And you didn't get no money, either. Seems like a waste, don't it?"

Earl didn't answer. He was still thinking of what Novak had told him. Colored people could drift in and out of places like smoke. That's what Novak had said. . . . Nobody saw them. A colored man carrying a tray or wearing overalls could go anywhere. White people went through whole days without seeing who brought them their coffee or shined their shoes or swept their cigarette butts into the gutter. That was the big part of his plan. Ingram drifting into the bank like a wisp of smoke. . . .

A great plan, he thought with a weary confusion and anger. Ingram was in the clear. Novak was in the clear. Even Burke was in the clear. Dead and out of it for good. They only wanted him, the wounded animal. That's who they were hunting for.

The old man was smiling with pleased, secret knowledge. "How'd the colored fellow fit into it?" he said. "How come they didn't talk about him on the radio?"

Earl stared at him in silence.

"It's funny, ain't it?" the old man said. "They just talked about you. You suppose the colored fellow knows they don't care about him?"

Earl stood slowly and limped toward the old man's bed. "That's going to be our secret, Pop. You understand me?"

"Oh, sure. I wasn't going to tell him nothing. But it's funny, ain't it?"

"No," Earl said. "It's not funny. It's just something to forget. You want to enjoy the time you got left to live, Pop? Or are you tired of lying under those stinking blankets?"

"No, I ain't tired of it," the old man said quickly. The look in Earl's face frightened him; every minute and hour of his life was as thrilling to him as money to a miser. He savored time greedily, exultant with pride when he opened his eyes and found his old heart pumping faintly but steadily within his frail breast. But here was a man who could take all his treasure away with one twist of his hand. "Sure, sure," he said, "it's our secret, mister. I wouldn't ever tell him nothing."

"Remember that," Earl said.

CHAPTER TWELVE

It was after nine o'clock when Sheriff Burns left the bank and returned to his office in the Municipal Building. He hung up his wet slicker and told Morgan to post himself at the bank to keep traffic moving through town. Already there was a congestion of curiosity on Main Street; people exchanging garbled versions of what had happened, cars from a dozen miles around converging on the excitement. "Keep it all moving," the sheriff told Morgan. "I want that street clear. If the truckers get tied up we'll have a jam all the way back on the highway to Middleboro."

When Morgan left, the sheriff studied the large county wall map on the wall behind his desk. He had done all the routine things; calmed down the people at the bank and taken their statements. The wounded man had registered at the hotel as Frank Smith, and the sheriff had checked his room, finding nothing but a damp overcoat and a soft fedora. They belonged to the colored man, he knew. The dead man was at the morgue in MacPherson's Funeral Home. A beefy man in his late forties. That's all he added up to at the moment. There was nothing revealing in his clothes or wallet. This was routine. Now the harder job started—hunting down the Negro and the man who called himself Frank Smith.

The sheriff knew he had half failed tonight; he had stopped the robbery but two of the men had got away. That was his fault. He accepted the failure without guilt or remorse; it was a simple distasteful fact that he didn't try to evade or reassess to his own advantage.

Footsteps sounded in the outer hallway. He turned as a tall young man in a damp gabardine topcoat walked up to the counter.

"Sheriff Burns?"

"That's right."

"My name is Kelly, sir." The young man opened a small leather card case and placed it on the counter. "FBI."

"Well, well." The sheriff studied his photograph with care, then stared at the agent, noting his reddish-brown hair, sharp blue eyes and square, cheerful face. He didn't have to look down at the man and that was an uncommon experience for him; six two or better, he judged, with enough bulk to give authority to his height. "You got here pretty fast," he said pushing the wallet back across the counter.

"Our office in Philadelphia picked up the State Police alert about eight fifteen," Kelly said. "The SAC sent me out first. There'll be more men here soon. From Philly and Harrisburg. We'll have riot equipment in an hour or so, and there'll be two planes standing by at dawn if we need them."

"A regular convention, eh?" the sheriff said. "What's the SAC by the way?"

"Special agent in charge," Kelly said.

"This is your show now, eh?"

"Practically every bank job is a federal case, Sheriff. Deposits are insured by a federal agency and that brings us into it. But we're here to work for you. You know the area. We'll co-operate any way we can. That sound okay?"

"It sounds fine," the sheriff said, underlining the middle word faintly but unmistakably. He had an idea of what co-operation meant—a polite way of taking the reins out of his hands. "Come on in. You got some idea about what our next move should be?"

"There's no identification on the dead man?"

"Nothing yet."

"I'll print him and Philadelphia can wire the information to Washington. When we know who he is it may lead us to the other man."

"There's two other men," the sheriff said.

"The State Police just mentioned one. How come?"

"Nobody saw the other fellow." The sheriff explained to Kelly what he had learned of John Ingram and the man who called himself Smith. "I called the State Police from the bank as soon as the shooting was over," he went on. "I told them what I'd seen—not knowing the colored boy was in on the job. Everybody in the bank took him for a regular delivery man. When I got the whole story pieced together I decided to let the first report stand for a while."

Kelly raised his eyebrows.

"Well, you may not agree with my reasoning," the sheriff said dryly. "But it figured those two fellows will hear that report on the radio. The colored fellow may feel free to cut out on his own. And the other man—he's wounded, remember—might try to stop him. It's going to put pressure on them and that might prod them into making a break for it."

"How long can we keep it quiet?"

"Until tomorrow morning, I guess. There'll be talk in town about what really happened, and the reporters will be on our backs then."

"You say they might make a break for it. You think they're holed-up somewhere by now?"

"Come here a second." The sheriff took a pencil from his breast pocket and walked over to the county map behind his desk. "Ingram and the wounded man drove out of town on Cherry Street. That took them into open country in four or five miles." He drew a crude circle around the area southwest of Crossroads. "The State cops have roadblocked all that territory. But there's back roads those fellows can use to slip around our roadblock. All we can do is plug up the likeliest holes—the main highways, the bridge approaches and so forth. And we'll watch the buses and trains. They're in a noose, but it's awfully big and awfully loose."

"What kind of country is it?"

"Farms and woods, twenty-five square miles of it. Lots of houses, barns, outbuildings, old mills and so forth. We know their car, so they can't travel. And they can't stay outside in this weather. Likely they'll move in on somebody. That's why I want to make 'em run for it. Get 'em into the open where we won't run the risk of killing innocent people."

"Is the area too big for a house-to-house search?"

"We could try, but it would take a lot of time."

"Have you alerted all the doctors around here to be careful?"

"We did that first thing."

"The call might sound pretty innocent," Kelly said. "An old familiar patient with a touch of stomach trouble maybe. But talking with a gun at her head."

"We reminded them of that," the sheriff said. "They'll check with us before they go out on any calls tonight."

"Good." Kelly belted his topcoat. "I'll get those prints into the works. You've got everything running along fine."

"Why, thanks," the sheriff said, deadpan. He was human enough to have enjoyed this little session; there was very little the FBI was going to tell him about affairs in his own backyard.

Kelly stopped and glanced at him from the door. "You've got some fox-hunting down this way, I think. Is that right?"

"The Chesterson hounds. Why?"

"Well, just an odd thought. It might be a good idea to ask them to keep their eyes open. A hunt covers a lot of territory, and they might stumble across something interesting. A car hidden in the woods, or smoke from a deserted house." Kelly shrugged his wide shoulders. "Can't hurt in any case. I'll see you." He waved and walked out.

The sheriff stared after him, scratching his chin. Then he smiled reluctantly. He should have thought of the fox hunters; they trooped through the back country in all kinds of weather, completely isolated in their small, intense world of horses and trails, hounds and foxes. He'd give the master of hounds a ring in the morning; it wouldn't hurt them to keep their eyes open for something besides foxes for a change. Kelly was all right, he thought, still smiling a little.

Three more agents arrived fifteen minutes later, quiet, competent-looking men who introduced themselves to the sheriff and then went down to the coroner's office to check with Kelly. Within half an hour, Kelly returned to put in a call to the Department of Justice in Washington. "I sent one of the boys back to Philly with the prints," he said while waiting for the connection. "They'll wire them to Washington. We'll probably have something in a few hours."

"How do you know you have him on file?"

"It's a good bet. A man his age has usually been printed. Military service, defense work, civil-service application, any kind of arrest or jail sentence—that'll do it." He lighted a cigarette and perched on a corner of the sheriff's desk, filling the office with a sense of vital, healthy energy. When his connection was made, he said, "This is Kelly. That's right. Crossroads, Pennsylvania, the bank job. Now here's the right- and left-hand count on an unidentified male about forty-five or fifty. The prints are on their way to Philadelphia, and you should have them on the wire in an hour or so. All set?" Kelly took a notebook from his pocket and read a list of numbers into the phone. Then he said, "He's a high-arch, I see. That should help a little . . . Yeah. So long."

The sheriff hadn't understood what Kelly was talking about but he was reluctant to ask for explanations. Finally irritation at himself overcame his dignity. "How the devil can they start working in Washington before the prints get there from Philly?" he said.

"Well, they know where to start looking," Kelly said. "They'll pull the cards on one category—high-arch, in this case—and sift out the impossibles. Deceased and women and children. When the prints arrive they'll check them against the ones left—and they might have the field narrowed down to just a few hundred by then. It's not my specialty, but the experts in Washington read prints the way we'd read a newspaper."

Morgan came in a bit later and reported that the crowds had thinned out, and that traffic was flowing smoothly through Main Street.

The sheriff swiveled around in his chair and looked up at the circle he had penciled around the area southwest of Crossroads. Nothing to do but wait. The rain made any tracking impossible. But time was on their side now. They could sit tight: the hunted men would have to make the first move. . . .

After a few minutes he glanced at Kelly. "You had dinner yet?"

"I was about to ask if any restaurants are open."

"How about coming home with me? There's a roast waiting on the stove. With all the trimmings."

"I don't want to put you to any trouble."

"It's no trouble at all. In fact it might be a big help. Morgan, keep your ear on that radio. We'll be back in half an hour or so."

CHAPTER THIRTEEN

WHEN INGRAM RETURNED to the living room of the farmhouse, he was shivering uncontrollably, his legs plastered with mud and slime to the knees. He pulled on his clothes quickly, then crouched beside the meager heap of charred wood in the fireplace.

"You put it away okay?" Earl asked without looking at him.

Ingram nodded, too exhausted to speak; his bare flesh had been whipped by the wind, and the cold had driven into him like frozen needles. "Nobody will find it," he muttered at last. The words came awkwardly through his stiff lips. "If they do they'll need a crane to get it out."

"So we're stuck here now," Earl said, but he knew his anger was illogical; the car was no good to them. But now they were completely helpless. "Couldn't you park it on the side of the pit?"

"I wasn't worrying about the car," Ingram said. "I was trying to keep from freezing."

The old man laughed softly. "I told you it was a bad night. Didn't I tell you that?"

"You're quite a weatherman," Ingram said. "You hear rain on the roof and you know it's raining. You ought to go on the radio."

"Don't talk to me that way," the old man said shrilly. "You hear me?"

"Sure I hear you," Ingram said with heavy sarcasm. "You wouldn't need a radio. You could just open the window and scream the news. Right from your filthy bed."

"Don't talk to me that way."

"Both of you shut up, for Christ's sake," Earl said.

"Tell him to speak respectfully to me. I won't have a nigger talking down to me in my own home." The old man's hands were trembling with impotent fury. "Tell him, you hear?"

Crazybone came hurrying into the room, an expression of furtive dismay on her tiny wrinkled face. "What you shouting for, Pop? Dinner's on the way. Oatmeal, you hear? It sticks to your ribs all night long."

The old man lay back on the pillows, turning his face away from Ingram and Earl. "You got anything to go with it?" he asked her.

"You bet your boots," she cried in a crowing, triumphant voice. "I got a jar of home-made apricot preserves."

Earl felt his stomach turn; a spasm of nausea racked him,

and the wound in his shoulder began to pound with turbulent pain. "We got to do something," he said to Ingram. "We got to make plans."

Ingram shrugged. "Go ahead. Make plans."

Crazybone glanced at them with a puzzled smile, as if she had never seen them before. Then she skipped clumsily from the room, singing a wordless song in a high, sweet voice.

"We need money and another car," Earl said, pressing both hands against his roiling stomach.

Ingram smiled bitterly. "We tried to get some money tonight, remember?"

"You have any friends, Sambo?"

"Sure I got friends. They'd love to have me drop in on them. Can't you imagine how happy they'd be? I got three brothers, too. You think I should try them maybe?"

"We got to do something. Listen to me." Earl felt a rush of excitement go through him; Lorraine would help. She would stick. "I got a friend in Philly," he said, edging forward on the sofa. "She's got a car, and she can get hold of money." He glanced at his watch. It wasn't much after nine. Lorraine would still be at the store. "She'll help us, Sambo."

"You're dreaming." Ingram shook his head slowly. "You can't travel. Even if you could the cops would grab us the minute we showed our face. We're hot stuff."

"I'm hot, but you're not," Earl cried; the words slipped out of him in the excitement generated of hope—but it didn't matter. "I heard a broadcast while you were putting the car away. They're just looking for me. Nobody saw you. You hear me? You're free as the air."

Ingram looked thoughtfully at him. "And you weren't going to tell me about it, eh?"

"I just told you, didn't I?"

"Yeah, sure. When you thought about the car in Philly, and how nice it would be for me to get it."

"Don't take my word for it." Earl struggled to his feet and walked unsteadily across to the old man's bed. "Tell him what you heard," he said. "Tell him the police just want me. Tell him the truth."

The old man's eyes were bright with malice. "I ain't doing any favors for neither of you. Him sassing me, and you standing by. That's a fine way to treat a man."

"Tell him what you heard!" Earl shouted. "Tell him, goddam you."

"It's the truth." The old man's voice trembled with senile fear and indignation. He glared at Ingram. "They didn't say anything on the radio about you. It's just him they're after."

"Now you believe it, I guess." Earl limped up and down the cold, hard floor, trying to control his excitement and bring his thoughts into orderly focus. "There's a belt highway of some kind that crosses the main road and goes into Philly. I saw it this morning." He came to the bed and shook the old man's shoulder. "Isn't that right, Pop? What's the name of it?"

"The Unionville Pike. It's two miles from here."

"And it's got a bus line, right?"

"They go in every half hour nights. Takes in factory hands."

"Sambo, we're going to lick this deal," Earl said in a savage, exulting voice. "We're going to lick it, hear? I'll write you a note. If she's not at the store, she'll be home. She'll give you her car, Sambo. And money. Where's some paper and a pencil?" He limped to the mantelpiece and picked up one of the old, yellowing newspapers. "Now a pencil." He saw a cardboard box full of buttons, bits of string and dusty spools of thread. Emptying it he laughed triumphantly: there was a stubby pencil in the bottom of the box. He shook the paper open and found a page of advertising with wide margins surrounding the copy. "This is perfect," he said, carefully tearing out a square of paper. Moistening the pencil, he sat down and began to write slowly and laboriously, his lips moving in a rhythm with the point of the pencil.

"Now here's the deal, Sambo," he said, frowning at the message. "The Unionville Pike is northwest of here. I'll tell you every turn to make. You catch the ten-o'clock bus. You'll be in Philly by ten twenty or twenty-five. I wrote the address of the store down, and the address of our apartment. Go to the store first." He paused to underline a word in the note. "She's got black hair and she wears it long. You'll recognize her, don't worry. She runs the joint. You give her this note. Understand? She'll carry the ball from there."

Ingram was watching him with a faint smile. "You got it all figured out, eh?"

"It's our only chance, Sambo."

"Then we're in sad shape," Ingram said. "I'm not leaving here." He knew what it would be like outside; his imagination had been working as Earl made his plans. The rain and the wind, with maybe lightning searing the darkness and bringing the whole night world into a fearful brightness . . . And people staring at him, cops eying him while they swung their nightsticks in slow, speculative arcs.

"You don't trust me, is that it?" Earl said.

"You watch out for yourself. I'll watch out for me."

"Listen to me, Sambo. Use your head. Why should I send you out to get caught?"

"I don't know."

"You don't know! You don't know!" Earl mocked him bitterly. "Well, I'll tell you something since you're so goddam dumb. Without that car you're going to die. Get that into your woolly head. Burke is dead. We're facing a murder rap. Maybe you didn't know that, either?"

"I didn't have nothing to do with it. I got forced into this job."

"Do you want to die? Is that it, Sambo?"

"I didn't shoot Burke," Ingram said shrilly. "They can't blame me for that."

Earl said "Judas priest!" in a weary, disgusted voice. Then he sighed and shook his head. "Will you do me a favor, Sambo? Will you just be serious? Forget about the car. Sit here and wait for the cops. But be serious!" Earl's voice rose in sudden fury. "You're a murderer. So am I. The law says we're responsible for Burke's death. Don't talk like a fool. Is that asking too much?"

"I didn't know anything was going to happen to him," Ingram said. "I didn't even have a gun."

Earl settled himself carefully against the back of the sofa, and lighted a cigarette, his manner seemingly careless and negligent. He watched Ingram in silence for a few seconds, judging the texture of his fear with shrewd, instinctive accuracy. Then he said casually, "You ever been in jail?"

"No." Ingram shook his head quickly.

"I was in jail the night they burned a man. That's something you should know about. You'll be ready for it then."

Ingram looked away from Earl's bright, searching eyes. "I don't need any lecture about it. I can guess what it's like."

Earl laughed. "That's what people outside always say. But they're wrong. They get funny ideas from movies, I guess. You know the kind of stuff. Prisoners banging tin cups on the bars, colored guys singing spirituals, everybody solemn and scared." Earl shook his head. "It ain't like that, Sambo. You know what it's like? It's like the night they show movies. It's an event. Everybody gets all gagged-up and excited. There's a pool on the minute it's going to happen. You bet a half dollar and you can win a hatful. My cellmate won eighteen bucks. He was a lifer, a real lucky guy."

Earl straightened slowly and shifted to the edge of the sofa, studying the nervous fear in Ingram's eyes with clinical speculation. "But it's different for the guy they're burning," he said gently. "He's sure it won't happen. Right till the last. When the guards shave his head, he asks them if they've heard any gossip from the warden's office. Then the chaplain comes in. That makes everything just fine." Earl smiled at Ingram's trembling lips. "The chaplain tells you all your troubles will be over after they throw the switch. God's waiting for you, he says, waiting with a big smile on His face. You're heading for the big leagues and God's the manager who'll show you all the tricks and make you feel at home. You believe that, of course. You don't even mind what's coming you're so anxious to get up to the big leagues and be God's buddy. That chaplain's your best friend,

Sambo. He walks right up to the chair with you, telling you how great it's going to be up in the majors. He almost climbs into the chair to show you how easy it is—almost, but not quite."

Earl flipped his cigarette into the fireplace, and the flash of the glowing tip made Ingram start nervously. "They strap you in and put a metal cap on your head," Earl said quietly. "You jump because your skull is bare as an egg. Then they all stare at you, the guards, the chaplain, the warden, the newspaper guys, wondering how you'll take it. They make bets on it sometimes. One guy will fight the straps, trying to break loose. Others just start whimpering."

"Shut up," Ingram cried; Earl's words rang on his old, old hideous fears of being beaten and hurt, laughed at by merciless men.

"Then you just wait," Earl said softly. "Strapped into the chair, you wait. You don't know when it's coming. You stare at the guards and the chaplain, watching their eyes, ready to scream if anybody gives a signal. But you can't see the signal. They don't ask you if you're ready, if it's okay to throw the switch. If the warden doesn't like you he can let you sweat a while—make you start sobbing and screaming, waiting for the bolt of lightning to split your head in two." Earl settled back in the couch. "That's how it's going to be, Sambo. That's the straight dope."

"How do I know I can trust you?" Ingram muttered at last. "About the radio, I mean."

"I told you before: Why should I lie to you? What good will it do me to send you out to get caught?" When Ingram didn't answer Earl heaved himself to his feet and took the gun from his pocket. He checked the safety, then limped to the fireplace and extended the gun butt-first to Ingram. "Go on, take it," he said quietly. "I trust you, Sambo. I've got to. If we stick together, we've got a chance. So what do you say? You want to take it? Or do you want to fry?"

Ingram hesitated, staring into Earl's eyes. Finally he moistened his trembling lips and put out a hand for the gun.

CHAPTER FOURTEEN

INGRAM ARRIVED at the bus depot in central Philadelphia shortly after ten thirty. He went quickly through the crowded terminal, the brim of Earl's hat pulled down over his eyes, and within minutes had merged his thin body with the shadows of the city's side streets. His reactions were as instinctive as a fleeing animal's: fear had left him with nothing but the mindless tenacity to exist. He had walked to the highway in a protective cocoon of shock, mercifully oblivious to the rain and wind, and the dark trees swaying grotesquely above his head. The bus had been a dimly lighted refuge, a haven of darkness and warmth; he had found a seat in the rear, and pulled the collar of Earl's big overcoat high around his face. The motor throbbed like a powerful heart in the drowsy silence, and the soft lights fell like a blessing on the innocently sprawled bodies of the other passengers.

Ingram watched the level waves of water rolling down his window, staring through them at the pinpoints of yellow lights that gleamed from farmhouses set far off the highway. They had stopped once at a roadblock, and he pulled back in terror from the sweep of a flashlight across the window. Some of the other passengers had stirred and waked; questions were murmured while the driver talked to the police, and then the gears whined and they rolled slowly past a knot of troopers wearing long black rain slickers. There were no other stops. They roared swiftly into the city, the big tires whirring with a liquid power against the wet highway . . .

Ingram waited in the shadows for a streetcar to rattle by, then hurried on to the next block. The storm had driven pedestrians inside and thinned out motor traffic; lamplights gleamed on empty sidewalks and the high winds swept away the faint piping of horns, muted the heavy thunder of trucks and subways.

This was his town, his neighborhood. The familiar sights penetrated the defenses that fear had thrown up against reality. He stopped and leaned helplessly against the unyielding side of a building, a destructive wave of self-pity almost washing away all his strength. There was no hope for him. He was too sick and weak. Pain sharpened in his chest as a coughing fit shook his body. The cold and rain on his naked body had been too much . . .

He saw the delicatessen across the street, and remembered the smell and feel of the place, warm and spicy with Jewish foods, jars and cans shining on the shelves, the huge refrigerator filled with bottles of beer and milk and soft drinks. He used to buy sandwiches there to take home. The old man who owned the place made a sandwich that would do a hungry man for dinner.

But this was the dream world now. The delicatessen, the Chinese laundry, this street he had sauntered along in the past with a headful of crazy thoughts—those were the phantoms. The reality was back at the bleak, rain-soaked old farmhouse—Earl and Crazybone and the twisted old man.

Something moved and caught his eye. He saw a patrolman strolling along the empty sidewalk, the shadow of his swinging nightstick making a long, grotesque shadow up and down the street. The lights glinted on his brass buttons as he paused to check the door of a shop.

Ingram's breath came in rapid little gasps, silvering the cold air in front of his face. He crossed into the next block, his shoulders hunched against the sound of pursuit; a shout, or the pound of footsteps would have sent him into screaming flight . . .

In two or three minutes he came to the drugstore, slowing down to stare apprehensively at the bright plate-glass windows, and the huge neon sign above the revolving doors. It was a big, busy place, with a long soda fountain, magazine racks, a drug compartment and shiny glass cases full of toilet goods and cosmetics.

It looked like a trap, a bright neon trap . . .

Maybe they didn't serve colored people. Maybe he'd cause a commotion just by going in. Get himself arrested . . . the thought made a giddy laugh bubble in his throat. Rob a bank, okay. But don't go ordering a cup of coffee in a white restaurant.

But another thought dissolved this crazy, morbid humor: What about Earl's woman? Would she help him? Earl was sure of her, but Earl was a fool. He probably believed that any woman who slept with him was a slave for life. But maybe this woman wouldn't want any part of his troubles. Maybe she'd read the note and start screaming for the police.

But suddenly he was moving, heading for the revolving doors, his questions unanswered, his fears unresolved. He hadn't come to a decision, he had just started forward, crazily and defiantly. But he realized with elemental conviction that it was the thought of Earl which had sent him toward the drugstore, propelled him into this big, neon trap. He wanted to help the man; that was the fact of it, the senseless, pointless fact of it.

Everything at the soda fountain was clean and tidy; the coffee urns gleamed under bright overhead tubes of light, and the little groups of napkins, sugar bowls and mustard jars were lined up as neatly as a formation of toy soldiers. A blonde waitress took his order and wrote it carefully on a check; coffee and a sweet roll. She gave him a brief, impersonal smile before going away, and he felt his taut nerves relaxing, his body sinking into blessed lassitude. He put Earl's hat on the stool beside him, and opened the collar of his coat to let the warmth of the place soak into his bones. After a moment, he glanced around the store, trying not to seem furtive or nervous, making his survey slowly and casually. Several women were shopping at the cosmetic counters, and a knot of men were lined up buying cigarettes and tobacco. The short-order cook was slicing bread industriously and the blonde waitress stood staring with blank boredom at the rainy darkness beyond the bright windows.

Ingram heard an impatient voice say, "Now I want these magazines moved to the back of the store tomorrow. Circulation is our problem and goal, Lorraine. People leaf through books and block up the entrance. That's out from now on, understand?"

"I'll have them moved in the morning, Mr. Poole."

"Good. Now about that lunch menu . . ."

The voice faded slightly. Earl hunched over his steaming coffee, trembling with the excited stroke of his heart. Lorraine . . . that was her name. He waited a few seconds and then glanced around at the sound of the voices.

A man and woman stood together at the magazine racks near the door. The man wore an overcoat and had his back to Ingram. The woman was slim, with black hair and a pale square face. She nodded slowly as the man spoke to her, but she was looking over her shoulder at Ingram; he saw her eyes go wide and dark as they shifted to Earl's hat on the stool beside him. One of her hands moved to her throat, but she continued to nod thoughtfully at the man's urgent instructions.

"Yes, I'll watch that, Mr. Poole," she murmured as Ingram turned back to his coffee.

"Fine. See you tomorrow. Early."

Ingram heard the rubbery squish of the revolving door, and then the tap of high heels moved toward him on the tiled floor. She passed so close that he felt the draft of air caused by her body. Strolling toward the rear of the store she paused to realign a salt shaker, and then went behind the counter and talked briefly to the sandwich man. Ingram watched her from the corner of his eye. This was Earl's woman; black hair, dark eyes, a square pale face. High-strung and tense, with a flat slender body and neat ankles and feet. She looked cold as ice water. The thought afforded him a derisive amusement. Did Earl like that? No demands . . . asleep ten minutes after hitting the sack. Ingram's spirits were lifted and refreshed by his gleeful irreverence. But almost instantly he felt depressed and ashamed of himself.

She was coming toward him now, checking spigots and cutlery with professionally alert eyes. The waitress straightened and uncrossed her arms.

"Ann, I'd like you to see how many large-size mayonnaise we have in the stock room."

"I did already. There's six."

Ingram bent over his coffee. He heard Earl's woman say, "That can't be right. Check them again, will you, please?"

"Sure, but I know there's just six."

When the waitress hurried off Earl's woman stopped in front of Ingram. "Is everything all right? Would you like some more coffee?"

"No, ma'am. Everything's fine." She was carrying it off fine, except for her eyes; her voice was smooth and cool as ivory, but her eyes looked dark and hot, turbulent against her clear white skin. "Well, there is one thing you could help me with," he said, chuckling softly. "I've got myself twisted around in town." He took Earl's note from his pocket and placed it on the counter. "The address I want is written down here, but I can't find it no way."

"Maybe I can help you." She picked up the note carefully enough, but as her eyes flicked over the message the cords in her throat stood out like knife blades under her smooth skin. Ingram's nerves fluttered as he saw the sandwich man watching her curiously.

"Do you know where that address is?" he said, clearing his throat.

She nodded quickly. "Yes, it's not far from here. Tenth and Edgely. You go two blocks left, then turn left again and it's just after the stoplight."

"That sounds simple enough."

"You won't have any trouble. I—I keep my car near there, so I know the neighborhood." She was smiling, but her body looked as if it were being pulled to pieces; her shoulders were rigid with tension, and a pulse fluttered desperately in the silky hollow at the base of her throat. "You won't have any trouble, I promise you," she said.

"Well, thank you very much, ma'am. I'll hurry along then. The man waiting for me said not to be late. Good night, ma'am."

Ingram waited for half an hour in the shadows of a warehouse at the intersection of Tenth and Edgely Streets, stamping his feet on the hard pavement to drive some warmth into his body. She had picked a good place to meet him; the area was dark and silent, a neighborhood of garages, small factories and shuttered-up shops. But he shifted coldly and miserably in the shadows, without confidence or hope; the heat of the coffee had faded almost instantly, and when he coughed it roused up the heavy ominous pain in his chest. She wasn't coming . . . he knew that now. Otherwise she'd have been here long ago. Maybe she was sitting in a police station telling them what he looked like. He didn't know what to do, but he didn't have the strength to do anything but wait.

He tried to shore up his defenses, but his efforts were helpless and inert; he was just too cold and sick to care. Maybe she'd come after all. Maybe she'd just been delayed. Earl was important to her; he'd seen that in her eyes. But what good would a car be to him? With cops everywhere, with Earl wounded and sick?

He moved suddenly back into the shadows; a car had turned into the street a block away from him, its light flashing on the rain-black pavement. Ingram stayed deep in the shadows until the car slowed to a stop. He didn't move until the front window was cranked down, and he saw the blur of her pale face in the light from a street lamp. Then he hurried across the street, sliding into the front seat as she leaned over and opened the door for him. He sank wearily into the soft cushions, his body limp and grateful in the warmth of the car. As she twisted around toward him he smelled perfume in her hair, and saw the pale smooth flash of legs in the dashboard light. The womanly essence of her made him feel weak and helpless, almost like weeping.

"Where is he?" she said fiercely.

"A long way off. I got to get started back."

"How badly is he hurt?"

"Well, he got hit in the shoulder. It won't kill him, I guess, but he don't look good."

"Why did you make him do it?" she said, striking the steering wheel with the palm of her hand. "Why? Why?"

"I didn't make him do nothing," he said sullenly.

"He wouldn't do it on his own. Why didn't you—you bastards leave him alone?"

Ingram was wearied by her foolishness. "He's in it now, ma'am. Talking about how and why won't get him out."

"Where are you going to take him?"

"I don't know, ma'am. We don't have much choice. We just got to run. Try to get out of the state."

"He won't ever come back, will he?"

Ingram smiled faintly. "Not unless the government starts pardoning bank robbers. Give 'em civil-service jobs or something."

"I knew it was the bank," she said. "I heard the radio report. I thought he was dead. I felt it all through me."

"He's not dead. But he may be if I don't get started back pretty soon."

"I brought some whisky and food from the apartment. Luckily I shopped yesterday. There's a boiled ham, some canned goods, bread, butter and two bottles of rye."

"That'll help a lot."

"I'm going with you," she said sharply.

"He just wants the car."

"I don't care. He needs me." Her voice was coldly, harshly determined. "He's nothing to you. He's mine. Do you understand?"

Ingram let his hands fall limply into his lap. What the hell difference did it make? "You know where the Unionville Pike leaves the city?"

"Yes."

"That's the route. Let's go. . . ."

It wasn't until they were checked through the roadblock ten miles from Crossroads that Ingram's mood began to change; they had a chance after all, he realized with a touch of wonder. A chance. He sat in the front seat with the black countryside rushing past him and felt hope stirring warmly in his frozen body. With the girl at the wheel, they had a chance. She was cool and smart, driving easily and efficiently now, watching everything with her sharp eyes. Another woman might have wrecked the car, or got stopped for speeding. But not this one. She knew what she was after; he saw the determination in the set of her jaw, in the tight grip of her gloved hands on the wheel.

She had been cool as a cucumber at the roadblock. When the trooper flashed his light on the car she had rolled down the front window and said, "What's the matter? I'm in a hurry, officer."

Lying in the rear of the car, Ingram heard the trooper say wearily, "People are always in a hurry. Particularly when it's raining and the roads are dangerous."

"I'm an excellent driver. My husband says I'm more confident than most men."

"I'm glad you're confident," the trooper said. "It's a cheery thought on a bad night. Don't make any stops along the road tonight. Don't pick up hitchhikers. Don't pick up anybody. Got that?"

"But what's the matter?"

"We're just checking for somebody. You got nothing to worry about. Come on, get it rolling." The trooper walked back to the next car, his torch swinging easily in his hand. They weren't bothering too much about the traffic heading toward Crossroads, Ingram knew; it was people coming out they were watching.

But with the girl at the wheel they could get out; he and Earl could hide in the rear, one in the trunk maybe, and this girl could take them right under the cops' noses. They weren't watching for a woman, that was certain. . . .

Even his cough seemed better now. It wasn't even midnight yet and they would be at the farm in fifteen or twenty minutes. By tomorrow morning they could be two hundred miles away. He straightened up, savoring the feel of the warmth and strength in his body. "Kind of slow down along here," he said, watching the road carefully. "There's a town ahead, Avondale, I think. After that we make a turn and head into the country. It won't be long now."

There was a cheerful, almost arrogant lift to his voice. They had a chance, a damned good one. And because of him. Not Earl. Him. . . .

CHAPTER FIFTEEN

THE SOUND of the car woke Earl. He had been sleeping in fitful snatches for an hour or so, waking with sudden starts and then lapsing again into splintered and troubled dreams. There was no comfort in either state, little difference between nightmares and reality. He knew his wound was bleeding and that he was feverish, but the unnatural heat of his body didn't seem to warm him at all; he could hardly move his hands and feet; they were stiff and solid as blocks of wood.

He had been dreaming of a hot evening on a beach somewhere near Naples. The whole company had gone in swimming, trying to get clean and to scrape off their beards in the salty water. Then planes had come in low from the mainland with tracer bullets sweeping in front of them like the feelers of angry insects. The company had scattered, some men trying to pull on their clothes, and others running in naked hysteria toward the shelter of the rocky cliffs. But the dream was all wrong, Earl knew; there had been no planes that day. They had laughed and splashed around in the water like kids on a summer holiday. The planes must have been somewhere else. . . .

And he had dreamed of a cold afternoon in Chicago when a youngster playing in front of his house had asked him to come inside and look at his Christmas presents. But that was strange too; he had never dreamed about that before. It never bothered him in his sleep. It only bothered him when he thought about it.

He had gone with the boy into a big, warm house. He shook hands with a father, a mother, some people sitting in front of a fire. He called out his name like a railroad conductor shouting stops. They said "Who?" in huge, distant voices, their faces bright with suspicion. But they treated him fine. He was in uniform, wandering through a strange city on furlough. They gave him a drink and a cigar as big as a baseball bat. He ate in the kitchen with a maid, and in the dream he kept saying his name over and over again through the steam rising from the turkey stuffing. Outside at last he yelled his name at the windows of the house, but all the lights winked out and there was nothing left but the darkness, and the wind blowing the echo of his name into the silence. Why was he so anxious for them to know his name? That's what always bothered him . . . But he had never dreamed about it before.

When he heard the car he came fully awake, listening alertly and fearfully to the laboring engine. He looked around the cold, bitter room, cursing the weakness of his feverish body. Where was the gun? His hands moved stiffly over the sofa. The colored man had taken it away . . . left him there. . . .

The door opened and he saw Lorraine coming toward him, her face twisting oddly, and her heels sounded in a staccato clatter on the hard, cold floor. He knew he was dreaming then. . . . He raised himself on one elbow to ask her about the gun, but she didn't seem to hear or understand; she knelt beside him weeping, and the pressure of her body started an intolerable pain in his shoulder. The colored man stood behind her looking at him anxiously. "Why did you bring her here?" Earl said. The pain cut astringently through his drifting thoughts; his mind was suddenly dry and clear. "Why did you bring her, damn you?"

"I couldn't stop her."

"It's going to be all right," Lorraine said, rubbing her cheek against his forehead. "I'm going to take care of you."

"It's no good," he muttered. "It's no good, Lory." The reviving anger drained out of him and he closed his eyes. He felt himself drifting into sleep; the sensation was giddy and nauseating, as if he were swinging back and forth in space, with nothing below him but wind and darkness. "That kid was all right," he said slowly and distinctly. "Wanted me to look at his toys. His old man didn't mind. They gave me a turkey dinner. It was a nice deal."

"He needs a doctor," Lorraine said, turning on her knees and staring at Ingram. "You hear me? He's going to die. He needs a doctor."

"He can't travel, that's for sure," Ingram said. The hope that had sustained him was ebbing away; they were stuck here for good. They couldn't try to take Earl past a road-block. He'd be delirious soon, and there'd be no way to keep him quiet.

He shook his head slowly. The whiskers were blue against Earl's dead-white skin, and an oily perspiration gleamed on his cheeks and forehead. The man was in sorry shape. . . . Ingram felt fear prickling his body, but now the sensation was wearily familiar; he'd lived with it so long that he could hardly remember anything else.

"You keep him warm," he said to Lorraine. "Try to get him to drink some whisky."

"Where are you going?"

"I'll try to get him a doctor."

He glanced at the old man snoring under his mound of blankets. "While I'm gone you get him into the kitchen." Ingram nodded at the faded photographs on the mantel. "Get them out of sight too."

"Yes, I will."

She was smart, Ingram realized; she understood their problem. "And you stay out of sight too. Stay in the kitchen with the old folks, and keep them quiet."

"Yes—I understand."

"If the doc happens to know this place we're through. He'll blow a whistle for the cops the minute I take him back home. And lead 'em right to us."

She looked around quickly. "I'll put the lamp beside Earl, with a blanket around it. He won't see anything in the room."

"That's good. And you better give Earl a little whisky."

"Just get a doctor, that's all."

"Yeah, that's all. Just put one in my pocket and bring him back."

She caught the sleeves of his coat and shook him with a

fierce and primitive strength. "You've got to, understand? You've got to."

"I've got to try," he said wearily. He knew there was no hope for any of them unless Earl could travel. "I've got to try."

It took Ingram twenty minutes to drive back to Avondale, the small village straddling the federal highway ten miles south of Crossroads. He turned into a side street and coasted through the darkness for several minutes, driving around the sleeping town until he saw a doctor's shingle shining under a blue night light. Then he cut the motor and coasted to a stop in front of the house.

The rain had stopped and the night was colder; he could see the slick of ice on the pavement, diamond-bright under the street lamps. The name on the doctor's sign was Taylor—W. J. TAYLOR, M.D. Black letters on a white board. The house was white too, with a screened-in front porch and neat plots of grass on either side of a concrete walk. It was just like every other house in the block; tidy, substantial and proper.

If the police weren't looking for him there was a chance, Ingram thought. No reason the doctor wouldn't go with him. . . .

He studied the situation as he would study the cards against him in a poker game, analyzing the known factors and trying to guess at the imponderables. His lips moved as he rehearsed the story he would tell the doctor, whispering the words into the darkness. ". . . Friend of mine's hurt, Doc. Just down the highway. The jack slipped while he was fixing a tire. Caught his hand bad. I didn't want to move him. . . ." No reason why that wouldn't work. Doctors were used to such things. And a gashed hand was pretty much like a bullet wound. The Doc would bring along the right stuff to fix it. . . .

He realized that he was almost too scared to move. All he had to do was walk up to the doctor's porch and knock on the door. He'd have to go through with it then, talking, lying . . . But he couldn't make himself do it. He touched the handle of the car door, but pulled his hand away quickly, his fingers trembling with cold and fear. Five seconds, he thought desperately. I'll count to five. But his tongue was so dry he couldn't make a sound; it felt like a thick wad of wool in his mouth.

The key chain caught his eye; it was swinging slowly, glinting in the soft dashboard light. A star was attached to the ring. Ingram touched it with a finger, and tiny reflections danced on the five shining points. A Silver Star, he thought. He'd seen a couple in England during the war. You didn't get them for keeping mess halls clean. This was a medal you earned the hard way.

It was Earl's probably. And he'd given it to his girl to use as a charm for her key ring. The big hero. . . . Why didn't he have this end of the job? He was the tough man who slapped people around if they looked sideways at him. Why wasn't he here now? Instead of sipping whisky with his girl waiting on him . . . The big hero flat on his back while I got the job to do, he thought bitterly. He flicked the Silver Star disdainfully with the tip of his finger. Okay, hero, he thought, opening the door of the car. Okay. . . .

He rang the bell and waited for someone to answer it, shifting his weight slowly from one foot to the other, his hand tight and cold on the butt of the gun. A light flashed behind the old-fashioned transom above the door, and a floor board creaked in the hallway of the house.

The door opened and a slim man with graying hair looked out at Ingram. "Yes?" he said, tightening the belt of his bathrobe. The wind blew his hair about in disorder, and there was a sleepy, irritable note in his voice. "What is it?"

"My friend got hurt," Ingram said, speaking rapidly and nervously. "He needs a doctor."

"Where is he?"

"On the highway, Doc. We had a flat and he was jacking up the car. Something slipped and caught his hand."

"You mean he's pinned under the car?"

"No, but he's hurt bad."

"Why didn't you bring him with you?"

"Well—" Ingram's hand fluttered pointlessly. "I didn't want to move him."

"I see. Come on in." The doctor led Ingram into an office off the hallway and snapped on overhead lights.

It was a small, warm reception room, with a few chairs, a table with magazines on it and a neat row of hunting prints on one wall. A door opened into a smaller office where Ingram saw a desk, and glass-walled cabinets of dressings and surgical instruments.

"Where is your friend?" the doctor said, putting on a pair of horn-rimmed glasses.

"On the highway, like I told you."

"Yes, yes," the doctor said irritably. With glasses his thin features became sharp and formidable. "Whereabouts on the highway?"

"Well, about four miles from here, I guess."

"Which direction? North or South?"

"South," Ingram said quickly.

"That's about at the Texaco station," the doctor said. "Why didn't you call me from there?"

"Well, I didn't notice it, I guess. I was pretty excited."

"I see," the doctor said, nodding slowly. "Well, I'll have to put some clothes on. I won't be long. Sit down and make yourself comfortable."

As he opened the door to the hallway a board creaked above their heads, and a woman's voice called softly and anxiously: "Walt? Who is it, Walt? Do you have to go out?"

"Yes, dear. You go on back to bed now."

"Has there been an accident somewhere?"

Ingram saw the perspiration shining on the doctor's forehead, saw the tension in his face. The man was no poker player; he was suspicious and he couldn't hide it. Ingram stepped in front of him and closed the door. In the same motion he brought the gun up from his pocket.

"Take it easy," he said sharply. "Stay nice and quiet."

The doctor stared at the muzzle of the gun, breathing slowly and deeply. "Put that away," he said. "You're making a big mistake."

"Tell your wife there's been an accident. Tell her so it

sounds all right, Doc. I mean it." Ingram pulled open the door and nodded toward the hallway. "Tell her."

"Walt?" The woman's voice sounded clearly now; she had come to the top of the stairs, Ingram realized. "Who's down there with you?"

Staring at the gun the doctor said, "There's been an accident over on the federal highway. They need me right away."

"Well, bundle up good, Walt. It's turning a lot colder."

"Yes, dear. You get back to bed now."

"Do you want me to make a cup of coffee?"

"No, there isn't time. Good night, dear."

The doctor swallowed with an effort as footsteps sounded above their heads.

Ingram closed the door of the office. "My friend's got a bullet in him," he said. "You're going to take it out. You won't get hurt if you do just what I tell you. So start moving."

The doctor stared at Ingram for a moment, his mouth hardening into a stubborn line. "Just like that, eh? Well, supposing I tell you to go to hell. You use that gun and you'll wake up the whole town. Don't you realize that?"

"I don't know, Doc. I'm too scared to think straight. That's honest. You tell me to go to hell, and I might start running. I don't know."

"I'm not going with you."

"I'll bring you back safe. I promise, Doc."

"There's no room for bargaining. It's a flat 'no.' You can shoot or clear out."

Ingram resisted a crazy impulse to laugh. The man with a gun called the turns; it was practically an American institution. Everybody knew that. The gunman didn't wheedle or whine for people to do what he wanted; he just waved his gun and they jumped. Ingram wondered fleetingly how many gunmen had watched this myth explode in their faces.

"All right, Doc, turn around."

"What for? Don't you have the guts to slug me from the front?"

"I've got to shoot you, Doc. So turn around. Otherwise

you'll get it in the stomach. I got to do that. You see that." Ingram spoke quietly, but the weary conviction in his voice brought a startled look to the doctor's face.

"Now wait a minute," he said quickly. "Shooting me won't do you any good."

Ingram realized that he was prepared to pull the trigger, and the knowledge made him feel cold and sick all over. The gun did call the turn, he knew then; it dominated the man who held it as well as the man it was pointed at.

"Don't shoot," the doctor said, all his hard confidence dissolving. "I'll come with you."

"That's fine," Ingram said, letting out his breath slowly.

"Tell me what you can about your friend's condition. When was he shot, and where did the bullet hit him?"

"The bullet's in his shoulder. It happened four, maybe five hours ago."

"Around eight o'clock." The doctor stared at Ingram with a sudden tense understanding. "The bank at Crossroads?"

"That's right."

"Well, your friend's got a .38 from a Police Special in him," the doctor said. He was very pale. "Did the wound bleed much?"

"I didn't look at it. But he seems weak, kind of delirious."

"That's shock, of course." The doctor looked uncertainly at the glass-walled cabinets of the small, inner office. "I don't have plasma, but I can take along saline and dextrose solutions. He'll need it. And what else?" He checked the items on his fingers, speaking in a soft, hurried voice. "Novocain, penicillin, tetanus antitoxin—and let's see—Demerol of course, and secunesine to calm him down. I've got all of that. How long will it take us to get to him?"

"It's quite a ways."

"I see," the doctor said, after a little pause. "Well, I'll pack up what I need. . . ."

After stocking a bag with drugs and instruments, he glanced down at his robe. "I can't go like this," he said. "My clothes are upstairs."

"Don't you have an overcoat down here?"

"Yes—on the halltree."

"That's good enough," Ingram said. "I'll get you back here as quick as I can. I promise you that, Doc. Just one thing: you put a roll of gauze in the bag. I'll have to blindfold you with some of that when we get out of town. You're not going to be hurt, I swear it. But I don't want you to lead the cops back to us. You see that, don't you?"

"Sure," the doctor said bitterly.

Ingram ushered him into the hallway, staying a few feet behind with the gun held at his hip. The doctor was pulling on his overcoat when Ingram heard a car stop in front of the house. As the echoes of its motor faded in the silence, he turned and stared at the doctor's thin pale face. "Who's that?" he whispered.

The car door slammed and footsteps sounded briskly on the sidewalk leading up to the house. Ingram felt his nerves tighten cruelly. "Who's that?" he whispered again.

"I don't know."

"Get back into the office." Ingram hurried the doctor ahead of him and closed the door, standing with his back to it and pointing the gun at the doctor's stomach. "You better level with me. Who is it?"

"I don't know, I tell you. It might be anyone. A man with a sick wife, anybody."

"Why don't they ring the bell?"

The doctor's face was haggard; deep shadows had darkened under his eyes, and his lips had begun to tremble. "I don't know, I don't know."

Ingram put his ear to the door. He heard low, murmuring voices, and a teasing rise of laughter. Then a latch clicked, and high heels tapped in the hallway.

"Dad?" It was a girl's voice, soft and husky with excitement. "Dad? Are you still up?"

"She's just sixteen," the doctor said, whispering the words frantically. He stared at Ingram in helpless anguish. "Sixteen, you hear?"

Ingram's face was hot. "I can't help that," he said, shaking his head. "How can I help that?"

"Dad? May I come in for a minute? We had a super time."

"Tomorrow's a big day, honey. I think you'd better turn in. I've got some—work to finish up."

The knob turned slowly. "I just want to tell you one thing, Dad."

"No, go to bed!"

"It's too late, Doc," Ingram said sharply. "Keep still." Holding the gun at his side he opened the door and said, "Step in here," to the young girl who stood in the hallway. She smiled uncertainly at her father as Ingram closed the door and leaned against it. "I didn't know there was anyone with you, Dad. You didn't say—"

"I'm sorry," Ingram said, bringing the gun into sight. "Now don't scream, don't even talk. Just stand nice and quiet."

"Dad!" She whimpered the word. "Who is he?"

"It's all right, Carol," her father said in a tight, unnatural voice. He put an arm about her slim shoulders. "His friend is hurt. I've got to go and take care of him."

"We've all got to go," Ingram said. "You see that, don't you, Doc?"

"You can't take her!"

"I've got to."

"What kind of a man are you? Or are you a man at all?" The doctor's voice was trembling with impotent fury. "You're some kind of animal—that's closer to the mark, isn't it?"

"I don't know, I don't know," Ingram said helplessly. "But I've got to do it, Doc." The fear in the girl's eyes and the anger in her father's face cut him like whips. "I've got to help my friend. I've never done anything bad in my life before this. I'm in trouble. I don't look like a man to you, but I swear to God you or your daughter won't be hurt. You fix up my friend, and I'll bring you right back. I swear it, I swear it. You got nothing to be afraid of."

"I'm not afraid, Dad," the girl said in a soft, little voice. "Really I'm not. Don't worry, please." She was small and slender, just a child in a pink party dress and high-heeled silver pumps, but she stared at Ingram with level, sensible eyes. "He won't hurt us," she said. "I believe him, Dad."

"You won't be hurt," Ingram said, with sudden heat in his voice. "I swore that, didn't I? Now, let's go. . . ."

CHAPTER SIXTEEN

THE LANE twisting into the farm had frozen solid; Ingram had to fight the wheel as the car bumped over ruts and ridges, the long headlights bouncing crazily over the stone walls of the old house. He had driven back in a wide circle, making a half-dozen unnecessary stops and turns; it was essential strategy, but the trip had used up precious time.

He climbed out of the car and shivered as the wind struck his body. The night stretched wide and dark and empty around him, silent except for the wind screaming like something caught in the branches of the big bare trees. He helped the doctor and the young girl from the car, and led them up the porch. They had said little during the long, circuitous drive, but after he had stopped and bandaged their eyes Ingram could feel their straining attention to the evidence coming to their other senses; the distant throb of a plane, the heavy, wet-earth smell of a mushroom house, the transition from concrete to dirt roads—they were soaking it all up, he knew, trying to figure out where he was taking them. Now as they stood on the porch, the doctor's hand touched the door jamb, his fingers moved appraisingly over the porous stones of the old walls.

"Why don't you just relax?" Ingram said quietly. "We aren't worth your worrying about. Come on now, watch this step here. . . ."

Earl was stronger than when Ingram had left him, propped up on the sofa with the whisky bottle beside him, his cheeks bright with unnatural color, and a hard, weary light flashing in his eyes. "Who is she?" he said, staring at the girl. "Why'd you bring her?"

"She's his daughter. She came in from a party, and I had to bring her. How're you feeling?"

"Pretty good. Just cold."

Ingram took off the overcoat he had been wearing, and put it across Earl's legs. Then he took a quick look around the room; Earl's woman had done her job well. The old man was out of sight, the photographs were gone from the mantel, and except for the area around the sofa the room was lost in shadows. The doc would know he had been in an old house out in the country—nothing else. Ingram guided the girl to a chair, then removed the gauze bandage from the doctor's eyes. He blinked and looked around for his daughter. She sat with her hands folded in her lap, her childish lips composed in a firm little line, incongruously sweet and innocent in the cold, dank room, with the pink skirt spread about her knees and a faint light gleaming on the tips of her silver pumps.

"I'll be quick as I can, honey," the doctor said to her. "Don't worry about anything."

"I'm not worried, Daddy."

"Let's go, Doc," Earl said.

The doctor looked at him for the first time, his eyes clinically alert. There was no compassion in his face, and very little interest. He glanced at the whisky bottle, and said, "How much of that have you been drinking?"

"Three or four swallows. Why? Is that bad?"

"It probably won't hurt." The doctor bent over and looked into Earl's eyes for a few seconds. Without turning around, he said, "I'll need some boiling water, and a table or a couple of chairs."

"I'll get 'em," Ingram said.

The doctor removed scissors from his bag and unbuttoned Earl's shirt to cut away the bloody cloth. Ingram winced when he saw the wound; it looked like a purple eye squeezed between layers of swollen, discolored flesh. "I'm going to give you a local first," the doctor said, putting his bag on the chair Ingram had shoved over beside the sofa. "Then something to keep you quiet. After I clean up the surface area, we'll see what we're up against."

"How does it look? Bad?"

"I don't know. I can make a guess after I've taken your blood pressure. Have you coughed up any blood?"

"No."

"Maybe you were lucky. The bullet entered the pectoral muscle, but obviously missed the lung." He had filled a hypodermic needle as he talked, measuring the liquid with frowning attention. "Okay, give me your arm."

"How long's this going to take?"

"Half hour to an hour, depending on what I find." He hesitated then, and looked up at Ingram. "I'm going to do my best, but I can't promise a damned thing under these circumstances. I should have a sterile operating room and sterile instruments. In a wound there's the danger of shock and infection, in addition to the rupturing effect of the bullet, and the damage done to flesh and bone, capillaries and arteries. I'll try like the devil—that's all I can promise."

Earl put a cigarette in his mouth, studied the doctor with a little grin. "How do you rate yourself as a sawbones?"

"I'm good."

"Well, don't worry then. I'm tough. I took a town in Germany once with a bullet through my leg. Had the Krauts making coffee for me when the rest of the platoon showed up. So start chopping away."

The doctor loosened the rubber band he had strapped to Earl's arm. "Your blood pressure is good," he said. "It's damned near fantastic."

Earl grinned. "I told you, Doc."

The doctor worked with swift, efficient precision, taping tubes to Earl's arm for intravenous feeding, cleaning the surface of the wound and dusting it with sulfa powder. "The bullet was deflected downward," he muttered. "Probably grazed a rib without shattering it. Turn over a little. That's it." He probed Earl's side with the tips of his fingers, alert with professional curiosity. "Here it is," he said at last. "I can cut it out easier than going down the bullet track after it."

"How about me having a drink?"

"Well—" The doctor shrugged and nodded to Ingram.

"Give him whisky with a little water. If he can hold it down it might help."

Ingram shifted his weight from foot to foot as the doctor picked a scalpel from the saucepan of boiling water he had brought in from the kitchen. Earl's face was damp with sweat, and the muscles were tightening in his throat, but he made no sound at all, just sipped whisky and stared without expression at the doctor's intent, frowning features.

With the bullet out, the doctor turned back to the chest wound, packing it with powders and salves, then strapping dressings in place with broad lengths of adhesive tape.

"How do you feel?" he asked Earl.

"Kind of tired."

"Any pain at all?"

"No. I feel fine."

"When can he travel, Doc?" Ingram said.

"If he were in a hospital, they wouldn't let him out for a week. He needs rest."

"Balls," Earl said. "I got hit twice in the Army and it hardly slowed me down."

"You were a lot younger then."

"What do you mean younger? I'm only thirty-five now."

"That's a long way from twenty."

"Of all the crap," Earl said. "Look at Ted Williams! Supposing you needed a hit, who'd you send up? Williams or some twenty-year-old jerk of a kid?"

"I'd go with Williams, I suppose," the doctor said, shrugging. "But not if he had a bullet in his shoulder." He worked quickly for another three or four minutes, stitching and dressing the incision in Earl's side.

Finally he rubbed the back of his hand over his forehead and said, "Well, that does it. You're loaded with penicillin in a beeswax solution. That will keep you going for twenty-four hours. Then you'll need more. And you'll need to have those dressings changed. I've done all I can for you."

"You're good," Earl said. "You called it. Damned good."

"And you're tough," the doctor said, repacking his bag. "I'll give you that in spades." He straightened and glanced at his daughter. "Okay, honey. We're ready to go now."

"I'll have to put the blindfold on you, Doc," Ingram said. "Then we can start."

"Now hold it a second," Earl said gently. "They're not going anywhere, Sambo."

"What do you mean?" Ingram said. "I promised them I'd take them home."

"The minute he gets to a phone he calls the cops. Didn't you think of that?"

"What can he tell them? Just that he's been riding around somewhere in the country. He and the girl were blindfolded all the way. And they'll go back like that."

"No," Earl said, shaking his head slowly. "They're staying here till we pull out. That's final." He felt charged with confidence, ready to run this show. It was like the Army, he thought, where everything went smoothly if one guy made the decisions and the rest snapped to and carried them out.

The doctor stared at Earl without fear or anger, a stubborn ridge of muscle knotting along his jawline. "Now you get this," he said slowly. "We're going home. I've patched you as well as I could. Now I'm going home and I'm taking my daughter with me. Get that through your head."

Earl shook his head again. "You're staying, Doc. Until we leave."

"They've been decent to us," Ingram said hotly. "He saved your life, you know that. We made a deal, and he's done his part. Now I'm doing mine."

Earl laughed softly. He was feeling fine, light and heady. The gun was close to his hand; that was what made him laugh. Ingram had left it in the overcoat he had thrown over his knees. "You're way out of line, Sambo," he said. "I told you I was running this show, didn't I?" He sat up on the sofa and pulled the gun out from the pocket of the overcoat. "You're careless about weapons, Sambo. In any army you'd get court-martialed for that."

"What in hell is wrong with you?" Ingram said angrily. "Stop talking about the Army. This isn't no goddam barracks."

The girl stood uncertainly, a little cry of terror coming through her lips. "Dad? Dad, where are you?"

The doctor put an arm tightly about her shoulders. "We're going home, baby," he said. "I promise you."

"It just can't be, Doc," Earl said, letting the gun swing lazily in his hand. He felt great; the combination of drugs and alcohol had started a bland confidence flowing in his veins. "I've got to keep you here. You're a smart guy. You understand."

"Now listen," the doctor said in a tight strained voice. "If we're not home soon, my wife will call the State Police. Is that what you want?"

"Well, we can't have her doing that," Earl said thoughtfully. He nodded at the doctor. "You think way ahead, don't you?"

"I'm trying to be reasonable. You won't gain anything by keeping us here."

"Yeah, that's right," Earl said. "Keeping both of you is no good. So we'll just keep the girl. That's better, isn't it, Sambo?"

"You're talking like a fool."

"What would I tell my wife?" the doctor said wearily. "Can't you think, man?"

"You could say she stopped for the night at some friend's house."

"Her mother would know I was lying."

"Then tell her the truth," Earl said. "That's reasonable, isn't it? Just tell her to pretend nothing is wrong. Just call her school and say she's sick or something like that. We'll keep her here until we're ready to leave. You won't go running to the cops then, will you, Doc?"

"My wife hasn't been well," the doctor said. "I couldn't tell her the truth. The shock might kill her."

"That's your problem," Earl said harshly; anger was building up inside him, pounding for release. "She's your wife, not mine. Tell her any damned thing you want. But keep her quiet. Otherwise you may not see this cute little kid of yours again."

"You filthy rotten scum," the doctor said in a soft but savagely bitter voice. "You're nothing but dirt—you don't have an ounce of decency in your miserable body. You're tough, sure—blood pressure normal four hours after being shot. It's the reaction you find in animals. Your guts come from that gun in your hand. Without it you're just something crawling through the mud."

"Shut up!" Earl yelled at him. "You say anything else and I'm going to put a hole right through your head. You think I'm kidding?"

He forced himself to his feet, swaying like a badly hurt fighter; a terrible weakness was suddenly spreading through his body. "You think I'm kidding, eh? You want to die in front of that little girl?"

"No—I believe you." The doctor's lips were stiff and dry. He took a step away from Earl, holding his daughter tightly in his arms. "Just relax. You're sick."

Ingram stepped quickly in front of the doctor. "You want to shoot somebody, white boy, you shoot me," he said in a soft, trembling voice. "Go ahead. You're the big hero with all the medals. Here's a chance to get another. Shoot me, and then shoot the doc who saved your life, and then the little girl. You'll get a big medal. But you'll be all alone then, white boy. Remember that."

"Get out of the way," Earl said. "Get out of the way."

"I'm taking these people home. I promised them that. Start backing toward the door, Doc. If he shoots anybody, it's going to be me."

"Sambo!" Earl cried frantically. "Who are you with?"

"I'm taking them home. That comes first."

"Well, goddam," Earl said, swaying weakly. "I should have expected this." The gun swung loosely to his side, the muzzle pointing at the floor. "You're ratting out." The words sounded thick and feeble in his ears. He sat down on the sofa, his body moving with sluggish caution, and his muscles and nerves cringing at the sick feeling fanning through his body. "All right, take 'em home," he said, breathing heavily. "Take 'em home, hear? Take everybody home. Everybody with a home should go home."

Ingram crossed the floor swiftly and took the gun from his limp hand. "I'll come back," he said, touching Earl's shoulder. "Don't worry." He wet his lips, trying to think of something else to say; all his anger had gone. "I'm coming back," he said. "You get some rest."

Earl lay back on the couch, breathing through his open mouth. He stared at Ingram with sick, glazed eyes, and nodded weakly. "I'll wait for you, Sambo. Nothing else I can do."

CHAPTER SEVENTEEN

AT THREE O'CLOCK in the morning the village of Crossroads lay sleeping in faint moonlight, its streets shining emptily and bursts of wind tugging with a lonely sound at the canvas awnings above the dark shops.

The all-night drugstore and the gas station at the bend of the federal highway were exceptions to the black silence; they were courageously open for business as usual, bright and defiant flags against the night.

At police headquarters in the Municipal Building, Kelly was sitting opposite the sheriff's desk, a cigarette burning in the ash tray near his elbow, and a sheaf of notes and reports in his hand. Morgan had gone off duty, and the sheriff and several of Kelly's men were working with the troopers at the roadblocks surrounding Crossroads.

Kelly swiveled in his chair and stared at the county map on the wall, focusing his eyes on the black circle the sheriff had drawn around the area southwest of Crossroads. It was a pretty big noose, he thought. Too big. The men were trapped all right; roadblocks sealed off the section efficiently. But they had a vast territory to move around in, and someone might be hurt, before the noose was jerked tight around their necks. They had to get them fast. That was the essential thing at this end of the job.

Washington was working on the other side of it. They had identified the slain holdup man. Burke, an ex-cop from Detroit, bounced for using his badge as the emblem of a private collection agency. It was all over for him now, Kelly thought. He'd tried for the big time and missed by a country mile. Washington was running down a man named Novak, who had been an associate of Burke's in the past few months. Maybe Novak wasn't part of the bank job. But they wanted to make sure. Dozens of agents were after him, along with the police departments of every state. Novak, whoever he was, didn't have a prayer.

That left the man inside the noose. John Ingram, a Negro. The police in Philly had run a cautious check on him. He hadn't been in trouble before. He was known as a quiet, good-humored fellow, a dealer in a gambling joint, one of four brothers with good records and responsible jobs. Ingram puzzled Kelly; he just didn't fit the picture. Bank robbers fell into categories. They were usually impulsive and reckless men, indifferent to risk or danger. Hard to stop, since banks seemed to challenge their outlaw temperaments, but very easy to apprehend; they inevitably spent their stolen money foolishly, drinking and brawling, and showing off until they brought the law down on themselves.

The white man, yes. They didn't have his name yet. Just the sheriff's description: big and rangy, with steady, sullen eyes. He fitted. Moody, restless, a man with a grudge.

The door opened and Kelly turned from the map, expecting Sheriff Burns; but it was his daughter, Nancy, bundled up in a hooded raincoat and carrying a large thermos in her arms. She said "Hello," rather awkwardly, and put the thermos on the counter. "I thought Dad would be here."

"He's out at one of the roadblocks." Kelly glanced at his watch. "Should be back pretty soon."

"Would you like coffee?" She put her raincoat over a chair and ran a hand nervously over her long blond hair. "I couldn't sleep—I wondered if you and Dad might like something hot to drink."

"That sounds fine," Kelly said. He leaned against the desk and watched her pour steaming coffee into the metal cups she unscrewed from the top of the thermos. There was an efficient haste in all her movements as if she were eager to get the job over and done with; he found it dfficult to imagine her doing anything at a casual, leisurely pace. Rush, rush, he thought. He was puzzled by this girl; there were contradictions about her that he couldn't understand. She seemed warm and cold, wistful and hard, pensive and indifferent—but all the same time, the emotions blended together in aggravating and illogical patterns. He had been thinking about her quite a lot since dinner—not simply because she was a young and attractive female, but because the incongruities in her manner aroused his professional interest in puzzles.

They sat for a moment in silence, Kelly perched on the desk, the girl studying the splinter of light moving on the glossy black tip of her pump. The office was warm and quiet, a comfortable coffee-fragrant refuge against the night pressing against the frosted windows. But the silence between them wasn't comfortable, Kelly realized; she seemed awkward and strained for some reason.

He couldn't imagine why. She was good-looking enough, he thought, studying her smooth profile. Just a little bit stiff and shy, but everything else was definitely all right; nice blond hair, fresh clean skin, intelligent eyes and mouth. No discernible flaws. She was wearing a soft beige sweater with a neatly pegged tweed skirt, and the full curving lines of her bosom and hips were very evident as she twisted slightly in the chair and crossed her smooth, slim legs.

So why wasn't she married? he thought.

"You say you had trouble sleeping tonight?" he asked her politely.

"Yes—I don't know why."

"You often have trouble sleeping?"

She glanced at him, a touch of color in her cheeks. "I'm afraid so."

"I'm a pretty good sleeper," he said. "If sleeping were a commercial activity, say like baseball, I'd be the DiMaggio of the league."

"What's the secret? Plenty of exercise, wide-open windows and so forth?"

"The open window is the real secret," he said.

"Does your wife mind a cold bedroom?"

"I'm not married," Kelly said. "But I have a future wife wandering around somewhere, and I hope she won't mind."

"It's an interesting way of looking at things." She laughed a little. "In fact it's pretty cockeyed."

"I don't know. Men torch for ex-wives. So what's wrong with me torching for a future wife?" He smiled at her. "Don't you ever daydream like that? About the guy you're going to marry?"

"I suppose I must have. I suppose everyone does." She stood and smoothed her skirt with swift, efficient gestures. "Would you like more coffee?"

"Yes, thanks." Watching her, he began to understand the incongruous thing about her; she didn't seem to realize she was attractive—she just didn't have the casual confidence in herself that was usually part of a good-looking woman's equipment. That puzzled him, too. Hadn't anybody told her she was pretty or amusing or wonderful? It seemed unlikely. Maybe someone had stopped saying it . . . that had the same effect sometimes.

She should be married, he decided finally; that would fix her insomnia.

Kelly wasn't insensitive, but his mind worked simply and directly. The obvious seldom escaped him, and the obscure always sounded a warning bell in his mind; the combination made him a difficult man to fool.

The phone rang, shattering the uneasy silence, and he said, "Excuse me," and picked up the receiver.

"Is Sheriff Burns there?" It was a woman's voice, high and shaky. "This is Doctor Taylor's wife."

"No, he's out. Can I help you?"

"Something has happened to my daughter. Something terrible—I'm sure of it." The woman's voice was rising hysterically. Kelly said, "Take it easy now. Just tell me what's wrong." He covered the receiver and looked questioningly at Nancy. "Doctor Taylor's wife?"

"That's Laura Taylor—they live in Avondale, about ten miles from here."

"Mrs. Taylor," Kelly said.

"I'm trying to be calm. My daughter went to a parish dance tonight. She should have been home hours ago. But she's not."

"Who did she go with?"

"The Metcalf boy. I've called him already. He was in bed—he told me he left Carol off at one o'clock."

"Did he see her go inside the house?"

"Yes, yes—he took her to the door."

"Have you checked the house carefully? She might have curled up on a sofa or something like that."

"She's not here, I tell you. I've gone from the basement to the attic."

"Would she have gone out to stay at a friend's house?"

"No—something terrible has happened. I'm sure of it."

"Is Doctor Taylor there?"

"He's got a call. There was an accident on the federal highway. I'm here alone."

Kelly turned and stared at the radio speaker. He was sure there had been no accident on the federal highway; he had been sitting beside the speaker all night. "Mrs. Taylor, I'm coming right out," he said. "Just take it easy. I'll be there in ten minutes."

"Please, please hurry."

Kelly reached for his trenchcoat. One of the hunted men was wounded, and a doctor had been called to a nonexistent accident—it could only mean one thing. . . .

"I'm going to get your father," he said to the girl. "Can I drop you on the way?"

"No, please don't bother."

"Why do you think it's a bother? Come on. . . ."

CHAPTER EIGHTEEN

INGRAM STOOD at the windows in the living room of the farmhouse and watched the first mud-colored light of dawn pushing back the darkness that hung at the top of the meadow. It was too late for them to start moving; by the time they got ready to go the sun would be up. He glanced at Earl who was sleeping with his head against the back of the sofa and his good arm resting protectively across his wounded shoulder. In the dim lamplight his face was a mask of weakness and pain; the hollows beneath his eyes were like deep purple bruises, and his whiskers had grown into a black furry smudge across his soot-gray skin. Looks as bad as I feel, Ingram thought.

They would have to sit tight here today, he decided, glancing to where Earl's woman lay sleeping. She had made her bed with the rear cushion from the car, and was lying with her knees drawn up under an old comforter she had found in an upstairs closet. There was something grim about the way she slept, Ingram thought. Like a fighter taking a last rest before going into the ring—her breath came deep and steady, and her flat body seemed purposefully and deliberately still, as if she were readying herself for some big ordeal. A tidy cat of a woman, too; pumps lined up neatly, bed made like a Girl Scout, and even a ribbon tying back her long, black hair. He could see the pale triangular blur of her face, and the rhythmic vaporings of her breath in the cold air. She was strong, he knew; tough and selfish. She was watching out for herself and Earl—and nobody else. Maybe that was right, he thought, feeling a surprising stab of loneliness. That was a woman's need—to guard the life she had with a man. He began to feel sorry for himself, pitying his body its lonely sickness and pain. A motherless child, he thought, trying to mock his mood. *Sometimes I feel like a motherless child, a long way from home. . . .* He shook his head with weary humor at the plaintive words of the song. *Just because my hair is curly, just because my teeth are pearly. . . .* How square could you get?

Earl shifted and opened his eyes. Ingram looked at him and said, "How're you feeling now?"

"Okay, I guess." Earl was staring at the windows. "It's getting light. We better get rolling, eh?"

"It's too late." Ingram sat down slowly in a chair facing Earl. "I figure we got to wait till dark. We can't get past the police in the daytime. They'll see you're hurt. At night you can sit with your coat collar turned up and they won't see you too good."

Lorraine stirred and Earl lowered his voice. "We just sit here all day?"

"I don't see any other way," Ingram said quietly. "We'll be okay. The old folks won't bother us, and the cops don't know where we are. We just keep out of sight and we'll be all right."

"Maybe," Earl said, moving his good hand in a limp, futile gesture. The pain in his shoulder was dull and slow, better than he'd expected it to be, but his mood was heavy and spiritless; his thoughts drifted with sluggish indifference about their predicament. He picked up a cigarette from the pack on the couch, and leaned forward to draw a light from the match Ingram struck for him. Inhaling deeply, he watched the smoke drift in thin, blue layers toward the ceiling. "How about the doctor?" he said finally. "Think he can bring the cops here?"

"I don't see how. Funny, he acted like he didn't even want to. He kept thanking me for—well, how everything turned out."

"Yeah, that is funny," Earl said dryly.

"But he doesn't know anything that can help the cops. He was blindfolded all the time. So was his daughter. And I drove in circles till they were dizzy with it. I figure our chances this way: nobody knows about your woman and her car. So when it gets dark we can drive right through the roadblock. I'm small enough to curl up in the trunk, and you can ride up with your woman. Why should they stop us?"

"It sounds all right," Earl said slowly. He was silent for a moment or so, drawing deeply on his cigarette. Then he looked curiously at Ingram. "How did you get into this deal anyway?"

"I was a fool, that's all," Ingram said with a weary shrug. "I was in trouble. So I went to Novak. He said he'd help me out, sure—if I came in on this job." He sighed. "It seems like a million years ago."

"What kind of trouble were you in?"

"I owed money to a man who wouldn't wait for it."

"Yeah? How much?"

"Six thousand dollars."

Earl whistled softly. "How'd you get into that kind of debt?"

"Gambling. Just plain foolishness." Ingram coughed and put the palms of his hands against the pain and pressure in his chest. "I got shooting craps with a friend of mine named Billy Turk. I was reckless. I didn't give a damn. You know how that is. Something goes wrong, and you just don't care what else happens."

"Yeah, I know what you mean," Earl said. He was watching Ingram with interest, seeing him in a sense for the first time. "So this friend of yours wouldn't wait for the dough. Is that it?"

"No, Billy Turk was all right. But he did a thing that jammed me up. He sold my paper at a discount to some boys who worked for a big shot named Tenzell. You ever hear of him?"

"I don't think so."

"Well, Tenzell wouldn't wait. He wanted the cash. And what Mr. Tenzell wants he gets."

Earl waved a hand irritably at the smoke drifting between them; he wanted to see Ingram's face more clearly. Until just now he couldn't have described Ingram beyond saying he was colored; he hadn't seen much else. This struck him as odd. He inspected Ingram carefully, puzzled by his own interest. The man was small and slender, he saw, with silky black hair and funny eyes—kind of childish, almost, as if he were watching for something that might make him smile. "I don't get it," he said. "What do you mean, this guy sold your paper at a discount?"

Ingram smiled. "Just that. I gave Billy Turk an undated IOU for six thousand dollars. I lost that much in twenty minutes, like a fool. Usually I don't gamble foolish. But that night I just didn't care, like I told you. My mother wasn't dead long, and I felt—I don't know—just foolish, I guess. I told Turk I'd pay him in a month. He knew I was good for it. But he got drunk that same night and sold the IOU to Tenzell's men. Next thing I knew Tenzell wanted to see me."

"Tenzell's a tough guy, eh?"

"More than that, man. He runs two wards in the south end of the city. On the side he owns a fight club, a trucking company, handles all the horse rooms and numbers. He's got cops working for him—there's guys like him in every city." Ingram shook his head slowly, his skin prickling with shame as he remembered his session in Tenzell's office. Tenzell, flanked by two of his men, his bald head gleaming under a cold electric light, had said gently, "You got forty-eight hours, black boy. Use 'em." Ingram had begged for a break, but it hadn't helped; Tenzell could stand anything in people but self-respect, and when Ingram's had diminished to a satisfactory nothingness, Tenzell had said, "I told you, forty-eight hours. Get out."

Earl frowned at the sick look in Ingram's eyes. "Why the hell wouldn't he give you some time?" he said. "What kind of a crud is he?"

"He just wouldn't. Sometimes he does things to remind everybody who's boss. And he didn't like colored people much. That was part of it."

"You should have caught him alone and put your foot through his stomach," Earl said bitterly. "Bastards like that aren't tough unless they're running in packs. Well, Novak fixed you up fine, didn't he?" Earl stared through the windows at the black trees swaying in layers of drifting fog. "He fixed us both up fine. Country hotel, all the conveniences."

"We're going to get out, don't worry."

"How about a drink? We might as well enjoy something."

"You want some water with it?"

"Yeah, just a little." As Ingram stood up Earl realized that he looked taller than he was because he moved so easily and lightly, his body always in balance. Everything he did looked as if he'd rehearsed it to music, he thought.

"Aren't you drinking?" he said, when Ingram handed him a glass.

"I don't like whisky much."

"You look like you could use a slug. You're coming down with something."

"It's just a cold."

Earl sipped the whisky gratefully and lighted another cigarette.

"How is working in a gambling joint? Is that a pretty good deal?" Both men were speaking softly, in almost conspiratorial deference to the sleeping woman.

"Good enough; I usually made around two hundred a week."

"You're kidding!"

"Some weeks I did better." Ingram was pleased, but curiously embarrassed by the look of respect in Earl's face. "I usually dealt and cut the pot for the house, you know. But sometimes the house would back me against the heavy betters—if I won I kept twenty-five per cent."

"You must play damned good poker."

"It was my job."

"What did your mother think about you working in a gambling joint?"

"It was a respectable place. The boss paid off the cops, and he didn't allow any drinking or loud talk." Ingram grinned a little. "But she never did like it. My brothers had nice jobs, she thought. One drove a streetcar, the other drove a truck, and the baby of the family was working in a market. I made as much in a week as all three of them put together."

"Women are dumb that way," Earl said, shaking his head. "Just plain dumb. A guy has to take his chances." For some reason talking about these things with Ingram made him feel troubled and restless. He stood and began to pace the floor, rubbing his good hand slowly up and down the side of his leg. He'd had chances too; had his share of breaks. The thought gave him confidence. "You know I damned near stumbled into something good once," he said. He limped back to the sofa, caught up in a kind of anxious excitement. "It was quite a while back, seven or eight years ago." He sat down and picked up his glass, watching Ingram with a frown. "I was working at a lodge in Wisconsin then, a place that had a gas station and a bar along with the hotel. A handyman, you could say. Well, there were two guys who dropped in most afternoons for a few beers. They were brothers, Ed and Bill Corley. They were builders, but they had a loan outfit and a big real-estate company, too. You ever met guys like that? With their fingers in everything?"

"They sound smart, all right."

"I'm telling you," Earl said irritably. "They were big guys. They were building thirty-two homes for a housing development. Does that give you an idea of how big they were?"

"That's quite an investment."

Earl finished his drink and put the glass on the floor. "Well, they liked me. I used to ice-up the bar in the afternoon, and I talked with them a lot. Later on I figured they must have thought I was pretty smart. Why would they talk to me if they didn't think I was smart?"

"Yeah, that's right," Ingram said. "Unless they were just kind of making conversation."

"It wasn't that way. They liked me, I tell you. But I let the chance slip right through my fingers." Earl shifted to the edge of the sofa, tense and excited by the memory of this strange defeat. "I let it slip right through my fingers," he said. He could see Ed and Bill Corley clearly in his mind and smell the sweet-sour smell of the beer in the pine-paneled barroom. The whole area had been booming, but he'd missed the chance to cash in on it.

"Well, where did you fit in?" Ingram said, puzzled.

"It's plain enough for Christ's sake. I could have saved up a few hundred dollars, say, and just plunked it on the table some afternoon. 'Cut me in for that much,' I'd have said. And they'd have done it."

"Why?"

"They liked me, I tell you."

Ingram shook his head. "You got some funny ideas about the business world. You think smart guys go around saying, 'Let's cut this youngster in for a piece, and let's give a chunk to the happy kid behind the bar.' It just doesn't work that way."

Ingram's skepticism angered Earl. "What's so funny about them guys liking me?"

"I didn't mean to joke about it," Ingram said. "But look:

just being around money doesn't mean anything. Rich folks aren't giving anything away—anymore than a twenty-year-old kid is going to give some bald old man his nice curly hair." Ingram leaned forward earnestly. "Look here. Somebody wins a thousand dollars on a number. So all his friends get excited, acting like they won something, too. They get a big kick out of just being close to luck. Then the man gives the money to his wife or pays some debts, and it's all over—the money's gone and the people who crowded around it feel they've been cheated out of something. That's what I mean—if you feel lucky-rich because you're around some money, you're in for a headache."

"But you didn't know these guys," Earl said stubbornly.

"Well, maybe they were different. Maybe they'd have cut you in."

"Sure, they would," Earl said.

But he realized suddenly and bitterly that the Corley brothers would have smiled and shaken their heads at him.

"It's what you do yourself that counts," Ingram said. "You plan something and you go ahead and do it. That makes you feel good. You can think about it later and get a kick out of it."

"Maybe you're right," Earl said tiredly. "I used to think that in the Army. We were doing something we could remember later. But who in hell remembers?"

"You do," Ingram said.

"It isn't enough for one guy to remember it," Earl said. He wasn't sure of what he meant, but he felt he was getting at something important. "If a lot of guys do a thing together, and only one of them remembers it—well, there's something wrong with that."

"It didn't mean the same to everybody, that's all."

"That could be it." Earl nodded slowly, absorbing Ingram's explanation. "Maybe you're right." He lighted a cigarette and flipped the match into the fireplace. "We're going to have something to remember, Sambo. If we get out of this in one piece, we're not going to forget it."

"Not if we have beards all the way to our knees."

"What did you use to do in your spare time, Sambo? I mean, did you go to ball games or what?"

"I never was much interested in baseball. I slept days and worked nights. Maybe that's why."

"Have you ever been to a ball game?"

"Oh sure."

"And you didn't like it?" Earl shook his head, exasperated for some reason. "You didn't see anything pretty in a pickoff play? Or a long throw coming into the plate to cut off a run?"

"Sure, that's all interesting." Sambo's tone was politely enthusiastic; he didn't really know or like baseball.

"Interesting!" Earl said. "That's like saying Marilyn Monroe is a girl!" He couldn't understand his irritation and disappointment. "You come with me to a ball game, and I'll show you what to look for."

"Fine," Ingram said. "But let's get out of here first."

Earl poured himself a little more whisky. Why was he thinking of taking Ingram to a ball game? He couldn't take him to a restaurant or a bar, that was for sure. But they could sit together and talk at a ball game. Lots of colored people went to the ball parks. They would get bleacher tickets and sit in the sun and drink beer. And they could talk about this thing. What they'd done together was stupid and wrong, okay. But you couldn't always pick your memories. If you never did anything good or smart, what in Christ's name were you supposed to think about? You had the right to remember the wrong and stupid things if that's all you'd ever known. Maybe they were important, anyway. He and Ingram had done something together and they had the right to keep it alive.

"We'll go to a ball game," he said, nodding at him. "Don't forget it."

"After we get out of here, okay."

"Don't worry about that. I got a hunch our luck is changing." Earl smiled and took a pull on his drink. "That's your influence. You know what they say about colored folks. Changing luck, I mean."

"Yeah, I know," Ingram said slowly.

"It's just an expression. I didn't mean anything."

"That's all right." Ingram shrugged and smiled; Earl's apology made him hot and cold all over, grateful but uneasy at the same time. "Do you feel up to eating? I put some soup on while you were asleep. That's my real hobby. Cooking."

"No kidding?"

"It's a fact. I was the oldest boy, so I ran the house while my mother worked out. I got pretty good at it."

"Where was the old man?"

"He took off when we were kids. There wasn't any work. I guess it was all he could do."

"He could of stuck around," Earl said. "But it's six of one, half a dozen of the other. My old man stuck around, and I wished to God he hadn't."

"Well, things turned out okay for us. We kept out of trouble. And after my brothers were married I set the old lady up in a nice apartment. I used to come over weekends and cook for her." Ingram stood up and rubbed his chest with the palms of his hands. "This is the coldest place I've ever been in."

"You ought to take some whisky, I'm telling you."

"It just doesn't set right with me. I'll get your soup. It's canned, but it smells good. Chicken and rice. You like that?"

"Sounds fine."

When Ingram left, Earl settled himself cautiously back on the couch and lighted another cigarette. Dawn was pressing against the windows, but the trees bordering the fence line were almost lost in the heavy rolling mists. The ground was black and wet, and he could hear a lonely wind sweeping over the fields and veering away from the old stone walls of the house. Lorraine was still sleeping quietly. Earl felt the warmth of the whisky dulling the pain in his shoulder and lighting all of his thoughts with a glow of hope. They would have to leave in a few hours, of course, trusting themselves to the coldness and the night, and to the lonely, hostile roads. But now they were safe; the fog and rain were like friends hiding them from the police. Ingram was right; tonight they'd have a good chance. He felt a curious, tentative respect for Ingram. The man was smart, no doubt of that. He had been right about the Corley brothers. But Earl didn't mind being wrong. What difference did it make?

Ingram returned in a few minutes with a bowl of soup, and placed it on the table beside the sofa. "You get this inside you and you'll feel a lot better."

"You better try some yourself," Earl said.

"I don't feel hungry yet. I'm going upstairs and keep an eye on the road. If anybody comes poking around back here we want to know about it."

"You better take my overcoat. You'll freeze."

"All right, thanks."

Earl patted the portable radio. "I'll check the news. Maybe Russia declared war or something, and they've forgotten all about us."

"Well, our draft boards would be after us then," Ingram said. "We just can't win for losing, man."

CHAPTER NINETEEN

WHEN HE finished the soup Earl snapped on the radio. Music filtered through the static with a distant, unreal sound, and Lorraine stirred restlessly in her sleep. Earl cut the volume down but her eyes opened and she sat up glancing alertly about the room.

"It's all right, Lory. It's just the radio. Try to get back to sleep."

She was still looking about the room. "Where is he?" she said quietly. This ability of hers to recover instantly from sleep always surprised him; she came awake with a clear head and clear eyes, her senses quick and responsive. No snuggling under the blankets or mumbled questions—like a machine when the switch was thrown, she began to hum immediately.

"Where is he?" she said again, pushing the comforter aside.

"Sambo? Upstairs keeping an eye on the road."

"Why didn't he wake us?"

"It's too light. We've got to wait until it's darker to travel."

Lorraine smoothed her long black hair and stepped into her pumps, wincing a little at the touch of the stiff leather against her feet.

"He made me some soup," Earl said. "There might be some left in the kitchen. That'll warm you up."

"We're going to spend the day here?"

"There's nothing to worry about. Ingram thinks we've got a good chance."

She studied the marks of pain in his face with appraising eyes, as if they were factors in an equation she was pondering thoughtfully and privately; the suggestion of compassion in her mouth was a truant reflex eluding her tightly disciplined emotions. "How do you feel?" she asked him. "How far do you think you could travel without resting?"

"I'm okay. Once we start you won't have to stop for me."

She sat down beside him and lighted a cigarette, her expression composed and thoughtful. The radio music bounced brightly around the cold room, as empty and pointless as an idiot's laughter.

"How about that soup, Lory?"

"Not just now."

"You're quite a girl." Something in her silence and manner made him uneasy; she seemed miles from him, absorbed in her own thoughts. He rubbed her thin flat shoulder blades with the palm of his hand. "No tears, no yelling—most women would go up like skyrockets in a spot like this."

"This is the easy part. The tough part is ahead. Don't you realize that?"

"Sure, but we've got a good chance. Ingram in the trunk of the car, you and me up front. Why should they stop us?"

"That's how he figured it out?"

"What other way is there?"

"That's what I've been thinking about," she said. "You'd better think about it, too."

"I don't understand you, Lory."

"Just think, that's all. About me. About you. Nobody else. Do you understand?"

Earl felt a tiny, unnatural chill go through him. "We can't dump Sambo," he said. "We can't, honey."

"Even if it's his safety or ours? His life or ours?"

"But it's not like that." He tried to smile. "There's no point talking about 'ifs.' We're in this together."

"I'm in it with you. Nobody else." She tightened her fingers in the sleeve of his jacket, watching him with eyes that looked as hard and cold as marbles. "I threw away everything to come here," she said. "I stood in our apartment tonight and said good-by to it. The furniture I bought, the refrigerator, the television set, the Venetian blinds, my job at the store, the bonus I was getting next month—that's all gone. I threw it away, do you hear me? I gave all of that up for you. Not for some colored man I never saw before in my life."

"I didn't want to drag you into this."

"But you did—you did drag me into it," she said softly. "It's no good saying you didn't want to. You played on the fact that I love you."

"I didn't want you to come here," Earl said with weary, restless anger. "I wasn't even thinking of that—all I wanted was a car."

"But you knew I'd come. You couldn't have lived with me and not known that. You've got to think of me first now—you owe me that, Earl. I begged you not to do this thing, you can't deny it. I'll go to jail if we're caught. Haven't you thought of that?"

"Honey, I can't think—I'm just living from minute to minute. But you come first, I swear it."

"I've made plans," she said, speaking in a low, tense voice. "We'll go to California, traveling by night and sleeping days. We can go into Mexico without passports. My driver's license is enough. I can get a job there. A friend of mine works in a big department store in Mexico City. She's asked me to come down a dozen times. They're desperate for people who know bookkeeping and American techniques. I've shown you the letters from Marge Lederer. You remember, don't you?"

"Yes, sure," he said vaguely.

"We can get identity cards, live in Mexico as long as we want. We'll have everything we've lost—a home, a life together, all the things we want."

"Okay, okay," he said tiredly. "It sounds great. I'm lucky you're doing the thinking. But we don't have to worry about Ingram. The cops don't even want him. He's in the clear."

"The doctor may notify the police. You know that."

"Well, maybe he won't. Ingram saved the guy's life, practically. The doctor may give him a break."

"You're talking like a fool. A stubborn fool."

"Stop riding me, Lory. He dragged me out of the gutter and got me here. He kidnaped a doctor to patch me up—those are things you got to remember."

"Remember it then," she said in a sharp, rising voice. "I'll remember I was safe and free last night—and that now I'm going to jail."

"Lory, you're stewing about things that haven't happened," he said. "You think we've got to rat out on Ingram to save our skins, but that isn't true. He's in better shape than we are, if you want to know. We might need him to—"

The music faded and an announcer's voice said crisply, "Good morning, everyone, Derby O'Neill with a bit of cheerful breakfast music, and of course your morning news. We have a bulletin from the State Police in connection with the attempted holdup of the National Bank in Crossroads. In the confusion it wasn't established until early this morning that. . . ."

Lorraine quickly twisted down the volume until the announcer's voice became tiny and distant, blurring out and merging with the cracklings of static.

"Hey, what's the idea!" Earl said.

"Keep still!" Lorraine glanced at the ceiling, then leaned forward and put her ear close to the radio.

". . . the third bandit has been identified as John Ingram, a Negro in his middle thirties. Ingram, who gained access to the bank in a waiter's uniform, was mistaken by employees for the regular delivery boy. It is further reported that Doctor Walter Taylor of Avondale was taken at gun point, along with his sixteen-year-old daughter Carol to perform an emergency operation on the man wounded in the holdup. There are no details on this report just now, but it is known that both Doctor Taylor and his daughter have been questioned at length by agents of the FBI. It's a big story, and we'll have details for you as soon as they come off the wire. Meanwhile, let's return to the music—"

Lorraine snapped off the radio and stared at Earl in the sudden silence, her features pale and expressionless. "Do you suppose he could hear that?"

"Sambo, you mean? Don't worry about him. You wouldn't think it, but he's got guts."

"You fool. Don't you understand?"

"Understand what?"

"The police want him now. Not only for the bank but for kidnaping. You heard. The FBI is here! They execute everyone connected with a kidnaping!"

"Sambo took the guy back home," Earl said anxiously. "We didn't hold him for ransom or anything, for Christ's sake."

"Earl, listen to me." Lorraine took his face in her hands, forced him to meet her eyes. "We can't tell him about this broadcast. Do you understand?" She was fighting to control her voice, speaking with the desperate clarity of a mother giving life-and-death instructions to a helplessly trapped child. "We must get away from him. The police are searching for a black man and a white man—we've got to leave him. We couldn't go into a restaurant or a hotel or a drugstore with him. Even stopping for gas would be dangerous. We'd be stared at, talked about, questioned. People would remember a colored man traveling with a white couple. Don't you understand that?"

"But there's just one car. You expect him to make it on foot?"

"I don't care, I don't care. Just so we're rid of him."

"You can't expect him to buy that deal."

Lorraine shook him roughly. "Will you listen? He will if

he doesn't know about that broadcast—if he thinks he's still in the clear."

"Good God, we can't do that! The cops want him. We got to tell him that much for his own protection."

"If you do he'll stick to us like a plaster," she said in a vicious whisper. "Tell him you heard the broadcast. Tell him the police aren't looking for him—just you. Don't say anything about the doctor. Maybe he'll think the doctor gave him a break. You said the doctor might—you said that yourself."

"You think he'll believe me? He's no fool, Lory."

"You've got to make him believe it. Darling, darling, how can I get this into your head? We're not taking the easy way out. There *is* no easy way. For him or us. If he travels with us we'll be caught—all of us. Maybe he can make it on his own, get to his own people and find someone to help him. And maybe we can reach Mexico. We have a chance. But if we stick together, there's no hope at all."

"I hadn't thought of it that way," Earl said slowly. He rubbed his hand up and down his leg, trying to force some heat into his body. "I hadn't thought of that, Lory."

With a movement that caught him completely by surprise, she stood and picked up the radio. "Tell him he's still in the clear. Tell him he can go on alone." She raised the radio high above her head, then let it drop to the iron-hard floor.

The plastic case cracked with a sound like splintering ice, and shining screws spun around his feet in giddy little circles.

"You tell him he's safe," she said. "Tell him you heard that just before I stumbled against the table and knocked over the radio. Do you understand?"

"All right," he said very quietly. It seemed important to conserve all his strength now; his wound ached dully, and he felt suddenly weak and empty, without weight or guts of any kind. "I guess I have to."

"Yes, you have to."

A shrill laugh sounded behind them, and Lorraine turned quickly, a hand moving to her throat. Crazybone stood in the kitchen doorway, the light glinting on her rimless glasses, and a childishly malicious smile brightening her tiny face. "Time to make Pop's breakfast, dearie," she cried with a pointless air of triumph. "Want to help me drag his bed back where it belongs?"

"Yes, I'll help you," Lorraine said in a stiff, unnatural voice.

"He fusses if he's around the food," Crazybone said, jerking and twisting her head about like a confused hen. "Tries to get at it." She laughed and patted her thin gray hair with a coquettish gesture. "I never had the meanness to teach him manners, starve him a little bit. It would be easy in the winter when he can't move around. I will sometimes, I swear. Just starve him a little." She moved her head in a pecking gesture at Lorraine. "Oh, I'm bad, all right. Bad and sinful. But I don't go around breaking up folks' furniture. Not without cause. Come on now, help me drag Pop's bed in here. Lend a hand, dearie. He'll want his Bible, too, because tomorrow's Sunday. And his medicine for his sores. Oh, we've got lots of work to do. Come on, dearie."

Lorraine forced her dry lips into the semblance of a smile. "Yes, I'm coming. . . ."

CHAPTER TWENTY

INGRAM CAME downstairs at eight o'clock, his body pinched and shrunken within the folds of Earl's big overcoat. He rubbed his hands together and crouched by the small blaze that Lorraine had started in the fireplace. Without looking at him, Earl said sharply, "You should drink something. You'll freeze to death."

"I'm okay, just cold." Ingram could hardly feel his hands; they were hard and dry as weathered bones.

The old man was back in his customary place, snoring feebly under the mound of gray blankets. There was a worn

Bible under his bed, beside a jar of medicine which generated the foul, acrid stench in the room.

Lorraine stood close to the fire, hugging herself tightly; she had washed in cold water, and now her skin stung uncomfortably and the sinuses had begun to throb behind her forehead and cheekbones.

"Maybe you better go upstairs for a while," Ingram said to her. "We can take turns. It's too cold to stay up there all day."

"Of course."

"I'll come up when I get warm. We want to keep—" He stopped and stared at the splintered case of the radio. "Hey, what happened?"

"I turned my ankle and stumbled against the table," Lorraine said, watching Earl's frowning face. "We heard the six-thirty news, and I was just turning off the radio."

"Well, that's too bad," Ingram said slowly. "But you heard the news, at least."

"We heard it," Earl said without looking at Ingram. "I told you I'd listen, didn't I?"

"Sure, that's right," Ingram said, wondering what had got Earl into this mood; he was staring at the floor, his face hard and drawn with tension. Maybe his wound was hurting a lot.

Lorraine walked across to the kitchen door, but stopped there and looked back at Earl. "Tell him what we heard," she said.

"Yeah, let's hear it," Ingram said, puzzled by the insistence of her tone, and the restless anger in Earl's face.

"It's your lucky day," Earl said, limping over to the windows.

"What do you mean?"

"The cops don't want you, that's what I mean. I'm the only one they want."

So that's what's bothering him, Ingram thought. He glanced around at Lorraine, but she must have slipped through the door as Earl was speaking.

"But that doesn't make sense," Ingram said. "The cops

might have been confused for a while. But they'd get the real story quick enough."

"You're just lucky, that's all." Earl stared out at the broad, black meadow that swept up to a stand of poplars a quarter of a mile from the house. Everything was cold and lonely; the very earth seemed beaten and helpless and forsaken. Crows winged through the damp gray air toward the bare trees, occasionally crying out pointless warnings against the silence. The sound tightened the sick, weightless feeling in his stomach, and made the muscles of his throat crawl with nausea. Say it, finish it, he thought. Lorraine was right. Who the hell was he? What did he mean to them? Not a goddam thing. A colored guy they'd never seen before. A loud-mouth, smart-aleck jig. Brush him off like a piece of dirt. . . . He tried to pump up his anger, but he was too weak and sick. . . .

"You sure you heard that news straight?" Ingram said dubiously.

"Yeah, I heard it straight," Earl muttered. "The delivery boy from the drugstore disappeared after the holdup." The lie he had planned tasted bitter on his tongue. "He had a record. Did time somewhere. I guess he was scared the cops would figure he was in on the job."

"The poor bastard," Ingram said. "They will figure that now."

"Don't waste your sympathy on him. Worry about me, for Christ's sake." Earl turned from the window but he couldn't meet Ingram's eyes. "I mean something, too, don't I?"

"Yeah, sure," Ingram said. "We got to get you out of this mess. But how about that doctor? You mean the radio didn't say anything about him?"

"Not a peep. Your grandstand play paid off, I guess. You were the big hero, saving the doctor and his kid from me. That was smart, Sambo."

"You know I did right. You know that. If we'd kept them here the whole country would be swarming with cops. They wouldn't just be waiting at roadblocks. They'd be buzzing around our ears like hornets."

"Yeah, I suppose so," Earl said wearily and returned to the sofa. "But it saved your neck, too. The doc is covering for you."

Ingram picked up the radio and turned it around in his hands. "It's pretty funny, in a way. I rob a bank and kidnap a couple of people and nothing happens. I overpark ten minutes at home and a dozen cops jump me. It's funny." He took a penknife from his pocket and sat down, studying the radio. "I guess we better split up when we leave here. You think that makes sense?"

"Sure, you're in the clear," Earl said bitterly. "You might as well bug-out." His thoughts were angrily confused; he had wanted Ingram to suggest this, hadn't he? They'd stacked things so he'd leap at the chance to get away from them. So why chew him out for it?

"Hell, I'll stick if you want me to," Ingram said, unscrewing the back plate of the radio. "But a white man and a colored man traveling together attract attention. You know that. You and your woman will have a better chance without me."

"Okay, okay," Earl said shortly. "We'll split up."

"I can go on foot," Ingram said. "Hop the bus on the highway and be on my way. You and your woman shouldn't have any trouble getting out in the car."

"Okay, goddamit, we'll split up."

"We going to meet at the World Series?" Ingram asked with a faint smile.

"Yeah, I guess so," Earl said, rubbing his forehead. "We'll drink some beer and I'll tell you what to watch for." Why did he say that? he thought. Why keep piling up lies? "What the hell are you doing with the radio?" he said abruptly.

Ingram had arranged a number of parts in a neat pattern on the table. "Maybe I can fix it," he said.

"Yeah? What do you know about radios?"

"Can't hurt to try, can it? These old sets were made good and solid. Like those old dollar Ingersoll watches. You drop 'em and they usually work better afterwards." He peered into the radio, puckering up his lips in a soundless whistle.

"No good, eh?" Earl watched him closely, sick and weary

with a new fear: he didn't want Ingram to know they'd lied to him. Let him find out when the cops grabbed him. Not here. . . . "It's too busted-up, eh?" he said, unable to keep the hope from his voice.

Ingram glanced at him. "Maybe, maybe not." He went back to work. "If the rectifier tube is shot, there's no chance. But it might just be the speaker leads are pulled loose. Something like that."

"Where'd you learn about radios?"

"In the Army. I was in a communications section."

"Communications, eh?" Earl put a cigarette in his mouth and struck a match with a flip of his thumbnail. "That was a soft touch, I guess."

"No, sir. They worked us four hours on and four hours off for three days at a stretch. That was overseas, though. In the States it wasn't bad."

"Where were you overseas?"

"England. Near a town called Weymouth most of the time. But we got to London regularly."

Earl said dryly, "You call England overseas?"

Ingram grinned. "You show me a way to get there on dry land."

Earl stood and limped back to the windows, savoring a sudden, stimulating anger; it was a sustaining emotion, a hot thing that burned away all the doubts that had been nagging at him. The wise-cracking about the Army had triggered it; that's the way they all acted when they forgot their place. Puffed up, slapping your back and offering you drinks out of their bottle. Crowding close to you. . . . Earl knew this as a general truth, but he wasn't interested in general truths now; he was suddenly aware of a big truth; it was all right for him to hate Ingram. It was a responsibility, in fact, doubly important since Ingram had done him a favor. That was the essential thing. You treated people the way they ought to be treated—regardless of how they treated you. That's what took guts.

The thoughts beat warmly in his mind, suffusing him with a sense of virtue and confidence. It was okay to lie to Ingram; it was a duty. Earl wasn't sure how he had reached these conclusions, but their truth couldn't be denied; they rang vigorously through his whole body, drowning out the tiny voices of doubt and guilt.

"So how was it overseas?" he said quietly, standing rigid and tense with his back to Ingram. "How was the stuff in England, Sambo?"

"We didn't have it too bad." Ingram bent over the radio, frowning intently at one of the tubes. "We lived in barracks, and the CO was pretty good about passes."

"It sounds nice and cozy," Earl said.

"The Army's the Army," Ingram said. "Good deal or bad deal, it's still the Army. You know that."

Earl watched him with narrowed eyes. "You must have liked England, I guess. They went for you over there, I heard."

"The people were real nice." Ingram laughed. "You ask 'em for directions and they'd take your arm and walk half-way to where you were going, saying, 'You cawn't miss it, old chap, really you cawn't!'" Ingram shook his head. "They talk like that, no kidding."

"You've got the limey accent down pretty good. Somebody must have taught it to you."

"I heard enough of it, I guess." Earl limped back toward the sofa, staring at Ingram's bent head. "You got along fine with the people, didn't you?"

"Most of them were friendly to soldiers. You know how that is. They'd show us pictures of their sons off in Burma or some place, ask questions about America."

"You must have given 'em an earful," Earl said.

Ingram shrugged and managed a smile. He could feel Earl's anger beating at him like a blast furnace. What the hell was wrong with him? What had started him up like this?

"Well, how about the people, Sambo?" Earl said. "I'd like to know about them. I never saw anything but mud and Germans."

"Well, they were friendly and nice, like I told you." He knew now what Earl was getting at, and an old primitive caution stirred in his blood. "I didn't get to know any of them real well, but they were always nice to us."

"You didn't get to know any of them, eh?"

"Well, I knew one fellow pretty well," Ingram said. "Not for long, but that didn't seem to matter. He was the kind of guy you understood right away, if you know what I mean."

"I'm dumb, Sambo. I don't know what you mean."

"I met him in a bar one night in London," Ingram said. "He was just standing there with a beer and we got to talking."

"You went into the bars with them, eh?"

Ingram looked steadily at him. "That's right. We used the same toilets, too. That's what we were fighting for. Democracy. Community crap houses."

"So what about him?" Earl's eyes narrowed dangerously. "What about him, Sambo?"

"He was from Scotland," Ingram said, still staring steadily at the anger in Earl's face. "He was about sixty. He liked music. He asked me if I'd like to go to a concert with him the next day. I said fine. We went to the concert. Next day he took me and a buddy of mine around London. Out to neighborhoods where there were row after row of little brick houses with flower gardens in front of them. Then he took us to Piccadilly, and then to the East End where the people were so poor they never used up their Scotch and gin rations. All the little pubs had Scotch and gin. He knew a lot about history. He told us that an Englishman named Disraeli once said, 'The good things in life are for the few—the very few.' The Scotchman didn't like that idea. He dropped us at Paddington Station and we caught the train back to our outfit." Ingram let his penknife fall to the table. "That's the story of the people of England."

"Well, why did he pick you up? Was he queer?"

"You couldn't prove it by me."

"And how about the girls? How about the shack jobs, Sambo?"

Ingram shifted his eyes from Earl's face. He couldn't face the senseless anger there. Why? he thought bitterly. Why should I have to apologize for what my body did ten years ago? "I'll tell you this much," he said, suddenly contemptuous of himself and contemptuous of Earl. "I never took anything in England that wasn't offered to me. On a platter."

"A great war you had. You weren't in the Army, you were in heaven."

"They gave me a soldier suit and put me on a ship. What was I supposed to do? Jump overboard and swim to the front lines with my rifle in my mouth?"

Earl stood and limped back to the windows, embittered and consumed by his restless anger.

"You should have tagged along with me, Sambo," he said. "You'd have seen the war. I left the States a Pfc. Four years later I was platoon sergeant. There were only about a dozen guys in our outfit that made the trip the whole way. The rest were shot up in Africa or France or Germany. Anytime they got overstocked with Purple Hearts they'd send us back to the line."

"You were with the First, I guess."

"You heard about it, eh?"

"Sure. That was one of the real Glory outfits."

"You're frigging right it was." He limped up and down the room, inflated with belligerent pride. "They took the greatest bunch of guys in the world to make that outfit, then killed half of them to make a name for it. You know something? Every officer we left the States with was killed in action. The CO, his exec, four second looies. All killed in action." Earl moved to the sofa, feeling suddenly confused and weary. His mood was changing, softening; the cold knot of anger in his breast seemed to be melting. "One of our second lieutenants was just a kid," he said shaking his head slowly. "A guy named Murdock. He played football at Santa Clara. God, he was a hell of an athlete. He had everything. Good-looking, a big grin on his face all the time. 'He was never discouraged about things. He was an optimist, I guess you'd call him. He kept everybody cheered up. He got hit in France. A bullet went right through his helmet, in the back, out the front. When we turned him over a couple of guys started swearing—it was just wrong to see him busted-up like that."

Earl had forgotten Ingram, forgotten the bitterly cold room with its medicinal stink, forgotten that he would die if the police caught him; everything was crowded from his mind by proud, painful memories of the Army. It had been the best time of his life. There was no doubt of that. With all the mud and crap, the best time he'd ever known.

He'd griped about it then, like everybody else, because he had been ashamed to admit what he really felt. Even combat was different for him than for the other guys. It made him wild and giddy, but it wasn't like fear at all; it was a roller-coaster feeling, almost too exhilarating to bear. That's why he'd yelled and shouted like a madman at times. Just to release the thing. . . .

They had put together five big years, marking them with graves that stretched all the way back to Africa. They were an outfit, something you gave to and took from at the same time, something bigger than just one hundred and fifty foot soldiers. Then the outfit broke up and the guys scattered all over the country. And there was never a postcard or a telephone call from any of them, never a way to keep the memories alive. It was like the whole thing never happened.

Once, in Davenport, Iowa, Earl had met a man from the outfit—Hilstutter, a tough, savvy sort of guy, a good soldier. Hilstutter hadn't changed; he was a little fatter, that was all. They stood talking on the sidewalk, Hilstutter nodding at him and saying, "Yeah, that was a bad night," or "What ever happened to So-and-so, I wonder"—nodding as Earl talked on eagerly, recalling some of the big times in the Army. And then Hilstutter had said, "You haven't changed, Sarge. You look great." And he'd shaken hands after that and glanced at his watch. Had to get rolling, he said. Had to get home to his wife. . . .

And that was all. Earl had stared after him, watching the dumpy little man hurry off down the sidewalk, looking just like any one of a thousand guys you'd see in a crowded city. After soldiering together five years that's all it meant to Hilstutter: a hello, a hand shake, a good-by.

The real outfit was dead, he thought gloomily. The dead ones had made the outfit's record—the silent dead of the old First. It was funny, the dead ones kept the memories alive. The others didn't count. Scattered all over the country, watering lawns, growing fat and bald, forgetting the whole damned thing as soon as they got their discharge papers in their hands.

Ingram's hands were still; he was watching the pain and confusion in Earl's face, wondering about the man. He said at last, "How did you get the Silver Star?"

Earl looked at him curiously. "How did you know about that?"

Ingram dug around in his overcoat pocket and pulled out Lorraine's car keys. The Silver Star gleamed brightly on his brown palm. "I figured it was yours," he said.

"You figured right," Earl said, nodding a little. He was silent for a few seconds, a humorless smile twisting his lips. Then he shrugged and fumbled for the pack of cigarettes. "We got caught in the basement of a German farmhouse that night," he said. "Six of us. We thought it was a good place to hole up, but the Germans came back with tanks and cut us off. They moved their company headquarters right into the house. We could hear 'em talking up above us, getting food ready, posting details. I didn't know what to do. We talked it over and decided to wait until dawn, then slip out a basement window and crawl through the Krauts to our own lines." Earl lighted his cigarette, remembering the smell of root vegetables in the basement, the slick muddy floor and the growling sound of German voices above their heads. He laughed. "We made it too, out the window, through the yard and into an orchard. Everybody was on his own, taking off at half-minute intervals. It was just like a field problem. But only five of us made it—one guy was missing, a big clodhopper replacement who'd just been with the outfit a week. I didn't even know his goddam name. Monroe or Morgan or something like that. He was always picking his nose and stamping his feet." Earl shook his head. "You know the kind of guy? Useless. But I had to go back and get him. I found him about ten feet from the house, huddled on the ground, too scared to move. Frozen there like a big pile of crap. I practically had to drag him back. But this time our luck was no good. A guard heard us and started shouting. They all began yelling then and flashing torches around—you know Krauts blow sky-high if you take 'em by surprise. Greatest soldiers in the world when everything's going according to the book. But when things snafu they act like a bunch of crazy women. Anyway, I got this Morgan into the orchard and started shooting back. The trees were pretty good cover. Morgan or Monroe or whatever in hell his name was made a run for it and got hit. I kept moving from tree to tree and firing and the Krauts never charged. They must have figured we were a recon section. I picked up Morgan—that was his name, I guess—and dragged him back to our lines. And that was it." Earl drew deeply on his cigarette, then threw it at the fireplace. "So they gave me the medal." He stood up feeling bitter and ill at ease. "That and a dime buys a cup of coffee, I guess you know."

Ingram smiled and studied the Silver Star. "I got a Good Conduct medal. That's something, ain't it?"

"The medals were mostly a lot of crap," Earl said.

"I don't think so."

"To hell with it, anyway. You did what you were told, right? You said that yourself. You didn't ask them to send you to England—I didn't ask for Africa, France and Germany. They sent us, that's all. You did your job, that's all anybody can do. What's there to worry about?" He squeezed Ingram's shoulder as he limped past him. "Forget it, Sambo. You got as much right to be proud of yourself as a man with the Medal of Honor hanging around his neck."

"Well, that's one way of looking at it, I suppose." He grinned with a kind of foolish pleasure; the touch of Earl's hand on his shoulder had started him tingling all over. "Maybe you're right at that."

"Sure, I'm right." Standing behind Ingram, Earl looked curiously at his hand, a frown darkening his eyes. Then he stared at Ingram, exasperated with himself. "How're you coming with the radio?" he said. "You're a communications man. How're you doing?"

"It's useless," Ingram said, but he was still smiling. "It's shot to pieces."

"I could have told you that."

Ingram sighed and turned around to look at Earl. "You know, I don't understand you."

"Well, so what? What difference does that make?"

"You might be the last man I see on this earth," Ingram said. "That makes a difference. You're like a magazine serial story I may not have a chance to finish."

"So what don't you understand?" Earl was limping back and forth in front of the fireplace, staring at Ingram with tense, irritable eyes. "Am I some kind of a freak? Do I have two heads or something?"

"Why didn't you make something of yourself, that's what I can't figure out. You've a lot of good stuff in you. How come you never used it?"

"What do you know about it? You don't know me at all, Sambo."

"I've got eyes and ears." Ingram smiled. "You're not the smartest guy in the world, of course, but that's not too important."

"I get along. I always did okay."

"You don't have to pretend with me. You probably couldn't fool me if you wanted to."

"What do you mean by that?"

"We've been through something, that's all. I got a chance to know you pretty well."

"You don't know a damned thing about me. Get that into your skull." Earl's voice rose angrily. "Stop worrying about me."

"You know me, don't you? Why can't it work the other way round?"

"What the hell do I know about you?"

"You know you can trust me. How many people do you know that well? Enough to trust, I mean?"

"I didn't have any choice," Earl said, looking away from Ingram. "I had to trust you."

"Sure. And it turned out okay. You know, it might not be a bad idea if there was a law to make people trust one another. Everybody would probably be surprised how well things turned out."

"You're crazy."

"Okay, I'm crazy. But how come you never settled down to a good job? With your Army record and everything, you could have made something of yourself."

"Christ, I don't know," Earl said impatiently. "Nobody knows things like that." He limped back and forth in front of the fireplace, suddenly filled with a weary despair. "Nothing ever worked, that's all. I kept striking out. That just happens. Look at any Skid Row. You'll see people wandering around with eyes like balls of glass. What happened to them? You think they know?" Earl stopped and pounded his fist on the table. "Like hell they do. They'll tell you about a mother or father, or a girl maybe, but they can't tell you about themselves. They don't know what happened, they just don't know. That's why stories and movies are always about heroes. The life of a bum doesn't make any sense. It's just—" He shook his head with futile anger. "It's just a mess."

"But you're no broken-down derelict," Ingram said. "You're a big healthy man. You could have been a construction worker or truck driver or a lumberjack or something. Or maybe got in with a veterans' organization—with your record they could have used you for a showpiece."

"Ah, cut it out," Earl said wearily. "I was no good, that's all. And I knew it. That was the toughest thing. I knew it."

"Lots of people think that about themselves. Go into a bar where they're playing the blues and you'll find plenty of them. That's why the blues got sung in the first place. They aren't for heroes and good guys. They're for people in a mess."

"No, you don't understand." Earl was trying anxiously to organize his feelings into words. He knew it was important to be honest now; this was a chance to drive the thing into the open. He had never made the effort before; some guilty fear had always restrained him. "Now listen! I knew I was no good," he said, speaking slowly and quietly. "I don't mean

I was a drunk or a deadbeat or anything like that. What I did had nothing to do with it. What I did might be good, but I was no good." Earl swore under his breath, infuriated by the futility of his words. "I don't know," he said, shaking his head. Finding what he wanted to say was like picking up a pin with gloves on—a frustrating, hopeless task. "You understand?" he said desperately. "The stuff I'm made of is no good. That's what I'm trying to say. I'm put together with bargain-basement junk. That's the feeling I can never shake. Don't you see what I mean?"

"It doesn't make sense. Why should you think that?"

"You don't understand. You're not listening to me." Earl sat on the edge of the sofa and stared anxiously at Ingram. "Take a car that's put together with cheap, worn-out parts. And filled up with watered gas and dirty oil. What's going to happen to it? It's going to break down, fall to pieces. You can tinker with it, and keep it washed and polished, but it's never going to be any good. That's what I'm like. I always knew that about myself." Earl was breathing slowly and heavily. "I knew it. Sometimes I'd look at my hands and think about it. I'd see the skin and the veins and the hair, and I'd realize that none of it was any good." He stared at Ingram in a silence that was broken only by the feeble snores of the old man in the corner. The coldness and stench of the big bare room seemed to force them closer together, compressing them into a single unit of humanity. Earl's tension and fear lessened; he felt at ease with Ingram suddenly, understanding him, and depending on him for understanding. They were both in the same mess, he realized. Not just in trouble . . . it was more than that. They were alive and they were alone, he thought, but something helped him to realize that these terms meant pretty much the same thing; one stemmed inevitably from the other. There was no terror in this knowledge; the real terror was not knowing that everybody faced the same problem. That everybody was alone. Not just you . . .

"You see, Sambo—" He hesitated. "You mind me calling you Sambo?"

"It's as good a name as any."

"Well—" Earl stared at his grimy hand, studying the dirt-rimmed nails, and the hair coiling strongly on the brown skin. "I always knew I was no good. Because I knew where I came from. I knew my old man." There was pain in the admission, but no shame; it was just a hard, bitter fact.

"That's a load to carry," Ingram said. "But hell, you and your old man are two different people. He's him. You're you."

"I know," Earl said thoughtfully. "I just figured that out. And you told me I was dumb."

"Not dumb," Ingram said, shaking his head. "Just not smart. There's a big difference. Let's have a drink on it, okay?"

As he was looking for Earl's glass Crazybone came in from the kitchen humming softly under her breath. "The fox hunters are coming," she cried merrily. "I just saw one of their hounds in the meadow. Oh, there's a fine sight." She pirouetted slowly, patting the back of her head with both hands. "The gentlemen in their red coats, and the ladies so calm and fine leaping over the fences." She laughed shrilly. "Sometimes the ladies fall on their fine round tails, too. Oh, dearie me, it's a sight."

The old man stirred under the blankets. "You've woke me," he muttered petulantly.

"I better let Lorraine come down," Ingram said. "We've been gabbing here more than an hour."

Crazybone stared at the parts Ingram had removed from the radio. "Won't do you no good to fix it," she said, shaking her head firmly. "She'll just break it again."

"Who?" Ingram said.

"The woman. She's bad-tempered and destructive, qualities you don't find in true ladies. Ladies are sweet and gentle."

"What's she talking about?" Ingram said to Earl.

"She's crazy. It was an accident. Lory stumbled against the table."

"Ha, ha," Crazybone laughed gaily. "That's her story. But she picked it up and threw it down. And I know why."

Ingram stared at the cracked plastic case of the radio.

It was pretty banged-up for a fall from a table . . . The tiniest of doubts nagged at him. "Why did she break it?" he said slowly.

"She doesn't like music," Crazybone said promptly and cheerfully. "She isn't gentle and sweet. What a curse for a good man!"

Ingram sighed and smiled sheepishly at Earl; the suspicion he had almost entertained made him warm with embarrassment. "Rumors every hour on the hour," he said. "She'd go great in the Army."

But Earl wasn't looking at him; he was staring through the windows at the layers of white fog rolling over the wet fields. "You better go on upstairs," he said slowly. "Keep an eye out for those fox hunters."

"All right. Sure, Earl."

CHAPTER TWENTY-ONE

THE DAY cleared slowly and by the middle of the afternoon a patch of thin sunlight brightened the faded carpet in the living room of Doctor Taylor's home in Avondale.

Kelly stood at the window with his hands in his pockets, and the sheriff sat heavily on a straight-backed chair holding his wide-brimmed hat on his knee. They were alone but they had nothing to talk about, no speculations to exchange; the silence between them was a mark of their failure.

They had been working here on and off since dawn, questioning the doctor and his daughter, then returning to Crossroads to feed the information to the teams of agents and police working on the case. But so far they hadn't got on a definite lead.

They had learned a number of significant things, however. They knew the condition of the white man, they knew the Negro was feverish and ill. And they knew they were holed up in an old house somewhere in the country. And that they had disposed of the station wagon and were using a sedan now.

From the other sources they knew that the sedan belonged to a woman named Lorraine Wilson, a friend of Earl Slater's. Frank Novak had been picked up by police in Baltimore, and he had talked; he had given them Slater's name and address, and that had led them to the drugstore where the girl worked in Philadelphia. The counterman remembered that a Negro had come to the store the night before and talked with her. She had left the store after him. Now her car was gone, and her apartment was empty. The inference was obvious; the Negro had brought her back to the hideout. Then he had driven to Avondale for the doctor. Quite a boy, Kelly thought with reluctant respect.

The doctor was co-operating with them, Kelly thought. Trying his best, anyway. He had used his pulse beat to time the trip, and in his judgment it had taken the Negro almost an hour to drive them to the old house. But he couldn't recall the turns and backtrackings on the way. And his estimate of how long they had driven over concrete and dirt roads was no more than a thoughtful guess.

But with these facts and impressions a dozen police cars were probing the countryside southwest of Crossroads, in close co-operation with FBI agents in jeeps and commandeered delivery trucks. They had pinpointed the plane the doctor had heard; a commercial flight flying a southeasterly course toward New York. If the doctor's memory was accurate he had been west of the federal highway when it passed over his head.

But they still couldn't reach out and put their hands on the men. It was an exasperating and dangerous failure, Kelly knew. Slater and Ingram could probably make their move when it got darker, and that would mean trouble for anyone who got in their way.

Kelly glanced at his watch: two o'clock. If his assumption was right they didn't have much time left. The doctor had gone upstairs a moment or so ago to wake his daughter. He had put her to bed with a sedative, after they had questioned her. Kelly wanted to talk to her again because he had suspected something that hadn't occurred to the sheriff; the doctor and his daughter were unconsciously protecting the Negro. Without knowing it, they were in collusion to save him.

He strolled restlessly across the room to the fireplace. "It's clearing up," he said, looking at the sunlight on the carpet. "Be a nice day to go gunning."

"There's more rain coming," the sheriff said. Then: "You like hunting?"

"I don't have much opportunity anymore." They had talked about the case so long it was a relief to talk about something else. "But I went after turkeys last year in Georgia. That's pretty special. They run as fast as a horse, and can hear a twig break a thousand feet away. They settle into an oak or a pine twenty feet above your head looking as big as cargo planes. Then they disappear. Vanish. Their markings are green and gold and black, and they just fade out of sight before you can raise your gun."

"Sounds interesting," the sheriff said, taking out his pipe. There was both hope and skepticism in his tone, the reaction of a true hunter. "Our pheasants aren't anything special, but some pretty good shots go season after season without getting their limit."

"Your daughter told me about them. She's quite a booster for the area."

Kelly had stopped at the sheriff's house early that morning, and Nancy had made a quick breakfast for him. . . .

"I used to take her gunning when she was little," the sheriff said slowly. "I didn't know she was still interested. She was a nice shot." He rubbed the bowl of his pipe slowly between his big hands. "I thought she'd put all that away with her jeans and boots. Girls get into ribbons and skirts and they're not so keen about tramping through the fields with a gun anyhow."

"That's true, I guess." Kelly was tactfully noncommittal; he had sensed the stiffness between the sheriff and his daughter, and he wasn't planning to blunder into that personal area. This morning she had been at ease with him, attractive and confident in a white sweater and dark slacks, with her blond hair tied back in a pony tail. This was Saturday and she wasn't going to the office. They had talked about hunting and fishing, and places they knew in New York, and several other matters, the kitchen warm against the cold morning, their cigarette smoke mingling pleasantly with the aroma of bacon and coffee. He had listened to her with a stranger's capacity for direct, relevant compassion. She had wanted to talk, he realized. So he had listened. . . .

The sheriff was still rubbing the bowl of the pipe between his hands. "Nancy and I are pretty close in some ways," he said defensively. "But sometimes—" He looked steadily at Kelly, trusting him in this, but refusing to ask help of any man with averted eyes. "Sometimes I can't understand her. Maybe I'm too standoffish." The sheriff hesitated; in his code you didn't go whining to strangers with your personal problems. He liked and trusted Kelly, but he was nonetheless a stranger. "I don't know," he said, lowering this standard with a sense of defeat. "I'd like to talk to her, to help her any way I can. But I just don't know how."

"She's got to help herself," Kelly said. "You can hold her hand maybe, but that's about all. She's got to forget him—you can't do that for her."

It took the sheriff an instant or two to understand what Kelly meant. Then he said "Yes," and rubbed a hand roughly over his mouth, speaking against a painful constriction in his throat. So that was it. . . . Why hadn't she told him?

"She's doing fine," Kelly said, misunderstanding the bitterness in the sheriff's eyes. "If he wasn't smart enough to hold onto her, he's no bargain." He hesitated then, his cheeks suddenly hot. If the old boy didn't know. . . . "A stranger makes a good wall to bounce things off," he said, inwardly cursing his tactlessness.

"Why didn't she tell me about him?" the sheriff said so softly that Kelly had to lean forward to catch the words. "That's what I'm wondering."

Kelly felt like biting off his tongue. "I'm terribly sorry. Naturally, I thought—"

"Naturally. Naturally a girl tells her father. Who was he, by the way? Or are you supposed to keep her secrets?"

"There's no sense huffing and puffing," Kelly said quietly. "At her or at me."

The sheriff was slightly startled by Kelly's tone; not many men would use that voice with him when his temper was up. Then he smiled wearily, and said, "You're right. I'm sorry."

"He was a man she met in New York. They saw each other for a year or so. Then things changed. With him." Kelly raised his hand and let it fall. "Your daughter took it like a big girl. No scenes, no recriminations, no rebound nonsense. She just packed up and came home."

"I don't understand her," the sheriff said helplessly. "But that's not her fault, is it? It's mine. I just don't understand."

"You won't be the last man to say that about a woman." Kelly retreated gratefully into the protective cliché. He distrusted too-tidy explanations of emotional conflicts. And he distrusted people with quick solutions for them. Loose talk about Oedipus complexes and sibling jealousies made him uneasy. The amateur analyst might be right; that was the hell of it. Buckshot usually hit something. You could even hit a hornet with buckshot but that was no way to stop a swarm of them.

Things would work out. He believed in that philosophy because he was a hopeful man; he had learned to wait cheerfully.

So they didn't get along. Well, that would work out. The sheriff was a demanding man without knowing it. He had grown taller and taller with the years and now he was too damned far from the ground. He needed to be brought to earth—to change a few diapers, get a flailing little foot in the eye occasionally, stock up his wallet with some new baby pictures. Solving her needs would solve his, Kelly figured. Making her happy would make him happy. It would be a nice job for some guy. Two birds with one stone. A rewarding kind of job. But it couldn't be rushed; it needed patience and humor.

They heard footsteps on the stairs, and the sheriff stood up quickly, forcing the conversation from his mind. Kelly said, "Let me do the talking, will you? I know what their trouble is, I think."

The sheriff nodded; his respect for Kelly had gone up

considerably in the last few minutes. "You go ahead," he said.

The doctor opened the door and ushered his daughter into the room. "Sit down and get nice and comfortable, honey," he said. "This won't take long, will it, Sheriff? We've told you everything we can remember."

"We'll be quick as we can," the sheriff said. He smiled at the girl. "Feel better after your nap?"

"Yes, thank you." She sat on the sofa with her slippered feet tucked under her, looking sweet and young and rested; but Kelly saw the nervousness in her tightly gripped hands.

He took a sheaf of notes from his pocket, and sat down in front of her. "You know what the subconscious is, I suppose, Carol."

"Well, more or less."

Kelly smiled. "That's a good answer." He realized that behind this teen-aged poise and dignity was a very frightened little child; he could see the pulse beating rapidly in her throat, and the quick rise and fall of her soft bosom.

"I was once in love with a very beautiful girl," he said, with nothing in his voice to mark the comment as irrelevant.

"What?" the sheriff said, staring at him.

"This was quite a while ago. But she was a knockout, Carol."

"Oh?" She looked interested. "What was she like? I mean, was she a blonde or a brunette or what?"

"I don't remember," Kelly said. "I struck out with her pretty completely. There was another guy with looks and money—so she foolishly brushed me off like a speck of lint."

"How old was she?" Carol said doubtfully.

"She was ten," Kelly said, "and very flighty and immature for her age."

"You aren't serious."

"Yes I am, Carol," Kelly said quietly. "I'm being very serious. I don't remember what the girl looked like because I don't want to. Part of my mind simply hides her from me, so I won't worry about her. We forget things, Carol, without knowing we've forgotten about them—that's our safety valve, a protective device we all use without realizing it."

"But I'm not hiding anything from you. Really, I'm not."

The doctor patted her shoulder. "Of course, honey." He looked at Kelly. "But I know what you're getting at—and believe me, I've tried to be honest."

"You owe your lives to that Negro," Kelly said. "He made a bargain to bring you back and he stuck to it. Even at the risk of getting a bullet through his head."

"I know, I know," the doctor said. "He saved Carol's life and I can't forget it. But I've tried my level best not to let that influence me."

"I'm sure of it," Kelly said. "But think about this possibility: you may be unconsciously trying to repay him for saving your lives. You don't want to dredge up anything that might put his neck in a noose."

"I'll tell you this much," the doctor said sharply. "When he's caught, I'll see that he gets the best lawyer in the state to defend him. That man behaved with courage and honesty—in spite of everything else he's done."

"Fine," Kelly said. "Do everything you can for him. But think of this in the meantime: those men will move when it gets dark. They're armed and desperate. Someone will get in their way. Think about that person for a second. A police officer with kids waiting for him at home, a salesman or a housewife, a young girl, maybe. Whoever it is may wind up dead. And you can't help the Negro then. You can only help him now—before he's hounded into more trouble."

"I haven't held back a thing," the doctor said with a stubborn edge to his voice.

"Let's go over a couple of points anyway," Kelly said. "Forget about the car, the roads, the weather. Just concentrate on the living room of that house."

"There is nothing more I can tell you. Floor boards of uneven width. Hand-hewn beams. We've gone through all this. There are hundreds of homes like that in the country. Old, pre-Revolutionary houses with two-foot stone walls, and fireplaces you can walk into. That's what brought a lot of wealthy people into the area—the fun of renovating those old relics. I didn't see anything distinctive. I was treating a wounded man and wondering if my daughter was going to be killed before my eyes. Maybe I missed something that would help you find the place. But can't you understand that I wasn't in the best possible mood to be taking an inventory."

"And I was blindfolded," Carol said. "I didn't see anything."

"Yes, of course," Kelly said, looking at his notes. "But you both mentioned that there was an odor of food in the house. Something that reminded you of sauerkraut. You used the word 'reminded' each time we've come to this point. You mean it wasn't sauerkraut—but something similar? Could you pin it down exactly, do you think?"

The doctor was frowning. "It seemed like sauerkraut. Didn't it, Carol?"

"I don't know. I said sauerkraut because you did, I guess. But it wasn't like food at all—" She was frowning faintly, not looking at any of them, and Kelly sensed that her thoughts were searching for a memory buried deep in her mind.

"What was it, Carol?" he said gently. "It wasn't food, was it?"

"No, it was more like—well, the chemistry lab at school. It was something sharp and unpleasant."

"I think you're right," the doctor said slowly.

"Was it some kind of acid?" the sheriff said.

"No—I'm trying to remember."

They were silent for a moment, and Kelly held his breath. "Daddy, wasn't it like a mustard plaster? That's all I can think of."

"A mustard plaster?"

"Maybe there was someone sick in the house," Kelly said.

The doctor began to pace the floor, snapping his fingers rapidly. "Not mustard, not acid—wait a second." He stared at the sheriff. "Balsam Peru— Do you remember that stuff?"

"Sure."

"That's what it was—Balsam Peru. How that helps I don't know, but I'm certain of it. Balsam Peru!"

"What is it?" Kelly said.

"An old patent medicine, a cure-all like Doctor Pratt's Salve or Mother Mercer's Remedy." Excitement had brought color into the doctor's pale tired face. "You remember it,

Sheriff. Years back there wasn't a home in the county that didn't have a jar on hand. They used it for burns, aches and pains, damned near anything. Carol mentioned a mustard plaster, and that jogged my mind toward medicine."

"We may be able to trace that," the sheriff said. "There's not much call for it any more."

"We'll check the doctors and the drugstores," Kelly said, standing and looking at his watch. "Doc, can I use your phone?"

"Yes, of course. It's in the hall."

Kelly hesitated, looking down at the little girl's unhappy eyes. "Don't worry," he said, and touched her cheek with the back of his hand. "Believe me, you've done him a favor. You'll understand that someday."

"I wish I did now," she said, slowly.

The doctor pressed her shoulder as Kelly went into the hall and scooped up the phone.

CHAPTER TWENTY-TWO

At three-thirty Earl turned away from the window and pulled his overcoat about his shoulders. The weather was starting to work for them; clouds had come up an hour or so ago and rain was falling on the black earth and beading the windows with soft, gray moisture. Darkness was settling fast. The night would be cold and windy, with the rain lashing at everything. They could leave now, he thought, moving out under the cover of this murky weather.

"You better go up and get Sambo," he said to Lorraine. Earl limped to the table and poured himself a short drink, using up the last of the bottle. He felt cold and empty, but very calm. "When we drop Sambo we'll head away from the main highway. Go out the back way. I know the roads." He drank the whisky and stood perfectly still as the warmth spread slowly through him.

"The sooner we start the better," Lorraine said.

"Sure," Earl said. "We've got to roll. Wind 'em up." He

looked at her with a little frown shading his eyes. "That's the Army command for starting up truck convoys. Did you know that, Lory? Wind 'em up."

"Do you feel all right?"

"I'm fine. We'll dump Sambo and get rolling. Go get him."

Lorraine turned and went into the kitchen. Earl heard her heels clattering on the back stairs. She crossed over his head, going down the hall to the room where Ingram was watching the road. Crazybone had gone up an hour or so ago to keep him company.

The old man lay with his eyes closed, his slow breathing sounding like the wind rustling a pile of dry papers.

Earl limped about pointlessly examining the junk on top of the mantel, studying the sturdy old beams and floor boards, pausing once to frown at the broken radio on the table. I'll never see any of this again, he thought. Never see this room again in my life. Why should that bother him? he wondered. It was a cold, stinking dump. No man in his right mind would want to see it again. But leaving it reminded him of the other places he had left. He stood fingering the glass, while a dizzying succession of rooms and barracks and Army camps flashed through his mind. He was always the guy who had to leave, he thought. Everybody else stayed put, cozy and snug, while he hit the road. He never went back anywhere. There was no place on earth that called out to him, no stick or stone or blade of grass that belonged to him and nobody else.

Was it because he was dumb? Because he couldn't feel what other people felt? The confident peace he had known after talking with Ingram had deserted him; he was uncertain again, worried and tense, afraid of the shadows in his mind.

Talking with Ingram he had licked this feeling. Or thought he had. Everybody was alone. Not just him, everybody. But what the hell did that mean? How did knowing that help you? he wondered.

The old man stirred and peered at him, pulling the blankets up about his scrawny throat. "You fixing to leave, eh? Think you'll make it?"

"Sure," Earl said. The old man sickened him; with his stench, with the fun he took from probing at them. "We'll make it," he said. "Don't worry."

"Taking the colored fellow with you?"

"That's right."

"All three of you, eh? Good-looking white girl, and a white man and a colored man. That's a funny combination any way you look at it."

"Well, stop looking at it then," Earl said.

He heard Lorraine coming down the back stairs, and when she came quickly into the room, he knew something was wrong; her eyes were hard, and there was an anxious frown on her face. "He's gone," she said, staring at Earl. "You hear that! He's gone."

"What do you mean he's gone?"

"Just that. He's gone!" she cried.

"Well, that makes it easier, doesn't it?"

"Don't you understand? For God's sake, can't you think?" She looked close to hysteria; her face was gaunt and strained, as if her nerves were being stretched slowly and exquisitely to the breaking point. "God," she said, "God."

"Now, Lory," he said soothingly. "Sambo will be picked up by the police. And he'll know we've lied to him. So he'll probably talk. But that was going to happen anyway. I don't see why you're so worried."

"I'm sorry because you're a fool."

"This is no time to be riding me," he said slowly. "Just knock it off."

The old man tittered. "Shouldn't be fussing at each other this way," he said. "Look at me and Crazybone. Go weeks without a cross word." He smiled slyly. "Go weeks without any words at all. That's the best way."

"Lory, let's go. Nothing's changed. We're all right."

"Are you ready?" she said wearily.

"Sure, I'm ready."

"Have you got the car keys?"

"No, Sambo took—" Earl stopped short, dizzied and weakened by the sudden heavy stroke of his heart.

"Do you understand why I'm worried? Now, do you understand?" Lorraine cried furiously.

"He wouldn't take the keys. He wouldn't leave us stuck here." But the words sounded plaintive and foolish in his ears. "When did he leave, for God's sake?"

"That idiot upstairs doesn't know. He went out the back door. That's all she could tell me."

"Look, he didn't take the car. I'd have heard him starting it." Earl's voice sharpened with excitement. "I can get it going, Lory. I'll jump the ignition wires. Sambo didn't figure on that. I'll catch up with him someday, and–"

"Shut up!" Lorraine cried softly; a draft of air blew into the room, sweeping coldly about her ankles.

"What?"

She held up a warning hand. They heard the front door slam, and then Ingram came in, hugging his arms tightly against his body. He wore a short woollen coat that belonged to the old man and his hair gleamed with rain water. "It's getting awful cold out," he said, stamping his feet on the floor. "Goes right through you."

"Where've you been?" Earl said. "We're ready to leave."

"Just down to the road on a little reconnaissance. Everything seems quiet."

He watched Earl with a puzzled smile. "You people look like you just seen a ghost."

"Lorraine's a little nervous, maybe."

"There's nothing to be afraid of," Ingram said, glancing at her with the same puzzled smile. "You got a good chance of making it. The cops don't know about you or your car. Once you drop me off you're free as birds. Isn't that right?" he said, turning slowly to Earl. "The cops don't want me. And you two can make it in her car. Isn't that the way we planned it?"

"Yeah, that's right." Earl tried to smile but his face felt stiff and cold all over. "We drop you off, and away we go." The words came out as if he were drunk, twisting awkwardly on his tongue. "So what are we wasting time for?" he said, almost yelling at Ingram. "Everybody knows the deal. What are we yapping about it for?"

"You got it right," Ingram said softly. "Everybody knows the deal now."

He stared at Earl without explanation, without speaking, and the silence grew and filled the room with almost palpable tension. And then Ingram's face seemed to crumble, and a strangling little moan sounded in his throat.

"We all know the deal, buddy," he cried hoarsely. "The cops want me—they wanted me all along. But you didn't tell me. That was part of the deal I didn't know."

"Now listen, Sambo, you—"

"Shut up! Shut up!" Ingram's voice trembled with anguish and contempt. "You were going to let me walk right into their arms. You lied to me all along. I was heading for the chair, while you and her went free. That's what you planned, wasn't it? Goddam you, wasn't it?"

"What are you talking about?" Earl said. He wet his lips, and the taste of his tongue was like a distillation of corruption and shame. "You're not making any sense," he yelled furiously.

"Crazybone came upstairs to tell about the radio," Ingram said softly. "She thought I figured she was lying. She kept saying the woman lifted up the radio and smashed it on the floor. I told her she was imagining things." Ingram's smile strained the skin tightly across his shining face. "Sure, I stuck up for you, buddy. I felt like a heel for listening to her. But once you get a suspicion, it's hard to keep it from growing. All I knew was what you told me. Then the radio got busted. So we couldn't get any more news. It was hard not to start adding things up. I tried not to, buddy, I tried as hard as I could. But I started adding it up. And you know the answer I got."

The bitterness in Ingram's eyes and voice cut Earl like a whip. "She stumbled and knocked over the radio," he said. "You believe me, Sambo, or that old fool, Crazybone?"

"She stumbled, eh?" Ingram turned and stared at Lorraine, appraising her slender legs and neat, efficient body with deliberate contempt. "Does she look like the kind of woman who falls over her feet? No more than a cat does, buddy."

"You leave her out of this," Earl yelled. An illogical anger rushed through him. "Forget about her. What's she got to do with it, anyway?"

"She's part of the big lie, isn't she? Send him out to get his black hide nailed to the wall. Dumb colored bastard—what difference will it make to him? That's the lie she's part of. She's as rotten as you are."

"Now hold it. I'm warning you."

"Oh, pardon me," Ingram said, laughing bitterly. "I forgot my place, didn't I? You white folks were just sending me out to get killed—that's all. And I'm such a rude, low-down nigger that I got mad and forgot myself in front of a white woman. I surely am sorry about that."

"Don't take any lip from him," the old man cried, his voice emerging from under the blankets in a muffled cackle.

"Keep still, both of you," Lorraine said. "Ingram has a right to be angry, if he believes what Crazybone told him. But it just isn't true. I broke the radio accidentally, Ingram. I swear it."

"You should have broken them all, ma'am," Ingram said slowly.

"What do you mean?"

"There was one you forgot about—the one in the car I drove into the mica pit. I climbed down there and the radio was working fine. So I waited to hear the news."

Lorraine looked quickly toward Earl, her eyes dark and anxious, but he turned away, rubbing the back of his hand roughly across his lips.

"You know what the news said?" Ingram laughed shrilly and slapped his leg, his manner a cruel parody of cringing good humor. "The news said the police are looking for a colored rascal named John Ingram. Just listen to what that cut-up has gone and done. Tried to rob a bank, then went and kidnaped a doctor to take care of his wounded buddy." Ingram glared at Earl, but his eyes were bright and hard as diamonds. "The name sounded pretty familiar, so I listened real close. Ingram, they said, was about thirty-five, used to live on Arch Street near Maple in Philly. Well, imagine my surprise. That's me, I thought. Little ole me. Wanted by the police everywhere. The *po*lice, that's how us colored folks say it." Ingram continued to stare at Earl, his smile changing slowly, becoming bitter and cold and sad. "You can imagine how surprised I was, buddy. Can't you imagine it?"

"It's different than what you think," Earl said, making a weary futile gesture with his hand. "It's not all one thing or another, like you think. It's a question of what you got to do, of how things really are—" The confusion in his voice swelled into empty, pointless anger. "But you don't understand that, do you? It's all black and white to you, isn't it?"

"We've got to go, Earl," Lorraine said. "Get the car keys."

"Yeah, I was surprised by the news," Ingram said, as if he hadn't heard her; he was watching Earl with hurt, bewildered eyes. "After I saved your skin, after I brought your girl here and got a doctor to patch you up—after all that, you could go on lying to me. It wasn't hard for you—that's what I can't understand. It was easy. You smiled and lied to me like it was the most natural thing in the world."

"You don't know how it was, I tell you. You just see it one way."

"Get the car keys," Lorraine cried.

"We talked about going to ball games together, remember?" Ingram said, clenching his hands tightly. "Like buddies. Sit in the sun and drink beer. Talk about what we'd been through. You remember all that?" Ingram's voice was derisive and bitter, but tears were shining softly in his eyes. "Old times in the Army, baseball games, how you felt about your old man—no, I didn't think you were lying to me. That was a great snow job, buddy."

"Damn it, shut up!" Earl shouted.

"That's the way," Ingram said, in a tone of mocking approval. "Don't talk about it. Lie, cheat—but oh for Lordy sakes, don't say nothing about it. Treat people like dirt, but don't be crude and discuss it." Ingram laughed and pulled the car keys from his pocket. The Silver Star gleamed and flashed in the light. "But you want to talk about these, don't you? And saving your neck. That's all right. That's nice and clean, isn't it?"

"Give it here," Earl said, putting out his hand. "Give it here, Sambo."

"You need old black Sambo now, don't you?"

"Give them to me!" Earl's voice rose in a shout; Ingram's defiance justified the anger pounding through his body. He pulled the gun from his pocket. "Give 'em here," he said softly. "I'm not kidding."

"You can't shoot me," Ingram said, laughing at the hot anger in Earl's face. "Who'd you go to ball games with then? Who'll you talk about the Army with? You can't shoot your old buddy."

Earl took a quick, long stride toward him and jammed the gun into his stomach. When Ingram doubled up, gasping painfully for breath, Earl brought the gun barrel down on his head with an abrupt, chopping gesture.

The old man sat upright, his eyes bright with pleasure. As Ingram's body pitched to the floor, he cried, "That's the way to handle 'em. Put the iron to 'em."

Lorraine knelt smoothly and quickly and took the keys from Ingram's motionless hand. "Let's get away from here," she said to Earl. "Please, for God's sake."

Earl stared down at Ingram, the gun hanging limply at his side. "Why didn't he hide the keys?" he muttered. "Throw them away or something."

"Earl, please!" Lorraine's voice was shaking. "Please."

"Waving 'em around like a fool," Earl said. "Didn't he know better? Communications character. Didn't know nothing." He shrugged wearily. "Give me a hand with him, Lory. We'll put him on the couch."

"What difference does it make?"

"I don't know. God, I don't know. But give me a hand. Come on, move. Come on, Lory."

After they lifted Ingram's body onto the sofa, Earl looked at him for an instant in silence, appraising his heavy breathing and the blood running brightly down his temple and cheek. "I didn't hit him hard," he said to Lorraine. "Just enough to put him out for a while. That's all I did, I swear."

Lorraine pulled her coat tightly about her throat and hurried toward the door. The old man grinned at Earl who was still standing beside the sofa staring at Ingram. "Go with her," he said. "You got a long life ahead of you, son." He pushed the covers back and rummaged around under his bed, hanging over the side like a big gray crab. "Here it is," he said, as his clawing hand touched the Bible. "The Word." He flopped back into bed exhausted and triumphant. "Me and the colored boy will read some prayers for you. We'll shout till God hears us, and saves you from evil and death. Go on, leave us now."

Earl couldn't make himself move. "Sambo?" he said softly.

Lorraine looked back from the door and cried, "Earl!" When he didn't turn, she ran across the room and shook his arm roughly. "What's the matter with you?"

"I'm all right," he muttered. "I'm okay." He saw Ingram's eyelids flutter. "Go out and turn the car around, Lory," he said.

"Why won't you come?" she cried softly.

He jerked himself free from her desperate hands. "Do what I tell you. Turn the car around. Tap the horn when you're ready." He stared into her white, strained face. "Do what I tell you!"

She backed away from him, moistening her lips, and then turned and ran from the room, her heels sounding with a frantic clatter on the hard floor.

Earl saw that Ingram was staring up at him, his eyes bright with fear and wonder. "I'm going to leave you some dough," he muttered. He took out the money Lorraine had given him, worked three tens loose with his thumb and let them flutter to the foot of the sofa. "There's thirty bucks. It's not much, but it's all we can spare. With what you've got of your own, it's something, Sambo."

Ingram's expression was grave; he seemed to be searching for something in Earl's face, probing at him with soft wondering eyes.

"I can't give you any more," Earl said. He saw that the old man was watching him, the gloomy light shining on his gray hair and soft silvery whiskers. Night had fallen now, pressing with black finality against the windows. Earl shifted uneasily as he heard the wind clawing at the sides of the house like an angry animal. "You got a chance," he said, trying to force a note of conviction into his voice. "There must be some colored folks living here in the country. They'd put you up, wouldn't they? You got money to smooth your way with. Think about that, eh?"

Ingram didn't answer him; his eyes were full of speculation, but the line of bright, crusted blood was like a seal drawn across his dry lips.

"You think I'm ratting on you," Earl said bitterly. "Why don't you say it? Say something, damn it. You helped me, now I'm walking out on you—that's what you're thinking, I know." Ingram said nothing, and Earl came closer to him, and cried softly, "It's got to be this way, Sambo. Don't you see? Lory and me have got to take off. I've got to go with her. Everything I am makes it what I've got to do. We're running to save our lives. It's the way life is. It's rotten, maybe, but I didn't make up the rules. Well, did I, Sambo? Did I?" Earl heard his voice rising to a shout; he could feel the words swelling in his throat like filth he needed to eject from his body. "I didn't make up the rules, remember that! I didn't do nothing to you. You can't blame me. I'm not responsible for you, am I?"

"Read the book of God!" The old man intoned the words slowly and solemnly. "He's got the answers. Don't matter whether you're black or white, there's where to find the answers."

Ingram was sick and frightened, but more than that he was puzzled—he didn't understand Earl or himself, and that seemed more important now than his fears or his illness.

In some devious way he had led Earl to this last moment of shame. Why had he done it? To humiliate him, just to see this look of shame in his eyes? Was it that way with all colored folks, he wondered, with their smiles and head bobbings, their unctuous courtship of the most evil and arrogant things in people. Cultivating their faults till they grew so big they couldn't be hidden any more. . . . Was that all they wanted? To make white people worse?

If that's all he'd wanted, he was no better than Earl. The relationship had just been an exercise in deceit, with both of them using kindness and understanding as their weapons. There was no honesty in it at all. It would have been kinder to walk out on him and let him die. He would have died without shame, anyway. It was wrong to treat a man decently just to get the whip hand over him. It was scheming and vicious. Not just dumb and scared like Earl.

"Listen!" the old man cried triumphantly. "Here's *Ecclesiasticus.* Get this now: 'God created man of the Earth, and made him after his own image—'" He laughed shrilly, peering sideways at Earl and Ingram. "Ain't that rich? Ain't that a thought to tickle your ribs?"

"Haven't you anything to say?" Earl said, looking quickly over his shoulder at the door. "I'm leaving you some dough, Sambo. I'm doing the best I can for you."

"And listen here," the old man said. "Listen to this."

"Goddamit, shut up!" Earl yelled at him.

"Don't be cursing the Good Book. Go your way. Me and the colored boy will pray for you. You'll need it, son. You'll need it."

"I've got to leave you, Sambo," Earl said. "I got to."

"'Tarry not in the error of the ungodly, give glory before death,'" the old man cried. "'Give thanks whilst you're living . . . and thou shalt glory in his mercies.' That's old *Ecclesiasticus,* too, a-shouting and a-stamping for all he's worth."

Ingram understood himself at last. He hadn't tricked Earl. He was sure of that. In a confusing way he had been closer to him than anyone else in his whole life.

"'O what is brighter than the sun?'" the old man shouted in the imbecile voice of a man drunk with sound and rhythm.

The blast of a horn came from outside the front door, insistent and demanding.

"I got to go," Earl said. He backed slowly away from the sofa, watching Ingram with childish anxiety. "You understand, don't you, Sambo? Just say you understand."

"'Or what is more wicked than that which flesh and blood hath invented?'" the old man cried, his voice crescendoing into an evangelistic roar.

The horn sounded again, two sharp blasts, and Earl glanced guiltily over his shoulder. "So long, Sambo, so long," he said.

"'He beholdeth the power of the height of heaven; and all

men are Earth and ashes!' " The old man closed the book as the draft from the opening door stirred his thin hair in grotesque waves. He settled back, drained and exhausted by his exertions. "There's always comfort in the Bible," he said. "Remember that, boy. Remember it when the police come to hang you."

Ingram was too sick and weak to move. The pain in his chest was dull and heavy, a weight pinning him helplessly to the sofa. He turned away from the old man's vindictive eyes, listening to the whine of the car plowing through the thick mud. The wind came up furiously then, obliterating everything with its sweeping roar, and when it died down he could hear nothing but the faint echo of the throbbing engine. That faded swiftly into silence, and he knew they were on their way at last, pushing through the dark toward freedom.

The cold tears stung the crusted blood on his cheeks. He's just dumb, he just doesn't know what he's doing, he thought. Why couldn't I have said something to him?

CHAPTER TWENTY-THREE

At four thirty the phone on the sheriff's desk rang. He lifted the receiver without any suggestion of hope, and said, "Sheriff Burns."

The call was for Kelly. The sheriff gave him the phone, and Kelly listened for a few seconds, then said, "Okay, Smitty." He shrugged as he put the receiver back in the cradle. "That's a final report on West Grove. No Balsam Peru customers there." Kelly shook his head. Balsam Peru. He was beginning to dislike the sound of the words. There had been about sixty calls in the last hour from state troopers and FBI agents, all containing substantially the same message; no luck. Every doctor and druggist in and near Crossroads was searching his files and his memory for clients who had used Balsam Peru. But so far the search had been futile.

Kelly glanced up at the black circle the sheriff had penciled around the area southwest of Crossroads. Were the men still waiting inside that noose? Or had they started to move by now?

They had a delicate logistics problem facing them, Kelly thought. Earl Slater, Lorraine Wilson and Ingram, the Negro . . . Would they stick together? Or split up? There was danger in either choice.

Together they would attract attention, so they would probably split up. Kelly made a dollar bet with himself that the white couple would desert the Negro—and that the Negro would be an eager and angry witness against them. Okay, he thought, a dollar. . . . Still, catching them wouldn't be a snap. The police had identification on both cars, the sedan and the station wagon, but it would be a simple matter for them to hold up a motorist and take his car and papers.

Then they had a chance to slip through the roadblocks. Traffic was heavy on all roads and highways in the area. It was a difficult night to make a thorough check of every occupant in every car. If one trooper hurried his inspection or swung his torch a bit casually, the harm might be done. It could happen easily if the woman were a fairly good actress. *"What's the matter, officer? Well, do you think it's safe to go on? All right, thanks so much. . . ."* And away they'd roll.

The phone rang several times in the next few minutes, but all the reports were negative; no doctor or druggist knew of any customer currently using the old patent medicine.

"Maybe it's hopeless," the sheriff said a bit wearily. "With sulfa drugs and penicillin, why should anyone bother with an old-fashioned cure-all?"

"But someone has," Kelly said. "Unless Doctor Taylor is wrong, someone in that house was using it."

"It could be an old jar. Bought a dozen years ago."

"Maybe," Kelly said. "But a few agents haven't reported yet. Maybe the break is coming."

"Maybe," the sheriff said, drumming his big fingers on the desk top. "Maybe."

It was frustrating to wait. They were ready to explode into action, with every contingency anticipated and planned for; six of Kelly's men were standing by at a temporary headquarters in the Crossroads' post office, and state troopers in squad cars were posted at strategic intersections throughout the valley. When the break came dozens of experienced men were ready to reach for riot guns, walkie-talkies, tear gas, torchlights—ready to move out in a matter of seconds.

But the break didn't come; and all they could do was wait.

There was an occasional respite furnished by the regular run of office business: once a man stopped at the counter to fill out a dog-license permit, and a little later a woman in riding clothes came in to report a minor accident on Main Street. She had dented the fender of a parked car and couldn't locate the owner; what was she supposed to do?

"Just give me the license number, and you can make out the forms in the morning," the sheriff said.

"It was my fault, absolutely," the woman said, grinning. "I guess I thought I was still on a horse."

"Don't worry about it, Mrs. Harris."

The sheriff watched her as she left the counter, studying her black riding boots with a thoughtful frown. Finally he said "Damn!" in an explosive voice and turned quickly back to his desk.

"What is it?" Kelly said, coming to his feet; he could see the excitement in the sheriff's face.

"Horses, that's what. I'm a damned fool, Kelly. Balsam Peru was made for man or beast. Didn't I tell you that? Dogs, cats, horses— My dad always kept a jar in the stable for harness sores."

"I don't get it," Kelly said, as the sheriff quickly reached for the phone.

"Vets," the sheriff said. "Vets are more likely to peddle the stuff now than druggists. Why in the devil didn't I think of that? There's just two in the area, Doc Gawthrop and Doc Radebaugh."

Someone answered his call, and he said, "Jim? This is Sheriff Burns. We're trying to run down a lead. You still stock that old cure-all, Balsam Peru? Well, I figured you would. Here's what I want to know: You get any calls for it from around, let's see—" The sheriff looked up at the circled area on the map. "Well, around Landenburg, say. Or East End. Probably somebody without stock . . . somebody who uses it on himself or his family . . . What's that?" The sheriff's big hand tightened on the receiver. "What's that name again?"

Kelly grabbed the other phone and dialed his headquarters in the post office. When a crisp voice answered, he said, "This is Kelly. Hang on a minute."

The sheriff banged the phone down and reached for his hat. "Old fellow named Carpenter. Lives alone with a dotty wife back in the woods behind Emeryville. I know the place. You better tell your men to meet us in West Grove, that's six miles south on the federal highway. I'll flash the state police."

Kelly nodded and took his hand from the mouthpiece of the phone. "Okay," he said quietly. "Head for West Grove on the double. That's six miles south on the federal. . . . Yes, everybody. Fast."

CHAPTER TWENTY-FOUR

LORRAINE SLOWED DOWN to swing into a gas station that gleamed like a small yellow flare against the darkness. They were five miles away from the farmhouse now, spinning along smoothly on a narrow hard-surface road that would bring them eventually to the Unionville Pike. Earl had planned the route, plotting it with his still accurate directional instincts; deep into the country first, then around in a wide circle to the pike, traveling on a network of curving back roads. They might be able to sneak past the police this way, hitting the highway well beyond the roadblock area. It was a chance. . . .

The gas station was isolated against the storming countryside, with a single pump and a rack of lubricants shining in the faint light from a small lunch shack set back a dozen yards from the road. Rain blew in diagonal crystal streaks through the headlights of the car, and every now and then a slow roll of thunder shook the heavy air. The restaurant was empty; Earl saw the deserted counter and a cigarette machine as vague outlines behind the steaming windows.

A young man in a slicker and a rubberized hat ran out

from the shack with a flashlight swinging in his hand. Lorraine rolled her window down an inch and said, "Fill it up, please."

"Right, ma'am. Quite a night, eh?"

When he disappeared, she looked anxiously at Earl. "How are you feeling?"

"Fine. I'm fine."

"You haven't said a word since we left. You look terrible."

"I said I'm fine, didn't I? Fine's a word, isn't it?"

"I'm scared, Earl. If we're stopped—you won't shoot, will you? Promise me you won't."

"Let me worry about that."

"Give me the gun. Please, Earl."

"I need a cigarette. You got any?"

"No," she said. "Why don't you answer me?" She was speaking softly, but the fear in her voice trembled through the warm interior of the car. "Give me the gun, Earl."

"Go in and get some cigarettes."

"Can't you wait till we're out of this?"

"If the cops stop us I can put one in my mouth and keep my hand up to my face. It will help, Lory."

She hesitated an instant, staring speculatively at his hard, pale profile. Then she said quickly, "All right, all right."

Earl watched her run through the rain, her body slim and indistinct in the uncertain light and shadows. She stepped efficiently over puddles, her feet quick and sure on the wet ground. Like a cat, he thought. That's what Sambo said. Wouldn't stumble and knock over a radio. Not Lory.

"I'm fine," he said so softly that the words were lost in the sound of rain drumming on the roof and fenders of the car. It wasn't true; he was sick and cold and miserable. All through. Whatever guts he'd had were gone. He felt as weak and scared as a little child. It was a bewildering sensation, because he realized with despair that it was permanent; this was the way he'd be the rest of his life, cold and empty and sick. The damage done to him was final and lasting.

He became aware of a painful cramp tightening the muscles at the back of his neck. The pain spread up the base of his skull and around to his temples, squeezing his head like the jaws of a vise; no matter how he tried he couldn't turn away from his vague, ghostly reflection in the windshield. Something seemed to be pulling his eyes toward the empty driver's seat; a tiny light flashed in the darkness beside the speedometer, but he couldn't force himself to turn and look at it.

For some reason a name popped into his mind: Morgan or Monroe or something like that. What difference did it make? It was the guy he'd dragged away from the farmhouse in Germany.

He felt a weak, pointless anger growing in him; they should have busted me for saving him—instead of giving me a medal.

The idea made him flinch. What the hell? he thought guiltily and defensively. I can think about it. It's mine, isn't it? But he couldn't make himself look at it; the light that danced just beyond the angle of his vision was a refraction from the Silver Star on Lory's key chain. And he couldn't turn his head to look at it. Tears started in his eyes. He knew what had been destroyed, then.

"Damn," he said slowly and wearily; the viselike cramp in his neck was gone, and he slumped limply against the cushioned seat of the car. Staring at the medal swinging in the gloom, he frowned at his bitter, confusing knowledge. It's mine, I earned it, he thought. Like everything else in my life, I earned it. And like everything else I can't look at it any more.

He pulled the key from the dashboard and tried to remove the medal from the ring, but he couldn't get a purchase with just one hand. Finally he put the key on the floor, clamping it there with his heel, and then he wrenched the star loose with a twist of his fingers. He rolled his window down and threw the little star into the night, seeing it flash once in the air before disappearing into the darkness. The rain and wind beat at his flushed face and the sound of thunder came through the open window like heavy artillery fire on the horizon. Fine, he thought, fine.

He pushed himself into the driver's seat and turned the key in the ignition. When the motor roared up the attendant said "Hey," in a startled voice, but Earl swung the car about in a fast tight circle, managing the wheel clumsily with one hand. There was no confusion in his mind any more, only an innocent anger. He hadn't just left Sambo; he'd left himself back at the old farmhouse. The idea made him laugh weakly; and it was really funny. Now he had to go back and get himself. . . . The one thing he'd been proud of was back there with Sambo. He didn't know the name for it, but it was something clean and hard and it belonged to him and nobody else.

A voice screamed his name as he swung onto the road. Lorraine was running toward the car, her feet slipping and sliding in the mud, and the rain lashing her frantic face like cold crystal whips. "Earl!" she cried wildly, but his name was blown away into nothingness by the high, sweeping winds.

He hit the brake and rolled down the window. "I'm going back to get Sambo!" he shouted at her. "You wait here."

"No, you can't," she screamed, and he saw the mindless terror in her face. "For God's sake, don't leave me."

He felt sorry for her; she didn't understand. "I've got to, Lory. Don't you see?"

"He's nothing to us. You can't go back."

"It's no good if I don't. Nothing's any good if I don't. You and me, the whole world is no good."

"You're crazy, you're sick—you don't know what you're saying."

Crazy, sick— He began to curse; the words filled him with fury. You did what was right so you had to be sick or crazy.

"Listen to me," she cried, gripping the door with desperate hands. "Come inside and drink some coffee. We can talk. There's time, Earl."

Again he cursed: talk, talk, talk. Figure everything out. Look at this angle and that, check the whole deal from start to finish, and if you kept it up long enough you didn't have to do anything. Sambo needed him now; not fifty years from now.

"I'm going, Lory," he yelled. "I'm going now." He released the clutch with a snap and the car lunged into the rain and darkness, the sudden lurch unbalancing her, almost spinning her to the muddy ground. But she wouldn't fall, he knew; she'd land on her feet.

She could figure out something to tell the gas-station attendant. She'd say Earl had forgot to turn off a stove at home. Or something. She always thought fast.

The sky opened with lightning, and the road leaped ahead of him, shining blackly under the vast, glaring explosion. Darkness swept down again, but he had seen the rain pouring into the woods, and the trees swaying in the grip of the big angry winds. He laughed and jammed the accelerator against the floor boards. They'd never catch them on a night like this; it would take a genius just to stay on the road in this weather.

On a straight stretch he frantically wiped the windshield with the palm of his hand, then grabbed the spinning wheel before the car slid into the culvert. He settled down to his job anxiously; it was almost impossible to see landmarks or intersections. If he couldn't find his way back to the farmhouse, Sambo would really be up the creek.

The poor guy was probably scared to death by now. No frigging wonder. . . . But I'll get him out of there, he thought. He was glad the odds against them were long; he wanted to show Sambo just how good he was. No guy should ever pass up a chance to show his best stuff. Why hide it, for God's sake.

In the Army it was easy; you soldiered or you didn't, simple as that. A guy got hit and you hauled him to the medics. Regiment wanted a prisoner, you went out and got one. The Krauts tried to push you off a hill, you dug in and pushed them back. That was simple. It didn't take brains.

Earl felt pleased with his reasoning; it was shrewd and sharp. The trick was to keep on doing things you could be proud of; then you didn't have to torch for some cloudy time in the past when you had showed off your best stuff. Just keep putting it out, and you'd always have good, solid things to remember.

Okay, okay, he thought, leaning forward to watch the road. Don't worry about it now—just get there, for Christ's sake. He saw a barn flash behind him, and knew he was all right; now there'd be a stretch of woods and a little white house at the corner of an intersection.

The bouncing, swaying ride had started a heavy pain throbbing in his shoulder. Sweat broke out on his face and he was suddenly hot and cold all over; the fever burned in him like a furnace, but the touch of his clothing and the cold wind on his face sent shudders through his body. It was weird; he was on fire but his teeth were chattering. But fever was okay, he knew; a medic had explained it to him. You needed it to fight off sickness. It was like Popeye's can of spinach, or the U.S. Cavalry showing up in a Western movie. A little extra help in a tight spot.

Why in hell were they in trouble? he wondered. It was becoming difficult to keep his thoughts straight. Where's the little white house? Had he gone by it? Oh God, he thought anxiously, and leaned forward to peer out the windshield. Who the hell were they fighting? The war was over, wasn't it? The black sleeve of his overcoat caught his eye. No uniform—no pack or rifle. Damned right it was over. Over and done with. He didn't need this fever anymore. No can of spinach for him. Just get Sambo and they could go somewhere and rest. It was all clear again.

The white house flashed past him, and a little later he swung the car into the dirt road that led to the farmhouse, fighting the snapping wheel with his one hand. Shifting to second he gunned through the heavy mud, swerving around the treacherous lakes of water that shone under his headlights. Not much longer, he thought, exultantly. It wouldn't take a minute to haul Sambo into the car. Then it was all over. No more trouble.

The clarity of his thoughts filled him with a giddy confidence; he had figured it out perfectly. For once in his life he knew the score.

Earl almost overshot the entrance to the farmhouse; only his instinctive physical alertness saved him. He spun the wheel with reflex speed and efficiency, and the car slewed about and plowed into the narrow muddy lane. Everything was all right, everything was safe; the night was noisy with a clamorous reassurance.

The wind and rain shook him when he climbed from the car. He steadied himself with a hand on the fender, trying to pull the lapels of his overcoat around his exposed shoulder and chest; he had to wear the coat as a cape over his strapped-up arm, and the wind caught the loose sleeve and shook it grotesquely in his face. He stared around at the darkness, seeing nothing but the bulk of the old house and the tossing branches of the big trees.

"Sambo!" he shouted hoarsely, as he staggered through the mud to the sagging porch. "Sambo, let's go." He limped up the steps, his feet slipping on the wet boards. "Come on Sambo," he yelled. "Shake a leg. We got to move out."

Lightning broke all around him, flooding the porch with brightness, gleaming with a blue-white radiance on the wet stone walls of the house. "Sambo," he cried again, sagging against the shining door. "I've come back for you."

Someone answered him; a voice shouted behind him in the wind and rain. What the hell? he thought angrily. What's he doing outside? Dumb bastard should stay inside where it's warm. . . .

There was something queer about the lightning, he realized, thinking about it with an effort. Puzzled and vaguely alarmed, he stared at the brilliance that bathed the front of the house and outlined his dark figure against the gleaming door. It didn't go away; that was damned funny, he thought, frowning at the strong light on the back of his hand.

With an effort he straightened up and turned around; the light struck his eyes with bewildering force, and he raised a hand defensively to his face. Long, yellow lances leaped at him from the darkness, silhouetting his body starkly against the backdrop of the house. What in hell? he thought, his mind working slowly and laboriously.

"Cut it out," he yelled, swinging an arm belligerently at the probing beams. "Cut it out."

"Get your hands in the air," a voice shouted from the shadows. "Fast! There's twenty guns pointing at you."

"I'm going to get Sambo, that's all," Earl cried into the darkness. "I'm getting him, hear?"

"Get those hands up! You won't get another chance."

"I got to get him. Don't you know that?" Earl said furiously. He jerked the gun from his pocket and snapped a shot at the light on his left. It disappeared with a crash of glass and he yelled, "We don't want trouble, hear?"

Something knocked him sprawling to the wet porch. He hadn't seen the muzzle burst or heard the rifle shot; all he knew was the sudden pain in his leg and the sting of angry tears in his eyes. "Damn you," he said weakly, and fired from a sitting position at the second beam of light.

Darkness dropped around him and he worked himself to his feet, hearing the rain pounding on the roof above his head and a distant roll of thunder far off in the woods. Why did they shoot him? he thought, sick with pain. He was doing right, wasn't he? Oh Jesus, why did they have to shoot him?

Another light leaped out from the darkness. He couldn't explain anything to the shadows in the night. The words rose like a swarming flood in his mind. It was over, there was no need to fight. He had to get Sambo, that's all. He waved the gun futilely in the air, and a cruel heavy pain tore suddenly at his stomach; it was as if a spike had been driven into him with a sledge hammer. He staggered against the door, whimpering with pain. The gun in his hand thought for itself; the light disappeared in a splintering crash as he sprayed his last bullets into the shadows.

Then there was darkness again, and voices and the sound of booted feet on the wet ground. He found the doorknob and with a desperate, final strength pushed his way into the house. Now he was safe, he thought; the fury of the storm and the fury of the men were outside. He and Sambo could rest up a while, and then get started. . . .

"Sambo!" he cried desperately, lurching along the short hallway. Something gave in his leg and he went down to his knees, the living room blurring and fading before his eyes. "God," he said, wondering if he had been hit bad.

The old man had rolled off his bed and was lying huddled furtively within his heap of filthy blankets.

But Ingram was all right, he saw; Sambo was up on one elbow staring at him with big, white eyes. Sambo didn't look too good, Earl decided; probably just scared. Thought I'd run out on him. . . .

"It's okay, Sambo," he said, putting his hand against the

pain in his stomach. "I'll get you out. Nothing's going to—" Earl shook his head, wondering why he couldn't breathe; there didn't seem to be enough air in the room.

"Don't try to talk," Ingram said in a soft, whimpering voice. "You're hurt bad." He worked himself up to a sitting position. "Lie down, Earl, lie down."

"I'm fine, Sambo." Earl tried to smile but his lips were too stiff and cold. "I came back for you. You knew I would, didn't you?" Earl swallowed something warm and thick in his throat. He said pleadingly, "You knew that, didn't you?"

"Sure, I knew it, Earl." Ingram began to weep helplessly. "I knew it all along. Lie down—please."

"I shouldn't have left. . . . We're in the same outfit. Got to help—" Earl shook his head again, fighting stubbornly against a terrible weakness. "Got to get going, Sambo," he managed to say. Then he put his hand out in front of him and sprawled forward on his face.

"God!" Ingram moaned softly. "Oh God, Earl."

"Don't worry—" Earl raised his head from the floor and stared at Ingram. "Sambo—" He saw the tears streaming from Ingram's eyes and a lonely sadness welled up in his breast. "I didn't make it," he said weakly. "Didn't get back. Not all the way."

"You did fine," Ingram cried. He worked himself along the couch, and then reached down and squeezed Earl's hand tightly. "Nobody else could have done better, nobody in the whole world."

"Some things I could do okay," Earl said, resting his cheek on the cold floor. He gripped Ingram's hand. "We never made that ball game, Sambo. Never made it."

"Who needs a goddam ball game," Ingram said in a savage voice. "We got enough, man."

Earl heard the words, but he couldn't answer them; the light in the room was turning dark, and finally it was gone altogether. There was no white or black then, nothing but a weary kind of peace, and that was the last thing he knew before he died. . . .

Ingram stared hopelessly at Earl's glazing eyes, not feeling the sobs that shook his body, not feeling anything but a sense of lonely, irretrievable loss.

Voices sounded around him and the floor trembled under the tread of heavy boots. Hands took hold of him, roughly at first, then more gently as his body fell weakly against the sofa.

Someone said, "He looks about dead, too."

Ingram heard another voice. "The woman's not here. Send out an alert for her. She can't be far away."

The old man was talking shrilly to someone, and a little later Ingram heard a cackling outburst from Crazybone: "The colored boy had good manners, I tell you. Proper, he was. But the woman was a devil. Destructive and evil. Pop liked her, though. Always did like hussies. Used to say I was too ladylike. Expected too much fine treatment. Never dared lay a hand on me, he said. Afraid I'd—"

"All right, ma'am," someone said quietly. "There's nothing to worry about any more. Just sit still and rest."

A state trooper in a blue drill uniform was staring curiously at Ingram's tear-filled eyes. "What have you got to cry about?" he said. "You're not hurt."

"Never mind," a voice cut in quietly. Ingram recognized the voice of the big sheriff in Crossroads. "Let him alone." The authority in the sheriff's voice was unmistakable, but so was the understanding; the trooper turned away with a shrug, and Ingram wept in peace.

Later he was taken outside on a stretcher. The rain had stopped but a sprinkling of water from the trees mingled with the blood and tears on his face. Far above him he saw a single star shining in the sky. Everything was dark but the star, he thought. In his mind there was a darkness made up of pain and fear and loneliness, but through it all the memory of Earl blazed with a brilliant radiance. Without one you couldn't have the other, he realized slowly. Without the darkness there wouldn't be any stars. It was worth it then. Whatever it cost, it was worth it. . . .

The highway leading into Crossroads was a shining-wet ribbon under the headlights of the sheriff's powerful car.

Kelly sat beside him, smoking and thinking, a restless frown on his face.

Both men were grave; they didn't understand what they had seen tonight but they were honest enough to respect it.

"He came back for him," the sheriff said at last, articulating the thing they didn't understand. "Ten seconds more and we'd have made our move. But we heard him coming and let him walk into our arms. It's queer that he came back, isn't it?"

"I bet a dollar with myself he wouldn't," Kelly said, shaking his head. "That's how sure I was."

They were silent for another mile or so, and then the sheriff dismissed the puzzle with a sigh. "We've got work ahead of us. But how about stopping at my place for coffee when we're through? Nancy will be waiting up for us, I guess."

"You're sure it's not too late? You sure she won't mind?"

The sheriff wasn't a man for winks or rib-nudgings. "I'm sure," he said quietly.

"Well, good, then," Kelly said. "Thanks."

The sheriff touched the brake as they approached Main Street, slowing down as they swung into the peacefully sleeping village. Everything looked fine to his careful eyes; the street and sidewalks gleamed softly in the night, and only a stray cat prowled cautiously through the innocent shadows. Everything was fine. Everything, he thought.

blue murder

If you have enjoyed this book, look out for these other superb titles in the Blue Murder series:

WHATEVER HAPPENED TO BABY JANE?
HENRY FARRELL

The book that inspired Robert Aldrich's classic movie, starring Bette Davis and Joan Crawford. "True Grand Guignol, exquisitely calibrated." (*New York Herald Tribune.*)

ISBN 1-85480-032-9

THE BIG CLOCK KENNETH FEARING

"Narrated with force and speed and wit by several voices, it has lasting value as a record of metropolitan life, both inner and outer. In the years since it was written, its clean, brilliant style has shown no sign of fading. Its suspense still catches continually at the throat, and its jokes are still funny." (Ross MacDonald.)

ISBN 1-85480-042-6

SOLOMON'S VINEYARD JONATHAN LATIMER

Banned in America until the 1980s, this vivid portrayal of murder, violence and perverse sexuality is here published in its unexpurgated form. "A genuine hard-boiled classic . . . deserves to be ranked with the best. (*1001 Midnights.*)

ISBN 1-85480-076-0

SHOCK CORRIDOR   MICHAEL AVALLONE

First UK edition of the brilliant novelization of Sam Fuller's outrageous movie, a study in madness, hallucination, sexual fantasy and terror that grips from the first page to the last.

ISBN 1-85480-058-2

SOMEBODY'S DONE FOR   DAVID GOODIS

A rare and compelling crime novel by the author of *Shoot the Pianist*, "one of the most satisfying and original post-war hardboiled writers."

ISBN 1-85480-037-X

THE HONEYMOON KILLERS   PAUL BUCK

The novel of the ultimate midnight cult movie, based on the staggering *true* story of Raymond Fernandez and Martha Beck, the bizarre lovers who killed and killed, now published in a revised, expanded edition.

ISBN 1-85480-038-8

TEXAS BY THE TAIL   JIM THOMPSON

First UK publication for this hard-to-find classic by "the best suspense writer going, bar none" (*New York Sunday Times*). The place is Texas, the sun is high in the sky, *anything* can happen. And it does.

ISBN 1-85480-087-6

SCARFACE   ARMITAGE TRAIL

The *first* gangster novel, which inspired the classic gangster film and single-handedly sparked into being an entire genre, *Scarface* is truly a forgotten classic, now back in print for the first time in 50 years.

ISBN 1-85480-053-1

THE BIG ENCHILADA L. A. MORSE
Meet Sam Hunter, the LA private eye who 'makes Dirty Harry look like Mother Theresa,' in an up-to-the-minute case involving drugs, porno movies, violence, murder and lots of hot, spicy food!

ISBN 1-85480-092-2

STRAW DOGS GORDON M. WILLIAMS
The classic thriller that inspired Sam Peckinpah's notorious movie, starring Dustin Hoffman and Susan George. 'Tremendously well-told, with a fierce pace.' (*Sunday Times*).

ISBN 1-85480-098-1

SCORPION REEF CHARLES WILLIAMS
From the author of *The Deep* and, *The Hot Spot*, 'a grand thriller, with tensely shifting suspicion and some fine scenes of diving and sailing in the Gulf of Mexico.' (*The New York Times*).

ISBN 1-85480-043-4

Each title is published in paperback at £3.99

If you have any difficulty obtaining Blue Murder thrillers, please contact The Sales Department, Xanadu Publications Ltd, 19 Cornwall Road, London N4 4PH (Tel: 071-272 4895).

T-SHIRT OFFER! If you would like a stylish Blue Murder T-sirt (limited edition, black and blue, one size E–L only), please send £7.50 to the address above. Price includes postage and packing; allow 14 days for delivery.